T0354302

ENGLISH

Bruce Drake

authorHOUSE

AuthorHouse™
1663 Liberty Drive
Bloomington, IN 47403
www.authorhouse.com
Phone: 1 (800) 839-8640

Published by AuthorHouse 10/11/2016

ISBN: 978-1-5246-4300-3 (sc)
ISBN: 978-1-5246-4299-0 (e)

Library of Congress Control Number: 2016916544

Print information available on the last page.

Other books by Bruce Drake.
Lakin
Blue River
Shorty

ARTHUR DRAKE

Arthur was the leader of a gang of thugs that terrorized Londoners and shop owners in that area. In his part of town no one was safe, not even the Bobbies. (British policeman)

Most folks would stay out of his way and give him and his gang a wide berth. Even the tough members of his gang were afraid of Art for often times he acted crazy. Arthur had a reputation that was dark and gloomy. He would just as soon lay waste to anyone in his way as cook a meal and eat it.

This English kid left people cringing in his wake. He enjoyed watching ladies of the upper crust flinch when he would cuss up a storm, which he did so well. His mouth often spewed out words that would turn the air blue around him and he would use detestable language in front of anyone if he thought he could use it to his advantage.

The police tried diligently to keep him and his gang away from the better side of town with very little success. When they gave him orders to leave he acted like a wild man and fought like a lion. Most of the time people who messed with him got hurt and sometimes hospitalized.

Funny though he seldom ended up in jail and laughed and made fun of those that brought him in to the lock-up. When they tried to dress him down they'd see a big ole sneer like smile break out on his face and those pure blue eyes of his he kept pretty much guarded. Art seemed to aggravate most everyone he came in contact with.

This young lad had no family and lived on the streets with other kids his own age. He had no one to guide him along life's pathway and he did as he darn well pleased. Doing those things that seemed right to keep up his image as a rough tough thug. In the beginning of his life this English kid didn't have the slightest inkling of what his last name was so he took the name of Sir Frances Drake for his own.

Arthur Drake gave most folks the willies and they shied away from him. His clothes were repulsive filthy dirty rags. English had no real place to call home and slept outside on the ground many a night. The best home he had was a small hole in the ground with a dirt floor and a dirt and tin roof. A narrow tunnel was the doorway into his little underground palace.

Down deep inside Arthur had a hankering for a better life that no one else knew about. He'd heard of the Americas and hoped some day to go there. But that was a long ways off. He was saving some money to make the trip, but it was coming pretty darn slow.

Stealing was the game that kept food in his stomach. With a stroke of luck a man from the Upper East Side became his fence and took most of what he could pilfer. This rotten scoundrel of a man raised Art's standard of living in those troubled times of his life. On certain occasions he'd give Art a list of what he needed and Arthur would get what he could. This kid had light fingers and could pick a man's pockets with the best of them. He had learned the trade from his uncle who was long dead. This English kid had perfected his trade far beyond what he had been taught.

Breaking and entering is where he got most of the things his fence needed. Four or five of his gang members would stake out a few houses in an area. When no one was home they would move on it and strip it of all they could sell and make a sovereign or two. (One-pound sterling) they had a two wheeled cart that they moved their loot with.

A knife was his weapon of choice. That kid was mighty good with the blade. He had some natural skill and quick hand speed. The boy was chain lighting and that was the key to his success. Arthur was a regular ripsnorter in the London area. When big trouble came that he couldn't handle foot speed would get him free.

At the age of seventeen Arthur Drake was learning how to play draw and stud poker in the card room. In these card games most of his money was snookered away from him, until he caught on to their treachery. What he learned from that experience is when men sit in a card game they must see a patsy sitting there or know it's them. When light finally came to him at the card table with these scumbags, Art moved into action. One man ended up in the hospital with knife wounds. Another fellow had long knife wounds on face and chest, one of those cheats had his coat ruined and the last scalawag scurried for cover and got clean away.

Shortly after that episode things began to unravel in Art's life. His fence got caught with some hot merchandise and he fingered Arthur Drake to the police as his pick-up man. Claiming he didn't know it was stolen. He told the police the man they wanted was from the lower west side and produced his name. That is all the information the

London Bobbies needed, they all knew him quite well and proceed to do their duty.

Another stroke of luck came his way for Arthur heard that the Bobbies were a looking for him from a member of his gang and knew this time he was buckin' a stacked deck. The only chance he had was to clear out of town and do it quickly. For the first time in Art's life his luck had run out on him. He was in one heck of a mess and needed to skip out of there in a hurry.

He was getting his few belongings together and saying goodbye when he saw three Bobbies coming to roust him out and take him in. Like a flash that boy cut across the street, shot up the alley and lit a shuck on out of there. He had all his good duds in a carpetbag, hid out, and always ready to go at a moment's notice. The boy picked them up on his way to the waterfront.

Arthur for some time now had planned what he would do if this time ever came. He'd been formulating a plan in the back of his mind to leave this place in the dust. Today he knew it was time to put feet to his plan and leave England. Over the course of time he'd saved nigh on to a hundred pounds in cash and was thinking of America and a fresh new start there. He would steal about anything he wanted from folks along the road to the coast, that way he could pick up some more cash to tide him over once he got there. Arthur made his way toward a harbor along the coast and booked a one-way passage on a small ship that was headed for New York City in America. The ship was small but it was leaving right away.

He'd gotten free of London and the Bobbies and he felt kind of smug with himself in his narrow escape. Down deep inside ole English had a gut feeling that he was on his way to a much better life with a whole lot better prospect in New York City and the United States.

The little ship he booked passage on was the Downey Cruiser a small cargo ship (a tub) and Arthur was the only passenger on board other than the captain and his motley crew. After Art came on board the ship and just before the crew set sail the captain of this small tub was seen talking to a Bobby at the foot of the gangplank and some money changed hands.

Arthur looked like he was ready to make a jump into the scum covered water of the harbor below when the Bobby turned and walked away with never a backwards glance. Right then and there the ship's crew that saw this knew that Mr. Drake was in a whole lot of trouble for the captain was looking for a couple more mates to go along on this trip.

Everyone on board the Downey Cruiser knew that many hands made for light work. Art was a new hand and didn't even know it yet. The ship was a good day and a half out to sea when that boy's life of luxury came to an abrupt end. The captain and three men descended on his little cabin in the middle of the night and took everything of value they could find and left him with some old clothes that were left behind by some long dead sailor. Arthur was dragged kicking and fighting from his stateroom and received a whack on the head for his trouble and then thrown down into the hole of the ship, put in leg irons and for two days he got no food and only a dab of water to drink. He'd been bucking the long odds and he finally came to the end of his string.

This kid from London Town had a hostile and mean streak in him a mile wide and was brought up to be aggressive, unfriendly, resentful, conniving and shrewd in his own way.

Because of the choppy sea the poor boy was as sick as a dog and heaved his cookies all over the place. The kid was getting as weak as a kitten from all his loss of body fluids and had to be dragged up out of the hole. The Captain of the Downey Cruiser was trying to get him to submit to his authority. He didn't want him to die for he needed the extra hand. It took quite a long while for him to come around, but in the end he had to submit or die. The boy was not stupid he would bide his time and wait for a chance to jump ship and escape this rat infested tub.

I took time to study the young man really well and decided to be his friend if he would let me. This young man needed someone about now to show him the ropes and help keep him out of trouble. I let him know that we were all in the same boat and wanted off the Downey. "Son, ya got to play it cool and don't rock the boat or you'll never get a chance to shake loose of this tub."

Several members of the crew were waiting for the chance to separate themselves from this ole scow. Many of us had been shanghaied at one time or another and we spent our time in port, down in the hole of the ship. We'd been kidnapped to work on this rat infested tub on the high seas. The Downey Cruiser was sea worthy but small for an ocean going vessel and no one would hire on or stay for over one trip if at all possible.

This English kid was a fighter and held out for four days and three nights, he didn't give up easily. Even when he did you could see that he hadn't really. This stubborn kid never threw in the towel but was only playing a waiting game.

He was biding his time waiting for a chance to go over the side and escape this wooden bathtub. The captain knew it and whenever we were close to land some of us were thrown into the bowels of the ship and made to help unload the merchandise from down in the hole and when we finished the doors were locked for the duration of our stay.

You could almost see the wheels turning in that tricky little mind of his; English was always looking for a way to escape. He watched the captain and first mate real close whenever we got near land and made a mental note of what they did and how they acted. He hoped to use this information later on to help him escape. There were others that were looking for a way to free themselves from the Downey.

In our travels we played with Art Drake's last name and called him things like Quack, Quack, Ducky, Gander, Mr. Duck and anything that was pulled from the last name Drake. We even used English all in good fun. Because we were good friends he took it as a joke.

His plan was to get ready to jump ship when we came close to some shoreline. After six months he got his clothes back, that were stolen from him, when he came aboard. I found out later he had some money and a knife hid out in that cabin down below.

In the early part of the voyage Arthur Drake was assigned to me to learn the ropes and be a good sailor. As time went on Arthur became a topnotch mate but he always had that far away look in his eyes. At times he was an awful fright, his nerves made him as jumpy as a frog on a hot cook stove. He didn't trust anyone aboard ship, but the four of us.

My name is Harley MacDonald, from Scotland, but most of the time I was called Big Mac. Arthur only trusted me and three others on board the Downey Cruiser, Justin Jenkins (J J.) from Pennsylvania plus Dick and Tom Ames who were from Maine. The five of us became thick as thieves and had our heads together and talked a lot.

Our main topic of conversation, when we were alone and away from the others, was always how are we were going to escape this floating prison we were on. We pretty much wanted to get free of Captain Nelson Rodgers and this slow moving, ole tub the Downey Cruiser.

We preferred an English speaking port and hoped for America. We didn't care where we departed this bathtub we just needed to get off this dinghy on to dry land. The idea was for us to disembark this little two by twice craft and become landlubbers once again. This Arthur Drake was a good worker and over the course of time he settled into the ship's routine and became a good sailor. But in the back of our minds we all knew he was looking for a way to flee this slow moving scow. I'd been shanghaied four years ago in London, England and had all but lost my will to break free of this bathtub. Way too many lashes had taken that nonsense out of me.

But this kid from London, England took each beating in stride and seemed to grow stronger with each strike of the lash. Just being around him renewed my will to abandon this ship, if I got half a chance. This wasn't a defeatist attitude I was carrying around anymore, but a will to be free. This ole sailor drew strength from watching English fight his battles; in fact he gave me the will to fight this feeling of submission. At this point in our trip English had been on board ship nigh on to two and a half years. We kept our bags packed and our paltry wages ready to go in a moment's notice. This slow moving little scow of a ship was headed for land on the west coast of the Americas. We were pretty sure that it was the west coast of California. Just before dark I climbed the rigging and saw mountains in the distance. When I came down we made preparations to leave our prison. A twelve foot dinghy was packed with our stuff and some food and water that we'd saved for this trip.

Arthur looked for and found the money he'd hid in his cabin when he first came on board. He also picked up that two edged knife he'd brought along. We had to leave the biggest share of our wages with the captain or tip our hand to our escape plans.

Two of our five man party was on watch that night and it made it easier as we left the ship and headed south. Our little lifeboat would not strike for land right off, but sail parallel to the coast for a day or so then head for shore. This we hoped wouldn't allow the captain to find us and haul us back to the Downey Cruiser and string us up by the thumbs from the yardarm. To be caught meant death by hanging.

That my friend wasn't very appetizing to any of us, so we hustled as fast as our little boat could take us. The slight breeze was in our favor and moved our little dingy right along. We put lots and lots of blue green water between our little lifeboat and that ole tub behind us as we ventured south. Two days later we struck the coastline and made an easy landing on a sandy beach. A small Mexican fishing village was our home for the next couple of days. It took us almost that long to get our land legs back and working on an even keel.

We tried to buy a couple of horses with our funny money from England but no one wanted our English paper currency. We had some gold and silver coins that would spend. We did swap the dingy for a couple of old mules and an old rusty shotgun. The nags weren't much but they belonged to us. We were about as broke as any five men can get. Even if a big ole herd of large Belgium horses had trampled us into the ground we couldn't be any more broke.

For a long month and a half we split rails for fences to earn money enough to purchase six horses to ride out of here on. That gave us six horses and a team of mules

Our English paper funny money wasn't worth very much to these people. The locals had no faith in our English currency, out here in California, so we took a beating on everything we acquired here in California.

We sailor boys were all as green as grass; only three of us had ever ridden a horse before. The Mexican rancher and his caballeros got a good laugh as they watched these greenhorn swabbies try to mount these green-broke horses. We ended up on the ground on our backs way to many times in the next day or so. We finally got the hang of it or the mounts were tired of us climbing onto their backs.

With a little instruction and lots of bumps, bruises and bangs we were ready to leave and head inland to a new life. We had no idea what was ahead of us out there in this wild, vacant and desolate land. We had heard that Indians covered the land from the east coast to the Pacific Ocean and most were unfriendly. They told us we must head inland right away to avoid capture by the law and the Captain of the Downey Cruiser. We were five men on the dodge and we looked like it. But first we must try to exchange the remaining English monies for American currency. For that job we needed a fairly large town with a good size bank and not too far from the coast.

In the two plus years aboard ship Arthur Drake had mellowed out quite a bit. The ocean voyage had smoothed out most of the rough edges in his life. Don't get me wrong ole English could be a powder keg, but mostly he kept it under control. I saw some things in him that I liked a lot. He was devoted to the four of us and considered us his best friends. The words I-I-I had crept out of his conversation and he had replaced it with we-we-we. He often thought of other people and not of himself all the time. Yes, I'd say his time aboard ship had made a man of him.

His bad reputation and hard character was not recognizable in him anymore. He had gone from a ruthless regular ole ripsnorter to a kindlier, gentler person. But don't get me wrong with Arthur Drake it was better to have him on your side than against ya. Yes, Mr. Duck could be a mighty dangerous man if it was called for.

When we climbed off them flea bitten ole fur balls we were a sight to see. It looked like we were straddling a wooden barrel when we walked. It took a bit to get these ole legs uncurled and able to walk right again. Straddling those horses had done a number on us and our seat ends were as sore as all get out.

In the first small town we came to, on the main land, that took the English money that we'd saved from our ocean voyage, we slicked up and headed into town to turn our pounds in for American cash. After buying supplies we only had a hundred American silver dollars to our name. A hundred bucks wasn't much for all that time we spent aboard ship. Just a little over twenty bucks apiece. English told us he could play poker so we trusted him with our meager savings.

As the first night in the largest cantina in town wore on, our winnings begin to grow slowly. The second night Art held his own and maybe won a dab. Finally on the third night the cards came our way. When the really big hand came Arthur bet it for all it was worth and in that one hand he collected well over a hundred and seventy-five dollars in cash and a gold mine with a cabin on the claim and all its contents.

I wondered why we wanted a gold claim but everyone said it was well worth what was bet. Maybe we could sell it and retrieve some hard cash. Somehow that piece of paper changed our whole life and set a new course for us. English had lived on that boat but he never had a home of his own and he was excited about seeing it.

After leaving the saloon we were a jubilant bunch of swabs. The first thing we picked up was a lot more food, a thirty-six caliber Colt Revolver, three old muzzle loaders, to protect ourselves with, lots of shot, percussion caps and black powder.

We talked it over on what we should do with the gold mine. We'd heard that some workman up north had found gold earlier this year in California at a place called Sutter's Mill up on the American River, wherever that is. Sutter's mill they said was located north of here near an outpost called Sacramento and since the discovery of gold all kinds of people were flocking into the area, some good and some not so good, all with one purpose on their mind, to get rich.

We made a decision to give this gold mining business a try so we picked up some mining equipment shovels, picks, pans, hammers, saws, nails and such like. The man we got the gold mine from offered to join us as we tried to make the gold mine pay some kind of dividends on our investment. Without him I'm not sure we could even fine the claim let alone work the crazy thing. I myself didn't know what gold looked like in the ground. English picked up a small booklet that told all the things a greenhorn miner needed to know about the gold field.

We fired up those old muzzle-loading rifles to see if they were any good and just how straight they would shoot. Well to my surprise they were true to the mark. English picked up that revolver and fired it off at some old tin cans. That ole boy was astonishingly accurate with that thirty-six caliber short gun. At a distance of thirty feet it looked like he couldn't miss some tin cans we had sitting on a fence rail

The rest of us tried it and couldn't hit the broad side of a barn at thirty feet. The big surprise was that the two-edged stiletto blade of his went where he wanted it to; that ole boy was mighty accurate with that knife in his hands. At the same thirty feet he couldn't miss. This young man was a natural at about anything he touched.

At this time and in this area the gold fields weren't producing all that much. It was a little bit early for the people from the East to make their presence known. The men that happened to be in the gold fields now were from this region and actually lived in this vicinity before the first strike was made. Later on this year they expected people to come swarming in from all over the country and the world.

We were warned to hurry and stake out the best claims before they came like locust and cover the land.

With all the things that were swirling around in my mind since I'd left London two jumps ahead of the law it was hard to keep everything in perspective. For the first time in my life I had friends around me that I could trust and people that trusted me and no one else knew how that made me feel. These four men could be trusted and I never had that feeling before, not with anyone. Except for my newfound friend Jesus Christ who came down to where I lived and helped me turn my life around and made my new life in Him worth living.

I thank my Lord Jesus for all the love He put inside of me. Jesus found a better nature in my soul and because of Him love took root and allowed me to find these new friends. Before this trip I trusted no one. He makes a person feel quite secure and at peace inside himself. Before I found my Lord there was no contentment down inside of me and that made me feel as empty as an old whiskey barrel.

The five of us worked really well as a team. But the best part was we had a fondness for each other that went deeper than just friendship. Harley MacDonald (Big Mac) the man that took me under his wing and made me take a good look at Jesus, the lifesaver. My life wasn't worth living before I met Big Mac and his heavenly friend. Before you come to know Him there is no way you can understand the change He makes in your life.

ENGLISH ART

You should see this big city kid out here in the mountains of California. Man-oh-man was this place ever desolate. The awesome scenery was everywhere in these Sierra Nevada Mountains. The sight was breathtaking, wherever I looked and it kept me in awe. These awesome mountains were high and rugged and the trees were tall on their slopes and snow on the high peaks sparkled in the sunlight.

In most valleys there was a cold stream of water running down the center of them. In one such place we found our claim and a cabin that was about half large enough for the six of us. First thing Mr. Milburn showed us was our working claim and how to work it.

The six of us worked for more than an hour to produce an insignificant speck of gold. Mr. Milburn assured us that, that's the way it goes sometimes and that the next pan might produce a bonanza of yellow stuff and make us rich. He took time and worked with us and showed us the ends and outs of working our claim.

Mr. Milburn suggested that someone go hunting and see if they could bag some kind of wild game for us to eat. We were plum out of any kind of meat, except hard and dried out jerky. Our jerky tasted a lot like some salty shoe leather.

A funny thing happened, one morning early Mr. Milburn took his clothes and left. That was the last we ever saw of him. I guess he had his fill of greenhorns asking all kinds of fool questions and making all kinds of odd noises day and night.

Two of our boys could really raise a ruckus when they were snoring up a storm. I swear many a night the roof would rise up a good foot and a half and then settle back down with each breath they took.

Marty Milburn seemed to be a straight up man as far as I could tell. He warned us not to trust anyone that came near the claim and went on to explain all the things that some men would do to get your mine and gold away from you. He was talking to me but we all listened to what the man had to say.

"English, my boy, don't trust any newcomers an inch and watch those that seem to be your friend, for gold fever can take control of a man and change his whole outlook on everything. Be extra careful up here and be alert at all times."

In the week that followed we took very little gold out of the streambed or from the creek bank. Just to try something different Harley and I moved upstream to explore and look for a spot that might give forth a little more yellow stuff.

Slowly we worked our way upstream looking under rocks and in cracks and to our surprise we picked up a small handful of that heavy gold colored stuff and put it into our little leather pouch. Our spirits were high and we worked feverishly to uncover as much gold as we possibly could.

We hadn't gone much more than a half-mile in two days and the little bag was full and we had trouble closing it up so I took off a sock, without holes in it, and we started putting yellow stuff in it. But as quick as the stream started to produce it ended and there was nothing to find. Where did the yellow metal disappear to? All at once it just quit on us? No matter how hard we worked after that we found nothing, not even a little speck. This was a puzzler to all of us.

The next day all five greenhorns struggled around in the water trying to comprehend what was going on and why the yellow stuff disappeared so abruptly.

Had someone else worked out this part of the valley before we got here? That was the big question that was on our minds, if so why hadn't they worked the area we'd just panned out, questions, questions always questions and not any answers. Many a night the big Quacker would struggle through that book we'd gotten back in town to see if this kind of thing happened to other miners and why it just ran out on us without even a goodbye.

In the late afternoons the sun couldn't be seen over the high walls of the canyon. The shadows would be high up on the eastern wall. It would be getting dark in a bit so we moseyed back downstream toward the cabin and our registered claim.

We'd sit around on logs by the campfire and we would have long discussion on why this thing happened to us and decided that tomorrow all of us would take our time and slowly work upstream from our camp until we reached the spot where the gold petered out. It took us four long days of hard work moving the gravel in that creek bed to reach the spot where we lost the gold the first time up here. We'd lifted about the same amount from the stream that Harley and I had a few days earlier just hitting the good spots.

Our gold pokes had grown to just over two small bags and a tin coffee cup. We had done well for those few days but what was on tap for us now. We decided to work downstream from our cabin and see what the creek could deliver up, down there.

The mining book talked about a mother lode whatever that was and it said that all the gold in the stream had been delivered from it. Jeepers creepers who could understand all that gobble-de-gook in this book? The mining book suggested that a mother lode had given birth to all the gold in the creek bottom. This ole English duck couldn't make heads or tails of all this gibberish the book spewed out.

My lack of any formal education was holding me back from ciphering this out. An old woman in London taught me to read until she up and died on me. This ole dude was no more than a dummy trying to strike it rich in the Sierra Nevada Mountains.

The next day we figured to work downstream looking for the allusive gold. We worked hard for two long days and didn't recover enough yellow stuff to stick in your eye. This valley had petered plum out. There wasn't enough metal in this stream to feed a chicken his morning meal and we were getting a little discouraged.

Mac kidded me out of it and this ole English kid decided he wouldn't let that happen to him again. We all got our heads together and made plans to try our luck someplace else in some other mountain stream in some other valley. For now we kept our yellow money in a quart can in a gunnysack. As we talked my ugly mood started to slide downhill and this kid felt a whole bunch better than he had earlier.

The excitement of what could be on the horizon for us was thrilling me to no end. Tomorrow we would cut loose from this place and head for greener pastures. I didn't like leaving that little log and stone cabin behind us. It was my little home for the most prosperous and the most enjoyable period of my entire life, but more than that it was a roof over our heads on a bad day and a warm place to sleep on cool nights.

Big Mac had his King James Bible and we struggled through it not knowing all that many big words but learning all the time. We read a verse and speculated on what it said and then wondered what God meant by it. The verse that really got to me was the one that said "Know to do right and do it not, that is sin." That verse told it all and there was no way to wiggle out of it and still be true to His Word. That was a huge verse to chew on.

It kept me thinking on it in all my down time. The only way to weasel my way out was to say "what is right and what is wrong," but down deep inside I knew what was wrong. The more this kid learned from God's Word, the more he knew what was right and what was wrong. Thank God I was out here where the temptations were almost zilch.

God made it so easy for man to know what sin was. So many people were chuck full of poison and filled to the brim with hatred. This is one thing I must always guard myself against, for over my short life I've hated and disliked many, many people and now I can see that ain't what God wants. The problem the duck had was he had to get people off his hate list and on to his like list and that was no small job. For hate can rule a man in all he does. Hate can disrupt good thinking and take a level head and push it off kilter.

The next day we set out for God only knows where. There seemed to be many more mountains to the north with snow on them so that is the way we went. We loaded everything of value, that was in that cabin, onto our horses and mules. Then made some tracks out of the valley.

After two long days of walking we came into a valley that had a wide cold stream running down the middle of it. You could say it was off the beaten path. All five of us set up camp for the night. Early the next morning we set out to find us some gold, we hoped. The starting point was just out of the valley. From that point we started to work our way upstream toward the high up mountains. We covered about the length of a football field the first day and never found so much as a small grain of gold. The five of us fell into our bedrolls exhausted from the long hard day's work.

Time was on our side and we still felt like we were going to strike it rich. At this point we felt this stream was going to yield a bonanza of gold for us. That all changed after a long hard week of steady work without seeing even the smallest of profit. We hoped we would find gold with every pan full of sand we dug out of the streambed but it didn't happen.

The five of us were inside the valley now and our decision was to just hit the likely spots for gold. (Like in cracks in the rocks, in front of large stones and wherever the heavier gold might settle.) The slow pace we were going we would be forever checking out this stream and the valley if we continually work like this.

This bunch of greenhorns needed to work more efficiently to find if there was gold in this streambed. With our new tactic in two days we covered close to a mile and still we had no color to show for all our hard work. This mining business wasn't going to be as easy as we once thought it might be. There weren't any gold nuggets as big as your fist lying all over the ground, like we'd heard.

Being the best shot the fellows sent me out to find some fresh meat to eat; our meat was running a smidgen low. The guys would stay here and continue to work the valley up toward the mountains. The only food I found was an old bore porcupine, which would last about two or three meals in some soup.

Man-oh-man did I ever get picked on, by the guys. Right away I became the great white hunter and all that goes along with not being very successful on the hunt. It was all done in good fun and we had a good time with it. This was the first time I'd ever shot any wild game and it was kind of thrilling for me. I'd cut up and wounded men a few times, with a knife, but never tried to kill anyone or anything in all my life. If it wasn't that we needed the food I'm not sure if I'd like this hunting business.

I'm a guessing this ole English kid could get used to it. He kind of liked firing the rifles. It made a person feel that he was safe from all that wanted to do him harm. The very next day with a horse on a string I hit the trail for the high country again. In my mind this old duck worked on how he would reload quickly after each shot. In my mind I never knew if for some reason I might need to shoot a second time.

The higher I went the rougher and more rugged the country became. This hunting trip would be a two-day affair. I was leading both horses now and following a deer runway up the mountainside. My horse and I moved up and over the divide and started down into the next valley.

Something caught my eye and I stopped dead in my tracks, far off in the distance I saw a mining camp with three men down in the water working their claim. I kept my horses out of sight in the rocks as I watched from my eagle's nest. I wouldn't be going down there for folks were funny about strangers that came a visiting anytime of the day or night.

I wondered if they were taking any yellow metal from their streambed down there. While watching it looked like they were. In my mind I wished them well. While watching them for an hour or so and off on the far side of the valley something caught my eye, something or someone was slipping up on their camp.

It looked like a couple of small black bears. I'm a greenhorn out here but would six bears be sneaking up on the three miners. As this ole English dude watched he could see they were men. What in the world where they up to; it was no good I'm sure.

At any rate I must warn them, but how? As it came to me I pointed my revolver toward the miner's camp and pulled the trigger and the bullet exploded from the barrel. I waited a moment and heard the sound echo down the valley and the men stopped dead in their tracks and looked straight at me. Then on the dead run they started up out of the water heading toward their camp and their rifles. One man died in knee-deep water and one bit the dust as he made it to the river bank. The last man crumpled in mid-stride as he ran for cover near their camp.

As those yellow bushwhacking killers crawled out of their hiding places they looked my way. This ole boy shook uncontrollability while keeping himself hid and the horses out of sight. No way did I want them to know how many people were hiding in the rocks up here.

Mr. Milburn told us to trust no one and now I see why. What was that all about? Were the gunmen after the miners' gold or their gold claim? This was a new chapter in my life for I didn't really think that this kind of thing went on in America. In all my born days I never tried to kill anyone and this didn't sit very well with me. This kid had a bad feeling down inside of him, a loathing for those cruel snakes on the other side of the divide. As the Gander thought on it a cold chill grabbed hold of him and he shook all over. The funny thing was it isn't that cold up here on the hillside.

This ole dude scampered back over the divide and headed downhill, it was getting dark in the valley below. Then out of the near darkness I saw five deer moving downhill toward water. Ole English Art made his shot and downed a nice young buck with one horn missing. This buck had lost one half of his nice rack; that ole boy was getting ready for a new set of antlers.

He would supply our dinner table for quite a few days. Sometime soon before hot weather set in we needed to preserve the meat so it would last us a few weeks without spoiling. No one wanted or needed rancid meat to eat. By the time I had him field dressed and loaded on the second horse it was nigh on to dark in this place. Ever so slowly we made our way downhill in the darkness. No way would I quit until this young man got himself into camp.

My thoughts were still fixed on those evil men over the ridge and on the three dead miners. This was something I'd never expected. It was outrageous and it confused me to no end. Why would anyone murder someone for their gold when there were streams and places all over California where there might be gold? I understand that anyone can stake out claim here. Everyone had the same opportunity here in America.

This English man wondered about the dead men's families would they ever know what happened to them as they dug for the precious metal out here in California? From this point on this ole boy was going to look out for himself and his friends and try to live long enough to talk to my future kids about his experiences.

How would we combat the murdering claim jumpers if they came into our valley? Should we shoot first and ask questions later. The problem with that is regular miners might come here to investigate the valley. True visitors might be decent folks. This whole situation had me on edge. This I knew we had to be on guard at all times or end up like those poor souls in the next valley.

With the five of us we should be able to keep one man on guard duty at all times and still work the creek until we found something worthwhile. It was close to midnight and darker than the ace of spades when I meandered into camp. It was just like I thought everyone in camp was sound asleep.

The murders could have come sneaking in here, robbing and killing everyone in our camp with just a butcher knife. Out here in this California wilderness we needed to prepare for the worst and hope for the best. Life is way too short and precious to just give it away.

Harley MacDonald got up, stoked up the fire and helped me unload and hang the deer from a meat pole. I told him of what I'd seen over the divide. How three men were working their claim and how someone murdered them to get what they had taken from the stream. "Big Mac, treachery stuck out everywhere in that little deal."

Harley sounded kind of upset by the news. "Well it's started. I knew it would sooner or later. I've been expecting it and keeping a cautious eye on the side hills. Arthur you're right we must be wary and on guard at all times or end up like those boys did over the ridge."

In the morning we got organized and posted a guard above our camp. We didn't want anyone killing us in this creek for this stream had no gold hidden away in it. The men wanted me to travel back up this valley and check out the situation and see if the outlaws were working the claim or had they taken the gold and moved on to greener pastures.

We decided to hide the gold we'd taken from the stream that had the cabin on it and move it someplace back away from our campsite so that anyone thinking of doing us in wouldn't be able to find where we'd hidden it. The five of us sure didn't want to reward anyone for sneaking in here and killing us.

Big Mac and the Ames brothers started to work the stream as Justin Jenkins kept watch over the operation. With our best horse under me, I hot footed it on out of there heading upstream shoving lots of California sand and rocks behind me.

Three hours later I found myself at the top of the divide looking down at the dead men's operation far below. Not a soul could I see anywhere? It looks like the men that did the dirty work were long gone. My presence high up on the hillside and that shot I took must have spooked them pretty good.

I made the decision to go down there and have a look around. I let the nag have her head and she made her way downhill to that camp far below. A hundred yards short of the campsite and the stream, I stopped and watched for a movement at the stream and camp in the rocks below.

The two dead men were still where they fell. The one in the water had drifted downstream about fifty yards and got hung up on the rocks. The two miners up on the bank had been stripped of their boots and clothes and were lying face up in the sun.

Their tent and all their belongings were gone; tools, clothes and I assume their gold also. Those killers took everything that wasn't nailed down and everything that would get them some extra cash. I took a few minutes to check their operation They seemed to know mining a whole lot better than we did. They had a wooden sluiceway that they used to run their gravel through to separate the gold from the sand and gravel.

I looked it over real good and behind the cross pieces designed to trap the heaver gold I found some precious metal, not much but some. These dead miners must have found enough yellow metal to keep them interested

This Englishman had an uneasy feeling down deep in his guts so he got straddle that mare and headed uphill. Could the claim jumpers be paying my friends a little visit over on the other side of the hill? Someone needed to dehorn those back shooters and send those mangy maggots a running for cover.

As the Big Quaker traveled downhill he could hear gunfire echoing up the valley, long before he saw our mining camp. Those low down, no good, mean rotten killers were shooting at my friends. From my position I could see shadowy figures moving down through the rocks above and behind my friends, so that's the direction I took to get in behind them.

I left my horse in the shade of a big rock and slipped in behind the killers. Found a good spot above them and hunkered down and waited for them to make a move. I saw one scalawag rise up and head for another rock a little further downhill.

The man never made it to his next shooting spot my fifty caliber slug hit him hard in the middle of the back and it sent him plummeting head first into the gravel. Once he hit the ground he didn't moved one iota. The others quickly forgot about their deadly mission and were now looking for me and a way to escape their predicament for we had them in a cross fire.

Once they reached their horses it wasn't long and those boys were making tracks of their own out of the valley. This little deal of theirs had gone sour on them and it left a bad taste in their mouth. Right now their prospects had to be better someplace else. A Kansas blizzard offered more opportunity than this little valley did about now.

Mac and the boys weren't taking any chances and stayed hid, until I hollered down to them. As I moved to get my horse they came out of hiding and watched me from below. The terrain was steep and quite rugged and it took me a bit to get the dead man's things and his horse and meander down there.

This nervous wreck took some time to dig a shallow grave for the dead man, and then kicked some rocks and dirt over the galoot so he wouldn't start to stink up the place in a few days. We had enough of him without that.

Everyone in our party was jittery about the gang getting the advantage over us and wondered if they would be back to causes us more trouble in the future. JJ suggested we follow them and see where they went. Justin Jenkins and I volunteered to take up their trail and see what they were up to and maybe thin them out just a little bit more if we could.

If Justin Jenkins and I followed them we would be out numbered. With it being six men to two we needed to be extra careful. We didn't care much for dry-gulching people no matter who they were, but this is what these boys did for a living and that didn't set right with any of us in our party.

We'd picked up the dead man's rifle, revolver, horse, powder and slugs, his weapons to take with us. We stripped him of a small bag of gold, all his clothes, food and anything we could use. So primarily we put him in the ground naked as a jaybird. His bedroll would come in handy on these cold spring nights. We only did what they had done to the three miners over at miners' creek. We named it after the three dead men.

JJ and I left our friends with two rifles and a Colt Revolver. They had the same number of weapons that we took along with us. We took two riders and a pack mule, that left Mac and the Ames boys with a rider each and a pack mule.

TROUBLE

It was mid-afternoon when we pulled out on our ole hay burners. Justin Jenkins was hot to trot but I knew that was a good way to run head first into a rifle slug. These ole boys must suspect someone would be following them or they are naive.

We stayed on the horse tracks raising some dust of our own as we slowly loped along and ole JJ moved to where he could see if anyone was setting a trap for us. Our movements were erratic but deliberate as we followed them into the next canyon.

Those boys had not given up on their pursuit of evil and were looking for another miner's dig. This is the canyon where we got our start a few weeks ago. And the gold just flat ran out on us. Very slowly, with our horseflesh in tow, we scrambled from one rock to another, always moving higher and higher above the valley floor.

No way did we want this group of bad men to end up above us and be looking down on our little surprise party. We almost made that mistake for they had a man higher up in the rocks a waiting for us. His mistake was he was still moving and JJ spotted him. We altered our course and got above him. The problem was it was just about dark by then. Justin asked "what we gonna do about that man English?"

"JJ when it gets pitch dark and before the moon shines into the canyon I'm gonna slip down there slow and easy like and take him out of the picture. These bad characters need a good throttling and sent home with their tails tucked between their legs and we're going to do it to them before we call it a day."

The moon was already up when the sun dragged all the daylight off to the west and out of sight. That's when I moved out of my hiding place and in slow motion made my way in the darkness toward their lookout down below us.

I'd soon call on all my experience with a knife and make this man pay for all the men he has done in. This ole dude knew about where the man was and I sought him out. Once I located him I took my time and eased up on him. A man long ago showed me where to stick the knife to cause instant death and the man would never make a sound.

This was not an easy chore for me. This was the second man that needed killing in the last day or so. I didn't like it one darn bit but I didn't want to end up like those miners did. To these guys killing had become a way of life. Big Mac warned me time and time again to think on what I did with a gun and a knife. It's all too easy to condone killing in our minds and that becomes a trap.

"This kid remembers what God said in His word. 'Know to do right and do it not that is sin.'" So I struggle with what was right in this situation as my knife did its work. Could I let these men continue to murder folks? "Lord, I hope this man has no family waiting for him back home like a wife and small kids."

The man never made a sound and died on his feet. As I lowered him to the ground I said barely audible "I'm sorry sir and Jesus please forgive me."

Sounding like the western quail that lived in this area I whistled to Justin and it wasn't long and he came moseying on in. In a whisper he said, "I see you got him, what shall we do now?"

"We'll wait until the moon lights up the canyon floor and then we'll take his weapons and move on down there and see what's what. We must somehow put these outlaws out of commission right here. At this point I have no thoughts on how that can be accomplished." When the moon displayed its light on the valley floor we eased on out of here and made our way downhill toward that old cabin. That was the logical place for them to hold up for the night. It put a good roof over their heads.

There was only one way out of there so we planned to wait across the creek for them to come outside to relieve their dead friend in the morning then take as many of them dudes out at one time as we possibly can. Then reload these long guns as fast as we can. If they rushed us we have our revolver and the dead man's rifle to fall back on.

There might be one bug-a-boo in our plan, if they got wind of us before hand. If they found the dead guard that would alert them to our presence here. Those rotten renegades must suspect we would be looking for them. Thinking on our plan I was nervous that our horses were so far away so I sent JJ. to bring them in. If we needed them in a hurry I wanted them close by, without them at our side we could be in a mighty big pickle.

Jenkins no sooner got back with the horses then the alarm went out that the first night guard hadn't come in and must be asleep or been killed. Right then we got our chance, for they were milling around the front door of the cabin.

Justin in his excitement jumped the gun and shot before I was ready. They didn't retreat into the cabin but in nothing flat scattered in all direction. I did hit my man on the run as, JJ grabbed up the outlaw's rifle and fired again and missed.

That little maneuver of theirs didn't surprise me at all, but it sure enough wasn't what we wanted. We would have preferred that they ducked back into the cabin. Now we would have to ferret them out of the rocks and that could be dangerous for both of us. Rather than dog their tracks and have them wait in hiding for us, I think we'll let them come looking for us, it would sure be safer for us. That is if they want to take that chance.

The rest of this crummy operation needed to be played out by ear, and then we will see how it goes. At least they didn't rush us right off the bat. A good rush would have made us resort to our revolver at close range and them with their long guns still loaded. They could fire the long rifles way before they came into handgun range. My guess is they weren't sure how many there were of us and how many rifles we had.

We'd misjudged their number with two dead in front of the cabin and one up the hill they still had four men ready to fight or flee. As soon as they fled to better cover we left our ambush spot and moved higher up into the rocks. As we traveled higher into the rocks, long gun slugs ricocheted off rocks and whined off into the distance, each time we made a move to a different location we heard lead finding a home off in the wasteland. It seemed that no one in that group down there were sharp shooters.

With long guns reloaded we settled into our new hiding spot and waited for something to develop. Justin Jenkins had his big fifty resting on the rock as he watched the goings on down below. Then without warning an orange flame and a thunderous roar exploded from JJ's rifle barrel, sending a large chunk of lead into the valley below. In the early light, dust jumped off a rock near an outlaw's head.

In the poor light we could barely make out their horses hid in the rocks and trees across the way. At this point we paid a lot more attention to their mounts thinking they would need the horses to make good their escape, which is if they were inclined to cut and run. Would they be more interested in getting us off their tails or making good their escape? Who knows what those murders will do for sure. Whatever they do we must be ready for it and anything that they might fling at us.

We didn't have to wait very long as horse and rider made a frantic dash for freedom. After grabbing leather the lone rider sank spurs deep into flesh and ran like a scared rabbit. The man lay over his horse's neck as he made a mad dash for freedom. JJ made his shot and sent a lead pill down there and hit the horse in full stride, he staggered as if he was exhausted, then stumbled and went down and disappeared in a swirling cloud of dust.

The last thing the Duck saw of the rider in the poor light was that he kicked free of his mount and ended up on the dead run until he disappeared behind several large rocks. That shot will make them think twice before they try that again.

The outlaws now had men in three different areas across the creek all bent on putting us out of business forever. With that thought in mind we moved higher and higher into the rocks above us hoping against hope they couldn't get above us.

For a brief moment we took in their strategy as they spread out on either side and started to flank us, moving upward. Their goal was to get behind us if they could, where they might look down on us. Our goal was to keep that from happening.

The horses worked hard to climb the steep grade. We located an excellent spot at the base of a cliff, with lots of cover to hold up in. It even had a trickle of water seeping out of the sheer rock wall. It was enough to water our horses and for us to drink from. We had plenty of food in the sacks hung on our saddles.

We set up a defensible spot and settled down to wait. We could still see the cabin front door and the horses out back, but the men were nowhere to be seen and that had me worried somewhat. They will make their move sometime soon and I had no idea where they were or when it would happen. This little surprise party wasn't going quite like we planned it when we first set it up.

I could feel that old London hatred rising up in me for these men on the dodge, and what they were doing to people. That feeling started to slip down deep into my soul and I didn't like it one darn bit. Harley MacDonald had shown me in the scriptures, when we were sailors on the high seas, that we should not hate the sinners, but like our God we needed to love the sinner and hate the sin that they commit.

Sometimes it's hard to keep the two separated, sin and sinner the two seemed to go hand in hand. These ole boys knew they weren't doing right, killing and robbing folks for profit for it is surely a sin. Right then I made a conscious decision to keep the two separated. I must stay faithful to my heart and God's Word. It would be easy to slip back into my old ways and become like these men we were after.

Big Mac also showed me that there is a punishment by God and by man for the evil things we do. Today we'll try to take care of man's part of it and it will be up to God to take care of the spiritual part. That's His business anyway; He knows the devious, deceitful and dishonest hearts of some men.

Harley says, "Hate for mankind has no place in a man's heart. For hatred is morally wrong in God's eyes. Love the man and hate the sin is His goal for us."

We got our little camp site organized and we didn't have to wait very long before they tried to dislodge us. They'd worked their way up through the rocks trying to get a bead on us. For an hour or longer they sniped at us and finally they began to ricochet bullets off the cliff overhang and they mortally wounded our mule.

As fast as we could we wrestled the other horses to the ground and tied their legs together to keep them from getting up, then hauled them out of the way of the rifle fire.

Somehow they sunk lead into another horse and he thrashed until Jenkins put a slug in his head. That left us with only one mount to work with but only for the moment as shot after shot caromed off the back wall and buried themselves into the dust and dirt nearby.

Together we pulled and tugged on that ole Cayuse and dragged him away from the danger area. Then set about systematically returning their fire. There wasn't much to shoot at for they weren't aiming at us but at the rock wall above and behind us and they were bouncing lead off it. The outlaws' lead was coming mighty close to us but not close enough to make us move. We snuggled in close to a good size rock at our rear and let them waste their ammunition. Before they give up on killing us they wounded our last nag in the hindquarters. It was about an inch deep and eighteen inches long.

For a half hour more we fought on, then they moved off the hill, mounted and rode away with every last horse in Cabin Creek Canyon. We took two long shots with our muzzleloaders and hit nothing but dirt. We didn't have horse one to follow them with so we set about fixing up our lone injured rider.

Someone said you could stop a wound from bleeding by heating a metal iron red hot and slapping it on the wound. It didn't sound all that reliable to me, but we tried it just the same and low and behold it worked.

The outlaws did a number on us in this little scrap we had with them. Today, might didn't make right and we were lucky to save our skins and one ole fur ball. Tomorrow will be another day and maybe then, right will be right like it should be.

Being defeated was hard to chew and harder to swallow. We would like to follow those dirty rotten scoundrels but we had no horseflesh to ride after them with. Those crooked snakes would probably put a lot of ground between themselves and this canyon before dark. There was no one else here for them to steal from.

We would take as much of this dead horse flesh with us as we could carry on this wounded nag and maybe come back for the rest with better horses. Horseflesh really tasted good. It has a sweet taste to it and that's a fact. Some folks called it Belgium moose meat, after the Belgium horse. I loved the taste. The cold creek water would keep it from spoiling.

We could make jerky out of it and smoke some of the meat for later on this year. Later on we could supplement it with venison or some other kind of game. We still had plenty of flour and canned goods to see us through the summer.

The wounded horse could walk with some difficulty and we loaded the meat on the front quarters then made our way downhill on our wounded horse always on the alert for trouble. Before we left we checked out the dead horse of the rider that tried to escape earlier, it had some mining equipment on it.

We made a mental note of what was still here and where it was. We stashed our saddles in the shack. Then took our lone horse by the reins and hit the trail for our home base. Jenkins walked to my left as I lead that big mare toward our mining camp.

I wondered to myself if the boys back at camp had found any gold in the creek or was this going to be a dry streambed void of any yellow metal. If worse came to worse and we didn't find anything in the next week or so we might try the valley of the dead miners, and see what we might dig up there.

As that old Chinaman once said, "A long trip starts by putting one foot in front of the other and we started back." My mind got to wandering all over the place, about my life and what was ahead of me, would I always be playing around in the cold water in these creeks and digging in the ground? "Lord, I sure hope not. This mining for gold is not what it's cracked up to be and I've got a hankering to get on with my life."

As it begun to get dark we stopped for the night. It wasn't very long and this Drake dude hit the feathers for the night. I was dog-tired and needed some sleep. Mr. Jenkins took the first watch while this ole dude slept. We kept a guard just in case those menacing snakes reared their ugly heads again and made another deadly strike at us. Without any more trouble we came into our little valley the next day foot sore and ready to soak them in the cold creek water. The guys were curious about what happened out there and we filled them in as best we could.

The next day Big Mac and I took our fresh mounts and returned to our old claim on what we now called Cabin Creek and worked on the horsemeat there. We needed to prepare the meat before it spoiled so we had horsemeat hung on every rock and bush to dry out. We salted the dickens out of it to help preserve it. In less than a week it was ready to take back to our camp. The jerky tasted good so we loaded it on the horses' back along with the miner's tools, supplies and set off for our home base. All the horses were loaded down with meat and things left behind by the killers. One ole girl we saved for riding. So Big Mac and I changed off, each of us riding for a spell.

Talk about tired feet this ole gander had some. They'd barely recovered from the last long walk and here I am at it again with many, many twinges of pain hindering me in my little stroll. This ole Englishman was putting blisters on top of sore blisters.

We saw neither hide, horns, hoofs nor hair of those murdering slime balls that are on the dodge. Not since they disappeared into the swirling dust over a week ago. Without a doubt they were out there somewhere doing their dirty work on someone.

This Harley was a man to ride the trails with and I've grown to trust and love him. Love, now that's a strange word and even stranger still was to experience someone that cared for you. All these guys cared for me. When you've never known love in all your life it is a new experience to treasure and keep.

These young men were real men who cared for each other and relied on each other. That little boat trip forced us to find someone we could trust and who thought alike. This kind of stuff is all new to me and if I've got it straight these ole boys are more than worthy of my trust.

This kind of thing gives me a whole new outlook on life. It's like some wonderful thing I've been looking for all my life and didn't know what it was. Once you've discovered it, it's like a great trophy that you didn't even know was out there and now it's all yours. Having the friendship of four good men means a lot to me. It helps me to understand why Jesus Christ did what he did for me way back when.

Our valley was just up ahead and it wasn't very long and we were watering our horses in the stream. As we moved into the canyon we saw other miners working the creek where we'd already worked it. We were going to tell them but they wouldn't let us anywhere near them or their digs. So we meandered on by both mounted on the one horse and plodded on toward our camp.

The guys were way upstream and hard at it, but they stopped as we rode in. Their guns were close at hand and ready for quick use. They took a break from their wet work and we unloaded the meat by the tent and sat around talking about the operation. My question was, "is this hole producing anything at all?"

The Ames boys were fed up with this place and were just waiting for us to return. Dick the oldest said "We've busted our butts and for what? We ain't taken out one little piece of gold yet and we got nigh on to three weeks of playing around in the cold water. We decided to just hit the spots that looked like they might hold the pot of gold and we worked like eager beavers and didn't pick up a trace of gold for our troubles yet. I thought of an old saying 'a bird in the hand is worth more than two in the bush.' Well we haven't even seen one bird yet.

"Mac, I think it's time to look for another place to dig. You must know summer is getting on to half gone and we need to get a decent stake. So we can get ready for winter."

We made the decision to split up and three would move into the next canyon, Dead Miners Canyon, and two of us would work on up this creek and continue to hit the likely spots. If we found nothing we'd joined them later on. Because they were all sick of digging in this stream and finding nothing, we all decided to let Dick, Tom and Justin work Dead Man's Canyon and see if there was some gold over there.

Once they took a notion to leave they took the gold, we'd already lifted from the water, with them and a whole bunch of Belgium moose meat. Everyone had all the meat they could pack out of here on their horses. There wasn't much room for their mining tools to take the ride over the ridge.

Big Mac and I just worked the good looking spots and headed upstream toward the high mountains. We were making about a half a mile or more a day. And like the other men we didn't lift a single piece of precious metal in more than two weeks.

Now I know why Dick and Tom were so discouraged it could get ya down real easy, if ya let it. This feather brain wasn't going to let anything get me down, if I could help it. Maybe I was only playing around in the water but this is the best life I've ever had and way down deep inside, this duck was enjoying it and the prospects of finding gold around the next bend in the creek, thrilled me.

But this ole kid also remembered what those Ames boys said "we're busting' our butts and for what." Like them I'd much rather be hauling gold out of this streambed by the pans full. But somehow I don't think it's going to happen.

It wasn't but four more days and we were up against a sheer rock wall and our creek became a waterfalls. We back tracked ourselves and finally found a way up on top with our horses. Right away we found a little color, not much but a little. It wasn't anywhere near a bonanza but it kept us interested.

The problem we were having was it was a funny looking color and we wondered if it was any good. It was heavy and soft so we were sure it was gold. At this point we began to work the entire streambed with some success. I got to say this about Big Mac he was a hard worker and a great motivator for me. No way was I going to let him dig out more gold than I did, so we both moved a lot of gravel in our little game.

Every once in a while we hit a good pocket and loaded up a small change purse. There was one spot behind a big ole rock, which made a small dam across the creek bottom; we took out many small bits and pieces of this yellowish, pinkish stuff and one good size nugget.

We came to a fork in the stream, the right tributary gave forth no gold at all for a hundred yards so we worked our way up the left hand side of the brook and the gold nuggets got some what bigger the further we went upstream.

It wasn't long and we thought of putting our full sack in a bank so we buried it in a dirt bank a short way away from the creek by a large rock that had tumbled down from above.

We worked that stream for all it was worth and buried two more bags in two different banks by the stream. We did it just in case some money hungry galoots came looking for what we had lifted from the stream. This tributary and valley we called Falls Creek.

By naming the streams and canyons we could keep them straight in our minds. Our original dig was over on Cabin Creek, the place of our first claim. The next valley over the divide where Justin Jenkins, Tom and Dick Ames were we called it Dead Miners' Creek.

We wanted the other guys that we loved to share in this harvest so we decided to take a couple of days off and look for our three sidekicks and see if they were having any luck at Dead Miners' Creek. This ole duck was kind of anxious to see the guys again; I'd gotten use to having them around and I wanted to see them again. We left our gold where it was hidden and we headed downstream to the spot where I'd crossed over the divide a month or so ago. I knew the way we should go by heart so I followed my old tracks down to the canyon floor. Everything went like clockwork.

We rode into the area where their camp should be and they were not there. They'd pulled up stakes and moved upstream about a mile and were also pulling small amounts of precious metal out of the water. It wasn't near the amount we were getting out of Falls Creek but after the dry spell they went through them boys were happy to see some fruit for their labor.

We spent the next couple of days together and worked their claim with them. After that Mac and I decided to meander back up to our place of business and go back to work. In vain we tried to get Dick and Tom Ames to go with us.

Those boys were satisfied with what they were gleaning from their streambed. Dick said a bird in the hand is worth two in the bush any day of the week and twice on Sunday. We spent half a day trying to convince them to go with us to no avail. They were satisfied with what they were pulling from the knee deep water.

JJ, after much persuading was convinced and decided to throw in with us. As we were putting the seats of our pants in leather to leave, Dick Ames said, "You know if you leave now you will forfeit all the gold we have stashed away." I felt kind of sorry for those boys; Dick was trying to use the gold as a leverage to make us stay on as a group and I liked that about him. He truly did want us to stay together.

He didn't want to see the group break up any more than I did, but he wasn't willing to pull up stakes and come with us to see what we were pulling from our creek. We made one more plea for them to come to no avail. Then Tom said, "If you hold out over there when and if this place plays out we'll come up and give you guys a hand."

"Tom if you want to we'll split everything the five of us dig out of the ground or these creek beds. For we love you guys and want the best for you."

Dick Ames said "You keep what you get and we'll do the same and English we hope you guys do well over there. Keep your powder dry boys and we hope to see ya one day soon."

I guess that made it final, for me the friendship ring was broken and we went our separate ways. This was mighty hard on me. I didn't have that many friends that I could just discard two like that. My hope is that it wasn't broken but only bent a little. Maybe we could get back together when the gold fever had run its course.

Dick and Tom were good men and hard workers although they had some doubts when we told them of our find and the odd color of our strike. They wanted to see our gold that we'd buried in our banks. They weren't all that sure it was really gold.

We tried to fess up and tell it as we saw it and we didn't 'beat around the bush' and we didn't back pedal one iota. They needed to know we had a much better claim than they did. All they could see was what was right in front of them. The saying often came from their mouths "a bird in the hand is worth two in the bush." They'd often say "give me what I can see over what I can't see any day of the week and twice on Sunday." There was no headway in talking to these two boys. Dick had his mind made up and nothing was going to change it. I had this feeling down deep in my bones that our close friendship was out the window. I'd never thought that this day would ever come when we would split up and go our separate ways. It's a sad thing and it hurts me deeply.

It's like Dick said to us before we left, "I really hope you boys do well in all you put your hands to." My prayer for the Ames boys is that they receive the same thing many times over for what they wished for us. I still have a lot of affection for those two young men.

HEADED BACK

At this point in our trip home I had to guide my horse and not think about the separation that had just took place. Our mounts were scrambling up the steep grade so my mind became focused on that and away from our old friends back at their camp below. From the top of the divide I got a bird's eye view of their whole operation far below.

As I rode higher my two brother friends disappeared from my sight but no way were they forgotten. In my guts it felt like they had died. That is a feeling I don't want to lug around with me for very long. The rain hid my tears from Mac and JJ as we descended into our valley making muddy horse tracks in the slippery California mud. As we descended the mountain grade a lump came into my throat and my thoughts caused tiny tears to form in my eyes. As the horses worked their way down the steep rocky slope on the other side of the divide, all I could hear was the squeak of saddle leather and the thud of horses' hooves hitting the soft ground and stones.

This is the first time since I've been saved I wanted to swear out loud. With effort this fretting dude held it in and didn't offend his Lord. To let off some frustration I jerked my revolver and shot a small tree dead center and that helped for a moment. The looks I got were hard as I let out a full burst of air and let a long loud scream echo down the valley.

Dark thick clouds came rolling in and it looked like rain would soon be moving up the draw. The south wind pushed the clouds past us and on up the valley. Visibility was nigh on to nothing and rain started to come in torrents and in an instant I was sopping wet. This squirrelly duck stopped his nag and pulled loose his slicker from the bedroll and wore it as we made our way toward camp.

The horses' footing got awfully bad really quick and we had to unload leather and walk with our horses as they scrambled to keep their footing under them. After a bit we were at the foot of the waterfalls. Now all we could hear was the falls and the thunder that rolled up the valley toward us and the hard hitting rain as it pounded the outside of our slickers. The mud was sticky and stuck to our shoes and they were getting heavy to lift as we plodded on.

Our camp was not as we'd left it, someone was using our tent for their home. The white tent looked like a big lantern as the light inside made it glow. We only used the lamp at night when we cooked. These people, whoever they were, were wasting our fuel. As we surveyed the camp area we saw no horses, mules or donkeys. We wondered why anyone would just move into our tent unless they thought we were dead.

With frontier courtesy we hailed the camp and then again "hello the camp" Instantly the light went out and Big Mac in a loud booming voice said, "You're in our tent and we need it to get in out of the rain."

Someone inside said "it was your tent, it's now ours. You left it and moved away and possession is nine tenths of the law."

"Maybe but not where we came from so if you don't come out quickly we will come in there and throw ya out or shoot that tent full of holes. Which we don't want to do." We didn't think this was all that funny, anyway you looked at it.

With a lot of moaning and grumbling out they came. There were four of them and in the bad light they looked a little bit like the killers that were giving us a bad time a few weeks ago. Softly I said, "Watch them close Mr. Jenkins they look like trouble to me." I eyed them with my pistol light in my holster and my rifle fully cocked and cradled in my arm. The three of us spread out and got ready for any kind of trouble they might send our way.

From the lighted tent into the darkness they were blind as a bat for a moment or two. We could see very little in the dark night. Having the drop on them they changed their tune in a mighty big hurry. Those boys had no idea how many there were of us and that made all the difference in the world. Harley commanded them to drop their weapons. Reluctantly they laid them on the muddy ground. His first question was, "what are you boys doing up here in our tent? We just got back from our digs empty handed and you are in our tent using up our coal oil. What ya got to say for yourselves."

"Mister, we were working this stream and we came across this empty camp and it started to rain so we just moved inside to stay dry, we're sorry sir. We have a tent of our own, may we set it up right here in your camp for protection. We've heard there are some claim jumpers working this area and with two outfits camped together they are less apt to try to do us in."

"Sir, we don't want you even in the same area with us. Just in case we do discover something we don't want anyone knowing our business. So get your horses and hit the trail on out of here. Arthur will you and Justin unload their weapons before they leave?"

We fired all their single shot muzzle loading rifles into the air and handed them back to them. "You understand why we are unloading your guns don't you? It's like you said, 'ya can't trust anyone out here.'" They climbed aboard their mounts and headed for the falls in the distance. This ole boy mounted up and followed them until they dropped below the top of the falls.

This English dude sat his horse in the pouring down rain for the better part of two hours watching as lighting lit up the night sky and this ole boy kept watch to see if they would return. Being soaked to the skin I was also chilled to the bone. When the downpour slowed to a slight drizzle, I stayed where I was and watched for the men that had disappeared into the valley below.

This wet to the skin kid was worn out and was lulled by the slight breeze that stirred the pine trees, the thundering waterfalls and the stream close by. The near total darkness, the rocks and the trees gave forth an ominous sight to see in the canyon below and all around me.

This English kid stayed on horseback in the shadow of a lightning struck pine tree and waited for the coming of the new day. The dark rain clouds had dissipated and grayness started spreading across the eastern sky. Soon it would be dawn and later the sun would light up the sky. We had the promise of another beautiful day.

Soon the sun began to peek through the rain clouds, the pine trees and spread its light across the mountain peaks. As I sat my horse I watched a Mountain Jay fly from tree to tree. A ringing sound came to my ears from the horse below and

I heard echoes off the rocks, started by horseshoes striking a stone on the trail below. Instantly this ole dude was fully alert to all that moved on this mountain side.

My rifle came loose from its resting place and rested across the front of the saddle. I quickly looked down to check the nipple on the rifle to see that it had a percussion cap squarely in place. I sure hoped the caps on my weapons would fire when they were needed. The revolver was ready to go and I unhooked the thong that held it in place. I made sure that the rain water wouldn't hinder the weapons.

The sounds of horses were coming up the draw and ole English needed to hold the fort and keep them from gaining the heights. Then I heard another sharp ring and saw movement through the trees coming my way. As they came closer in the morning light this ole English dude saw that those down below were the men that killed the miners over the divide. Their number had grown to five again. There must be a big supply of bad men that want to ride the hoot owl trail.

I was high up on the trail that led to the top of the waterfalls and I was playing peek-a-boo down on them. They came out of the trees and started uphill. From cover I hollered down at them "hold it right there pilgrims." They stopped dead in their tracks and looked around searching for me. They were trying to locate me in the heavy cover on the hillside. Their eyes moved in my direction as I said "what you boys up to this morning?"

Still searching for my hiding place, the lead man said, "Were looking to mine this rivulet. We were working the water down below and we thought we'd try it up here for a spell.

"Aren't you the boys that we put out of our tent last night?" A sound came from behind me and now I was really worried. How did they out maneuver me and get in behind me. It was a horse and it was getting closer. I stayed as still as I could and strained ever instinct at my disposal to listen to their slow progress.

"Hey up there we don't know what you're talking about we're just a couple of miners looking for a strike. You got no need to be worried about us." When I didn't answer he started again. "Hey you up there what are your intentions?"

With them in front of me and someone coming up behind me, no way could I answer that question. I was the meat in the middle of a sandwich and I was about ready to be eaten alive.

"Hey up there, can we come up and talk face to face?"

Ole English just couldn't allow them to come up and couldn't say no with someone behind me. The horse at my rear was within fifty feet of me. Somehow I had to know who was back there, so ever so slowly I ducked down and turned my head and took a long peek and saw no one. I then dismounted as quietly as possible and moved through the underbrush toward the rider.

Yours truly saw two horses headed toward my position at a slow walk. First off I recognized Big Mac's big bay gelding and then Big Mac himself moving toward my position. Whew that situation had me going for a bit.

Right then the man down below said, "I don't think he's up there. Hey mister we're coming up, is that okay?"

The pause was long but I finally answered the outlaws questions "no sir, we don't want your kind hanging around here so get your things and skedaddle." Five horses had already started up the grade when I barked out "no sir,"

Someone down there said, "It's a free country and we'll go where we please."

"No Gentleman, I don't think so at least not tonight" My answer seemed to be the signal and five horses came up the grade on a dead run. The riders just a bouncing all over the place as the horses labored to make the steep climb up the soggy hillside.

They had six guns just a blazing a way at me as they came full bore up the hill. A big ole pine tree gave me some cover and protection from their wild shooting. That ole fifty caliber of mine barked once and the first man was flung from his saddle and trampled by his comrades as they worked those nags hard to get to me.

As the first man broke over the crest of the hill and his head turned back and forth while scanning the area and at ten yards my colt took the second outlaw out of his leather seat and set him on the cold wet ground. Then two more riders broke into view and two more shots sounded from behind me and made them disappear back over the lip of the hill.

Below by the stream the last man was in the middle of indecision, he was out of revolver range and he turned his horse and high tailed it away as fast as his mount could carry him. His horse raced away at a reckless pace until he was clean out of sight. Four men were on the ground dead from the impacted of the slugs that hit vitals parts. The impacted of heavy lead ripped holes into their bodies. These four dead men will not be bothering anyone else.

Those four boys had been bucking a stacked deck and ended up on the short end of the stick. The four dead outlaws' horses were up on top so I stayed in place for the time being and watched their back trail. After the last outlaw disappeared from view I saw nothing move except the gentle sway of pine branches as the soft wet breezes pulled and tugged on them.

Big Mac and Justin moved slowly toward my position as this big duck was reloading. The first words out of JJ's mouth were "did we get all of them? Did they all suck the mud, English?"

"All but one of those yellow dogs was dead. Those killers of men got what they deserved here tonight for their treachery. We need to be chasing down that last remaining outlaw, before he gets the gang to working again."

At this point JJ and I took up the chase, "we'll see ya later Harley we've got to catch that last man before he start this all over again." I gigged my horse in the flanks and eased him over the lip of the hill and started downward at a rather slow pace at first. The horses were plowing deep furrows in the soggy soil as downhill we went.

When we hit the bottom of the grade by the creek the horses stretched out and we covered some ground in a hurry. The drums of Justin's horse hooves were close behind me as we followed our prey downstream. We dare not let this man get away and maybe start his dirty business all over again.

We may expend considerable effort to catch him but catch him we will. As Harley often says "we ain't horsing around here today." Then he'd smile. The man ahead of us was riding dangerously downhill ahead of us. The sound of his horse's hooves echoed up the ravine as hooves struck stone. The man was moving quite fast as he rode like a bat out of Hades. We tried to keep pace but this man rode like a maniac. The speed he rode was outrageous. If we didn't catch up with him soon he would prob'ly kill himself or his horse in his wild dash for freedom.

We slowed our mounts to an easy gallop but kept up the chase just a dogging his heels. Could he keep up this outrageous pace for long? I don't think so it's a mighty iffy deal if you ask me. As it got lighter out the rain came in buckets again and we were wet to the skin and chilled to the bone.

He crossed the stream three times as he wound his way down through the narrow gorge and out on to somewhat leveler ground. His horse tracks in the muddy dirt were deep after the hard rain and it was easy to follow him. As we gave chase we'd passed two miners' camps at the lower end of the canyon. He'd stopped at the third for a moment and took off like a scalded dog as we drew near.

Four miners came out and blocked the way. They were pointing their guns our way as we pulled to a stop in front of them. "What are you fellers doing chasing that man?"

"Well `sir that no good scoundrel is a murderer of many men and we are going to run him down and kill him if at all possible. That man needs killing really bad. He's killed at least three men that we know of and tried to do us in this morning. You've got to let us go mister for we can't afford to let that scoundrel break free.

He dodged the bullets this morning but we can't let him do it again, he might start up his business a second time. Are you gentlemen ready to except the responsibility for letting him go? Earlier today we shot up his gang and now we need to finish it up once and for all or deal with him from now on. Well sir what's on your mind, are you going to let him get away and maybe kill some more folks or what."

"No English if he's as bad as you say he is, well go ahead have at him."

We left that little valley at an easy lope hoping to conserve our four-legged transportation and eat up a lot of landscape in the process. The man ahead of us was pushing his little horse way to hard and we could see its faltering tracks in the soft soil. Our slower pace left our horses with a lot more stamina and we were now closing the gap between him and us. His mount was giving him all he had, but he had worked his little mount way too hard to get clear of us in this chase.

We could see him now and he saw us and with passion this man was a flogging his pony again to get all he could from him. He was heading for some large rocks in the distance. We mustn't allow him to make the shelter of that rock piles below; if he did he might break free.

This old dude yelled as loud as he could at ole JJ. "Justin keep pushing him at the same speed. I will follow you at a normal pace. As we rode on in the mud I could see the outlaw's mount had missed a stride, stumbled, staggered, but righted itself and ran on. A moment later off in the distance his mount went down in a heap in the mud. The rider got clear of that mess of flailing legs and hooves and hustled on back to his horse and what little protection it would afford him in the gun battle to come.

The man's well-lathered mount floundered in the mud as he struggled to regain his footing in the soft soil. It then laid quietly for a spell. All that tired looking brute got for all his hard work was a bullet in the brain. The poor ole hay burner gave him all he had and in the end found rest.

As I pulled to a stop and watched this take place I could hear and see Jenkins ride up to me and stop. "Well English, how we going to work this deal out?"

"We need to split up and one of us work around until we can get a better shot at him. JJ don't get to close to him, just use your head and we will get him. If we send enough lead his way we are bound to sink some into his mangy carcass."

"Okay English, you go left and I'll go right. Arthur as you proceed use your horse for a shield. We don't want this guy to get lucky with a long shot."

The sky had cleared up and the sun was bright without a cloud in the sky, soon the moisture would be sucked out of the soil and it would start to dry up. Now all we had to do was take care of this gent once and for all. I didn't like this for it felt like murder to me but we had to put an end to all his dirty work.

JJ and I moved in a semicircle until the outlaw became exposed to Justin and with systematic rifle fire, Mr. Jenkins did him in on the sixth reload. This man received an eye for an eye and death took him like all the men he'd help lay low in their graves.

Again we took what we could from his goodies and buried him in a shallow grave. My hope is that this is the end of it. I'm getting mighty sick of the goings on around his camp. The three of us needed to spend all our time mining for gold in Falls Creek before winter sets in and we can't stand the freezing cold water any longer.

We made the long slow trip on our tired out nags back up into the valley and up to the falls. Along the way we picked up the outlaws' four packhorses loaded down with supplies and moved them up above the falls and tied them to a bush. Our uninvited guests had all kinds of mining equipment loaded on their pack animals and a tent that would come in handy to store our goods in. The big surprise was a good size sack of gold they'd picked up somewhere in their travels.

Big Mac had the riding horses tied up but hadn't laid one dead outlaw in the ground yet, so we had our work cut out for us. Those no good scoundrels had paid right through the nose for their mean, low down schemes. Someone has got to plant them boys in the ground and I guess we're elected to get it done.

In the morning we got right to it. JJ was in favor of just letting them rot where they lay but soon came around to my way of thinking so we got two shovels and a pick for the big job ahead of us. The rest of the day was wasted sticking them in the ground. We saved everything of value that they'd carried and kept it for our own. Now we had rifles and pistols aplenty, thirteen horses and all their equipment, saddles, pack saddles, bridles, halters, bedrolls, flour, bacon and lots of other food, dishes, shovels, mining pans and many other needful things.

One man had some fine cigars on his horse, a dozen of them and we savored them and made them last a good long while. Another man had stick candy; wow we were in seventh heaven with all this good stuff. Those boys knew how to live on their ill-gotten gains.

We put a cross made of limbs over every grave for now. We knew the names of every outlaw but one and the states they were from. Two were from right here in California.

Two of the men had mail from back east addressed to them at Los Angles wherever that is.

With considerable effort we took care of them and returned to our camp with all our booty. It was going to be a hassle taking care of that many nags this winter. Somehow we would need some hay or get rid of some of our livestock.

Higher up the creek about a half-mile was another falls and below it a half mile was a narrow place. We took some time to build a fence at the narrows and any place that might allow the horses to scramble up the sides. The sides of the canyon at this place were steep enough that the horses probably couldn't climb up out of there.

Now we had a small pasture for the horses until the snow came. It was the last of June and we still had July, August, September, October and on into November to work Falls Creek. In all that time we saw only four miners. They were working the creek below us that we'd already lifted the gold from. It wasn't long and they pulled out for I'm sure they got discouraged and left for greener pastures.

Dick and Tom Ames hadn't been heard from in all this time so I hoped they were doing well, no matter where they went or what they did. The three of us had lifted plenty of that heavy metal from Falls Creek and had gold stashed in spots all along the creek banks. We decided to put it all in one area before we lost track of some of our hiding places.

The nights were getting colder and we started thinking about a warm place to spend the cold months ahead. The little shack of ours captured our thoughts, but we needed some supplies to get us through the long hard winter months ahead. So lock stock and barrel we moved back into that little shack on Cabin Creek. Someone else had stayed in the small house for a spell occupying it while we were gone.

We had all kinds of mining equipment we'd taken off the killers, plus we sorted through our stash of gold and took out the smallest pieces to take with us. We didn't want anyone thinking we'd struck it rich out here in the Sierra Nevada gold fields. Harley MacDonald and Justin Jenkins would take the extra horses and mining equipment along with them and trade for food and whatever we needed. Some of the better horses would be used to pack the supplies back up here. The poorer quality horses we would sell in town if there was a market for them.

Harley and JJ would use only the minuscule bits of gold in their pouch to buy supplies with if they needed them. Gold didn't buy much in a gold camp. But things like food, mining equipment and horses really brought a good price. Horses up here in the winter could also be used for food if things got really bad. Big Mac had a way to get the most out of people for what he had to trade. In England we would have called him a wheeler-dealer. For sure he was a good trader and would get the wherewithal from our things to stock our food cupboard for the winter. The snow and cold could make this a mighty long winter up here.

After we got settled in we rested for the remainder of the day and early the following day my friends left for a small place called Buck Shot Creek Camp, a small mining settlement to the north to buy our winter supplies. It was about fifty miles as a crow flies to get there, but up and down and around the hills made it a longer trip, then if they were on level ground.

My job was to guard our camp and keep it safe until they returned. The cabin was ours, it was on our worked out claim; we'd won it last spring in that card game. But claim jumpers were all over the place looking to steal whatever they could.

Many would want the cabin for the winter if they knew about it. And out here possession is nine points of the law. Plus out here the saying was always true, "that might makes right." I'd found that out for myself a long time ago.

Bright and early the next morning they were ready to roll on out of here, we said our goodbyes and they rattled their hocks downhill. The dust swirled up around their horses and they disappeared in that small dust cloud. Soon even the sun lit dust that followed them faded into the distance.

Mr. Quack, Quack was left all alone with a whole bunch of armament to defend himself. I had to hold down the small log and stone fort until their returned. I was on my own without anyone to talk to in a wild and woolly land. It hadn't been long at all and they'd gotten clean out of sight.

As I watched that happened a lonesome feeling took control of me. To get through it I started to clean the cabin and reload all the weapon and sang those kid's songs that Harley taught me, like Jesus Loves Me and the B-I-B-L-E. It wasn't very long and this ole boy had his joy back and was I ever in a good mood. What still bothered me were those English ships which I thought I saw last night.

In the coal blackness of the valley floor I saw coal oil lights again and I could make out folks walking around down there. For a moment I thought I could still make out a prairie schooner in the mountains and that was plum foolishness. As I watched I thought I could see what looked like a covered wagon but up this high it was pure nonsense. Was I going out of my mind, that scene really seemed peculiar to me.

I started downhill to see if I was losing my mind or not. At a safe distance I hailed their camp and several folks came out to see who was out this early and calling out to them. I got a real shock for there must have been close to a dozen young folks looking my way. They had a Ma and Paw with them

I could smell food on the fire and did it ever smell good. I wondered if these folks knew anything about panning for gold or if they were as green as we were when we first landed here in California. They were up here in the mountains way too late to do much mining for gold. They hailed me in, so I went closer to their camp and introduced myself. They fed me and we talked about mining for quite a spell.

They were setting up camp so I didn't stay very long. I had things to do back at the cabin, so I said goodbye and headed uphill toward home. I worked around the place until it began to get dark.

AN ADVENTURE

In the late afternoon just before dark it started to snow and snow hard in the high country. Here at the cabin we got our share of those white flakes and the ground and trees were covered with a beautiful white blanket of snow.

The very next morning early when I checked on the livestock one of the horses the guys had left with me was missing. The missing mount was a fairly good gelding so I needed to go look for him. You could still see the faint signs of his hoof prints in the ankle deep snow. The gelding's prints had nearly filled in with new snow that came after he got loose and started uphill. He was headed for higher ground.

I took time to get my belly full, packed a light lunch and started uphill in pursuit of the runaway horse. After a mile or so I begin to wish I'd rode one of the other horses up here, the ground was slippery with the new snow. At times on the steep grade I'd slipped and slid all over the place. It put a lot of meaning to the phrase 'two steps forward and one step back.' That seemed what I was up against as I struggled uphill after the gelding. Off in the distance you could hear a pack of wolves howling to one another. The woods seemed to be alive with activity this morning.

Chickadees were on the move flying from one tree to another and a couple of Mountain Jays were making their racket as they were upset with my presence. They didn't want me here and I wished I were down below by a nice warm fire.

A fresh set of deer tracks in the new snow crossed the horse's path that I followed. Without a doubt it was headed for its bedding down place to spend the day resting. I'd keep that information stored away in the back of my mind for when we needed deer meat for food. I'd grown fond of venison since arriving here in California. Back in England I never got a chance to taste it.

The wind was quite still this morning; the temperature was just below the freezing mark and the snow made the world look new and fresh. The white stuff sparkled like a million diamonds as the late morning sun reflected off it. It was good to be alive here in the Mountains of California. This life was oh so much better than what I knew back in England or on that ship.

The snow got deeper as I struggled higher and higher up the mountain side. We'd got about a foot of pretty white snow up here and the pine limbs were heavy with snow. The tracks in the snow were getting harder to see in the winter white stuff. You could see where the horse had stopped in his upwards progress to paw the snow and feed on some dead grass and then moved on.

Twenty minutes later I stopped and studied the prints for right on top of the Geldings tracks were the biggest bear tracks I'd ever seen. I'd seen black bear tracks a few times but never the prints of a big ole grizzly. Those tracks were humungous in the snow. Should I return to the cabin and forget all about the nag that I followed? The horse would probably come back on his own later on today if he could.

In my mind the cabin seemed nice and cozy as I thought of the warm fire that still gave off plenty of heat down there. The big bear must be twice the size of a black bear and that was hard to comprehend. Up the trail fifty feet to my surprise a smaller bear track joined in the pursuit. Did a big black bear join in this deadly game or was it an offspring of a sow grizzly. I'd heard some outlandish things about the mighty brown beast that roamed the west raising havoc and all out war on unsuspecting settlers and trappers.

This ole English kid wasn't worried all that much for he had his trusty fifty-caliber Hawkins rifle with him and that would put anything down. All this dude really needed to do was get his rifle sites on it and that would be the end of Mrs. Grizzly bear. But what about that half grown cub with her, was it a threat to me? With only one shot in my muzzle loading rifle maybe that wouldn't be enough to bag them both. If not I felt my revolver would be the equalizer.

If I got that hairy lady in the sights of my rifle she wouldn't be bothering anyone else ever again. I was just hoping the big bear didn't put an end to the gelding's life. From this point on this ole gander must be very careful or he could become bear dung himself. These she bears were whacky sometimes and very, very dangerous with a cub at their side.

The first man that told me about the grizzly said he was told when he first came out here that 'when you're in the mountains you should wear small bells on the fringes of your coat, that way as you walked the bear could hear you coming and have a chance to get away. He went on to say that when you're in the mountains you should always keep your eye pealed for bear signs. Black bears would leave small piles of dung in the area that they traveled in and grizzlies would have larger piles with little bells in it' and then he laughed hard. He sure had my ear for a moment or two.

Pilgrims always got the who-rawing and joking around thrown at them, mostly in good fun. These mountain men thought it was their sworn duty to kid around with greenhorns. Well I for one liked their good humor.

Following the tracks in the snow I could see where all three animals began to run. Two were pursuing their meal and one was running for its life. I feared for that horse of ours. A little over a mile further up the trail, I stopped, then slowly stalked the bear and scanned the area ahead. After a bit I could see the dead horse and the two grizzlies, through the trees. The bears were feasting on the dead carcass. Well there is no way to save the gelding now but I must not allow the bears to do this again.

Once they feasted on horseflesh they would be looking for an opportunity to do it again and again. Horses would be easier to kill if they were tied outdoors somewhere. The bears just might start hanging around the cabin and causing us all kinds of trouble. No it must end right here and now or we could be in danger later on.

I looked for and found a good shooting position where I could see the outdoor banquet taking place through a small open place in the pine needles. I took my time and sucked in a deep breath, let some air out and squeezed off a shot. The female backed up a step or two upon impact, she then rose up on her hind legs and looked right at me.

A twig of a tree along the predetermined route of the slug had deflected it and changed its course. The wounded bear wasn't all that bad off. Now this ole boy was worried as he hurried to reload the fifty calibers Hawkins. With that wayward shot I'd made, what kind of a pickle did I get myself into? With one eye on the big bear and one on what I was doing, I worked franticly in preparing for whatever the bear would do next.

I had the required amount of gunpowder in the Hawkins barrel when she headed my way on the dead run. Thank God there was a good size pine tree right behind me. This ole dude tried desperately to carry that long rifle up the tree with him but it didn't work out for me and I had to leave the long rifle behind me at the base of the tree.

This kid was a bit nervous without the rifle but I did have my sidearm in my holster. My upward movement was a bit too slow to suit me. There were way too many limbs and they hindered my upward progress. As this ole gander climbed higher he watched that big bear circle at the base of the tree and then she commenced to follow this ole dude up the tree. Did you ever see a duck and a bear in a tree at the same time? I wish I hadn't.

With that wound I gave her and all the limbs she was slowed more than I was. I found a place to rest and reached for my revolver and quickly took a shot. The lead went through the limb just above her head. The slug did hit her in the skull but seemed to only bounce off her forehead. It only seemed to make her a little madder and added fuel to that fire I'd already started. That's when the worst thing you could think of happened to me.

This ole greenhorn lost his revolver as he started upwards again. I looked down and watched it as it caromed from branch to branch as it bounced its way down the tree. Now I really begin to worry as that bear kept following me upwards.

When is this surprise party going to end? Oh how I wish I'd headed for home while I still had the chance. The way the duck was breathing and his heart was beating he knew he was in big trouble. A while back I was told by a mountain man to exercise great care when pursuing the great grizzly. He said "haste makes waste." Well English was paying for all the haste that was in that shot, at mama grizzly.

Quickly I searched through my pockets and found my folded up jackknife. This was my last line of defense in my struggle to stay alive. The knife was one I'd taken off those dead bushwhackers earlier this year. It was a good one and I was mighty glad to have it on me today. I snaked that blade out and got ready to make a last ditch line of defense for my life. When she got close to me I stuck her in the paw and she made a squeal and a grunt at the same time. The deep cut only seemed to make her angrier.

Where I put the blade into her paw I could see blood seeping from the knife wound and the wound in her left shoulder spilled blood down the tree, as she watched me. With that rifle slug in the shoulder she was hurtin' for certain. The big right paw made a pass at me but only dug pine bark off a tree limb and missed by a whisker. In the process I'd made another cut in her paw as it went on by. For a moment she just looked at me as if to say what did you do that for.

I looked her right in the eye and asked that dangerous beast point blank "have you had enough?" She growled, so I said, "Suit yourself." Her hostility started popping out of her all over the place. I was close enough to look into her eyes and smell her breath and it didn't smell good. Then the battle moved into a constant thing her trying to get me and me trying to keep her at bay. It would only take one good swat with either paw and Ole English would be done for so I needed to fight her wisely.

All of a sudden right in the midsts of our fast and furious battle she stopped to listen, that's when I heard it too. The wolves I'd heard earlier were a whole lot closer and maybe moving in on that carcass where the half grown cub was feasting.

The grizzly looked at me and she looked like she was ready to leave. Truly she looked anxious as she climbed down the tree trunk. That lady was falling more than climbing as she descended the great pine tree. Once she reached the ground she took off full bore for the dead horse and her cub. I guess this duck dinner wasn't as important to her as I once was.

With one eye on the bear and one on what I was doing I followed suit, sliding and climbing down that tree as fast as I could go. On the ground I retrieved my revolver and long gun and nervously slid a slug into the barrel and rammed it home. Placed a percussion cap on the nipple and got ready to fire at that big brown beast. But before I could fire the wolves came on the scene circling the two bears and the dead horse.

The mama grizzly was not going to give up on the horsemeat that easily, but the circle around her got smaller and smaller until they could bite her on the flanks. They were making her day a most miserable one. As she chased off one wolf another one would chew on her backside. The cub rose up on its hind legs and watched its mother fight for all she was worth to save her kill and her half grown cub.

The wolves were relentless in their attack, attacking from all sides biting her and the cub. You could see the rifle wound was hindering her in her struggle against overwhelming odds. These wolves were mighty rough customers and their greed and hunger had forced them to invite themselves to the bears' banquet on the mountain.

She'd slowed noticeably in the war with the wolves and she finally gave up and retreated to the kill and the half grown cub and stood guard over them. The wolves weren't satisfied with this and continued to pursue her and her offspring. The pack of wolves looked like they weren't ready to give up on this giant meal they'd invited themselves to.

With the stabbed and bloody paw she connected with the leader of the wolf pack and rolled him head over heels in the snow. He got up slowly, staggered for a little bit then rejoined the pack in hassling the huge bears. All the time the other wolves kept up the constant harassment, biting her when her back was turned and confronting her and trying to lead her further away from the carcass.

Reluctant to leave her kill she'd always came back to the kill and her cub. I guess she thought she had first dibs on the horsemeat for she'd staked her claims first and wasn't about to give it up to these wild dogs to finish off.

Thinking her cub was in danger she cornered one wolf and got a mouth full of fur and dog meat, then hooked it and tossed it through the air. It hit a tree and lay stunned for a long moment. Then it commenced to slink off through the trees. The mama bear pursued another wolf and killed it. There was blood all over the white snow from the hurt and dying of the dead animals.

With the cub at her side and after much mistreatment she ran off a ways and stood looking back at the wolves settling down to a feast. Maybe she'd gotten her fill before all the hubbub started. This big lady was a force to be reckoned with up here in the mountains. I know this ya needed to be on your toes or you'd lose them.

With all the troubles that had beset the big sow she'd lost interest or had forgotten all about me and ambled off into the woods. This hairy lady and her cub were a formidable adversary for any dumb fool that tried to track them. This ole boy had plans of his own and they didn't include chasing down a wounded grizzly bear.

Before this little shindig started I was full of confidence in my ability to do away with the big brown bear but now I wasn't so sure. If she caused any trouble down below at the cabin we'd have to handle it later when I had more help.

My eyes were on two different groups now as I holstered my revolver and hoisted my reloaded rifle and started off down the trail. I'd just gone a short ways, always watching my back trail and my blood was pumping at a faster rate of speed as I went shanks mare downhill away from the fight scene.

To tell you the truth I'd been rooting for the wolf pack. They'd at least got that big brown beast off me when I didn't have much hope. Where would I be if they hadn't come along when they did? I'd be deader than a doornail. Tomorrow I'd be one of those big piles of dung without bells.

The gray horse was dead and gone and at this point I didn't care all that much one way or another. But this little white duck was still alive and that was what this ole boy cared about. All the gold we dug out of the water isn't worth anything if you can't spend it or use it for good. "Lord, I thank you for all you did for me today."

This ole boy wasn't a wasting any time getting back to that little cabin down below. The snow down here is almost gone, just a patch here and there. Man-oh-man was I ever glad to be home again. The topsoil for the last half-mile was a soggy gumbo mess and it stuck pretty heavy to my boots. At the door of our little cabin the mud was about two inches thick on the lower half of my boots. I had to pull the heavy things off before I went inside. Man-oh-man they must of weighed a ton. At least they felt like it. ___

About ten o'clock the next morning down at the mouth of this little valley we called Cabin Creek Canyon, of all things I saw two covered wagons come rolling in, again. They looked like two nester families. Someone that had come out here looking for a good piece of land to settle on and got caught up in this gold fever that everyone was catching.

In my mind I was thinking about this stream and where the gold had ended so abruptly last spring. Could the mother lode be somewhere close to that spot, maybe uphill a bit? Was there really a vein of gold waiting for us somewhere up the hillside or was I off on another wild goose chase in my mind? Was this half baked kid barking up the wrong tree? I guess only time and hard work would tell that story.

With a horse and a few days of hard work the wood was piling up around the cabin and it looked like we had enough to rough in a log lean-to and to keep a fire going all winter long. Now came the hard work of chopping and splitting the wood for the stove. We needed sleeping quarters for the three of us and maybe the Ames boys if they showed up later on. My hope is that they will come in here and stay the winter with us. This place belongs as much to them as it does to us. Besides that those boys are good friends and a lot of company. I wish they were still working with us, but they made the decision to strike out on their own and we must honor that decision.

I took our biggest tent and set it up over the spot where I thought maybe the gold vein was; that way at least the folks down below wouldn't come nosing around that spot and find the mother lode before we had a chance to explore my idea.

The Firth's had come into Cabin Creek Canyon just before that bear incident and were still nosing around. At this point they weren't anywhere near the place where I want to try to locate a mother lode this winter. I watched them across the valley working along the upper canyon wall and ever little bit they'd stop and dig a hole or two then move on. I watched them work with interest in hopes that I would learn still more on this subject of finding the mother lode.

On Wednesday we got more snow in the late afternoon and night. In the middle of the night I got up to stoke up the fire. About then I felt I needed to hit the outhouse out behind the cabin. So ole English pulled on his boots and in his long johns made quick tracks in the snow to the outhouse. Man-oh-man was it ever cold outside tonight.

Our outside toilet wasn't built all that well. It was solid enough but the snow blew through the narrow cracks and ended up on the toilet seat and the floor. I took time to brush the seat off and sat down. Man-oh-man was that thing ever cold, but when you've got to go you gotta go. We always carried a cloth to finish the job up and tomorrow I'd wash it out and dry it, then use it the next day. This was repeated over and over again. That was the way it was done in the West.

This cold bottom gent was finishing up the outhouse job when he heard a noise outside, our two grizzly bears were raising a ruckus outside. I stood up and took a quick peek through the cracks in the toilet door and couldn't see all that much so I sat back down again. No sooner had that cold seat touched my backside then I heard another grunt and it wasn't me. Our horses had broken loose and took off like a big bird in a wind storm and I knew right off the bat that it was that dear ole friend of mine that had caused all the commotion outside. That old sow grizzly bear was at it again.

This cold and desperate dude peeked out again and saw that cub of hers coming my way sniffing out my tracks in the new snow. He ambled right up to the outhouse door. I could hear him sniffing as his nose touched the boards of the outhouse door. You can bet it didn't take me long to get the trap door buttoned up on my red long johns.

What was this Drake kid going to do now; they were between me and the house and me without a weapon of any kind, not even my trusty pocket knife. The cub stood up and pushed against the door and it shook on the leather hinges. I thought to myself what am I going to do now? This kid gathered himself up and yelled at the top of his voice trying to scare it off and that cuddly little critter did turn and run off about twenty feet. It stopped there and looked back at the toilet where I was shivering up a storm.

Bruce Drake

The bad part was that noise and the cub's quick start brought mama bear our way on the dead run. That rifle wound I'd given to her didn't seem to slow her down one iota. She passed her cub and come to a skidding stop in the snow. That ole gal was eager to protect her young one from all harm. The she bear checked her offspring, and then turned toward my hiding place inside the outhouse.

She sniffed all around this little building and came back to the door. I was trying to hide but I didn't fool that pair one darn bit. They knew ole English was in here and that big bear was remembering our little set to up in the mountain. She pushed on the corner and the outhouse and it twisted and moved about a foot. Then she put her weight into it and she almost tipped it over.

The only thing that kept it up right was I threw my weight at the high side and it settled back down on its base. Things were getting out of hand and there wasn't a darn thing I could do about it. This ole boy knew he was battling for his life and all the odds were against him.

Right now all I was trying to do was keep them from getting inside the outhouse with me. There just wasn't room enough in here for them and me. In my peril I had to smile, all they had to do was ask and I would have let them use it. Now they must wait their turn. All I needed to know was that they wanted to use the privy and I would have let them have at it. The way she was acting she must really have to go bad. I really hated an impatient bear to be giving me a hard time.

Those crazy thoughts came to a sudden and abrupt halt when she hit the door and it swung in on its hinges and pinned me behind the door. Through the cracks in the door

I saw her stick her head inside the outhouse. That's when the duck shoved as hard as he could and the door banged her in the skull and she couldn't get back outside fast enough. She ended up running into her cub and nearly knocked him over.

They sat in the snow looking back at this little shack that had just bit her. She didn't know whether to run or stay put. What she did do was lick her gunshot wound for a moment and sat down and watched with lots of curiosity. You could see her twist her head back and forth and from side to side in wonderment at what had just happened.

That little knock on the noggin didn't hurt her very much but it sure surprised the stuffing's out of her. I'm happy for the short reprieve it gave me. In the dim light I searched every nook and cranny and there was nothing in this little outhouse to make any kind of a defense with. It was just me and that hungry bear in hand to hand combat.

Right now I wasn't thinking about the terrible cold temperature that surrounded the toilet anymore. I was thinking how could I get loose from this little shack and get back inside that warm cabin where my rifle and a hot fire were waiting for me.

Mama bear was up and strolling my way again; that ole gal gave me the willies. She was cautious this time, looking in all directions as she ambled on back. I tried to get ready for the attack I knew was to come. A couple feet away she reared up on her hind feet and placed those big paws on the edge of the roof and pushed. The outhouse reared up on that side and promptly settled back to the ground.

It caught my big toe under the edge of the building but I managed to pull it loose. I felt the weight and the stinging hurt and I sucked in a deep breath and stifled a yell of pain. I'd no sooner let out a long breath then up it went again and moved in a spiral movement to the right and settled back down again. It was a short trip but an exciting one for me.

Mr. Duck was sure thankful for whoever built this ole outhouse; it was a piece of work to hold together with all this abuse the bear put upon it. It didn't seem to be falling apart like it would have if I'd put it together.

Then mama bear made a lunge and over the john went with its back side down, with the door looking skyward and me holding the door shut with my feet and legs, "Lord, what am I gonna do now?" I could see her a-looking at me where the dirt floor should have been. I quickly got down behind the seat where I'd just done my job.

The hole wasn't large enough for her to squeeze through; it was hardly big enough for her head to squeeze inside. She got her head through the hole and propelled the little shack through the snow, along the ground on its side. Ole English just went along for the short ride hoping the toilet wouldn't come apart and let her in.

She finally gave up on that little exercise and then dragged everything back toward the cabin trying to get her head loose. In her little exploit, she stepped in the sludge hole and sank in a good foot and that movement sprung her head lose from her outhouse trap.

That's when the waiting game started in earnest, the problem was those two had a nice warm fur coat to wear and my red long johns were letting in the cold. It wasn't long and my teeth were a chattering and I was shaking all over. That seemed to confuse her and she pricked her ears in curiosity.

As that ole mama bear came close she shoved her head back through that hole again and watched me scramble to stay out of her reach. Those teeth were large and demanded respect. You can bet your bottom dollar this feather brain gave her all the room he could.

That is when I put all I had into a screaming yell. It exploded from my mouth and scared the willies out of her. She couldn't get her head out of there fast enough and almost rolled on her back in her haste, trying to spring herself free and get shuck of that little outhouse. If this whole thing weren't so serious it would be funny. I tried to yell and scare her again but it didn't do the trick. This time that lady just stood there and watched me intently. This thing was going nowhere fast; she wasn't concerned in the least at how much noise I made.

Arthur my boy you are going to freeze to death out here if you don't get back into the house soon and soak up some of that heat from the fire. It didn't look like she was going anywhere soon and neither was I. My teeth had stopped chattering for a spell, but started again as she took another short break. This trapped English man checked the door above his head and moved it a little bit, great; it still swung on its boot sole hinges. If I needed to get out of here fast, I could.

A half hour went by as I lie there with my teeth chattering and my body shaking like a maple leaf in the wind. She finally got up and wandered away from my little home away from home. This ole ma Grizzly and that cub of hers were playing the waiting game with me and as cold as I was I couldn't play this game to much longer or I might freeze solid.

Peeking through the cracks this cold dude could barely make them out in the dark shadows of the trees. The bears were about the same distance to the front door of the cabin as I was, but that ole fur bag could run a whole lot faster than I could. That hairy ole girl would catch me before I could make it inside, if I tried such a fool hardy stunt.

I thought on it for a spell and formulated a plan of escape. First off I opened the door enough to stick my head up and peeked out. Then surveyed all the logs I had piled all around the yard and picked out the path I intended to travel. As my head came into view, they didn't move but looked my way intently.

Next I opened the door all the way and laid it against the inside wall and stood up. That's when the big bear stood up. I ducked back inside and she lay back down again. MMMM that's interesting so I did it again and she repeated her part also. We had a little game going on here, you might call it peek-a-boo or hide and seek, but I was tired of it already.

I had to try something soon or freeze to death out here. I smiled to myself as I thought of all the jokes told about me freezing to death in the john. I crouched down low and then stood on the front part of the seat which was now the top and pulled that door wide open. I then jumped out and raced as fast as I could go for the back corner of the log cabin.

As I hit the ground running I glanced and saw the big bears getting ready to give chase, I could hear them coming as I rounded the first corner. They were closer as I moved past the second. When I got by the third corner and headed for the door I flipped the latch and slid through the partly opened door and slammed and latched it shut behind me.

Whew that was close, that ole girl was breathing down my neck as I'd scrambled through the front door.

The latch had no more them clicked shut then that big bear hit the door and the leather strap hinges just about came off the door post. From the two pegs above the door I snatched my rifle, cocked it and backed up to the rear wall. The rifle was ready to go and there was two more rifles leaning against the back wall that were charged and ready to fire.

Out loud I said, "Lord, please help me with this problem I'm facing." I'd no sooner got the words out of my mouth and the door came off its hinges and ended up flat on the dirt floor. As soon as I saw fur I pulled the trigger. Instantly the room was full of choking black powder smoke.

Like it was way too hot I dropped that rifle to the floor and snatched up another that leaned against the back wall. I saw movement and cut loose with another chunk of lead and heard her roar in pain and in frustration. Then came a long moan like she was expelling a big breath of air. With the last loaded rifle in my hand and my thumb on the hammer I waited to see her better but not let her get to me.

Through the thick smoke this scared rabbit could hear her struggling in the room and still I waited for her to make the next move. When I did see her she was up close and I jammed the muzzleloader into her mouth and touched it off all in one movement.

The big bear dropped to the floor like a sack of beans but that wasn't the end of her for she still struggled to get to me. This little jackrabbit ripped the powder horn off the back wall and quickly reloaded his weapon and before this ole dude made the final shot she stopped thrashing and lay still. Her brown eyes were fixed on me and they never left, as she died in her final defiant stare.

The warm room was cooling off fast and the door was under that big bear. I struggled to move the bear off the door. Gee-will-akers was that ever a hard task but I finally rolled her over, got the door out from under her and moved toward the doorway with it. Outside in the darkness about ten feet away stood the cub bear looking right at me. When I got to the doorway it turned and ambled off into the darkness.

With rifle close at hand and one eye on that big brown bundle on the floor I began to put more clothes on, then lit another lamp and set it by the door and commenced to re-hang the cabin door. I worked a good half hour to get the cabin door hung on its hinges and latched. In all that time ma bear never moved a muscle.

I got a blanket off my swinging bunk, put it around my shoulders and threw a couple of chunks of wood on the fire. Got the two empty rifles and charged them and made them ready to be used again. Out here in California in 1849 you must always be prepared with weapons loaded and primed. Inside I felt kind of sorry for the old girl.

Out back I heard the horses by the corral so I buckled on my gun belt, slipped on my heavy coat and hat, picked up my Hawkins Rifle and pushed through the doorway into the cold night air. Man-oh-man did I hate to be out here again so soon looking for trouble.

The horses were back and wanting some attention so this ole hay seed spent about fifteen minutes with them always watchful for that half grown grizzly cub. I assumed he's headed for the tall timbers of the high country. He'd be looking for his mother, I'm thinking.

I sure hope he can make it on his own now. I'm afraid we will be looking for him in a short while. Well I can't do any more tonight so I better get my tail end into the cabin and in that horse hide hammock. This little episode had taken it out of me, that's for sure.

While climbing into my swinging bed I thought I was a goner out there in the cold john. "I thank you Lord for seeing me through all those troubles outside tonight." The next thing I remember the sun was shining in through the small cracks around the door. When I put my feet on the floor my foot hurt something terrible. That big toe of mine, where the toilet lit on it was my problem. I wasn't going to do a whole lot, maybe hobble around in the shack and try to get something to eat. It took me most of the day to right the outhouse and wrestle that bear out of the cabin, skin her out and cut her up into steaks.

I took some of the meat and put it out to dry. This English man had bear steaks fried up and were they good. In the morning I'm going to take that hide and nail it to the outside wall to dry. Then just before dark I saddled a horse and headed downstream toward the Friths. I had loaded up some of that bear meat and went a visiting down the valley.

NEW FRIENDS

I didn't really know anything about that family down below but I hoped this would get me off on the right foot. Everyone needs a helping hand one time or another. Tonight I'll try to get to bed early. Harley MacDonald's, old saying is early to bed early to rise makes a man healthy, wealthy and wise. This morning when the sun was putting shafts of light into the house I saw dust dancing on the sunbeams.

In the evenings after dinner I moseyed on down there to have a look around and talk with them if they would let me into their camp. Sure enough that wagon had a plow and all kinds of farm implements tied to the side of the wagon. Just one glance at the wagons and you knew that they were farmers. The parents were a productive pair for I saw about eight kids in the family although none were really young children.

Mr. Frith and his family were out from Michigan with their brood of kids. They'd found a piece of land over near Sacramento and purchased it and then got the gold fever and left their new home place and headed into the mountains to strike it rich. They expected to return as soon as they struck it rich.

Talk about greenhorns, they were so green they welcomed me right into their camp again with open arms. They didn't know who I was or a thing about me. They had some mighty good looking young women folks and out here doing that was a no, no. I tried to explain to them that this was a no, no.

They didn't cotton to me talking to them like that, but soon their ruffled feathers were calmed down. Most evenings I got together with the Friths and talked and sometimes the girls and Mrs. Frith broke out some musical instruments and we sang until time to hit the hay. (Most folks in the west used straw or cornhusk mattresses and that's how the phrase 'hit the hay' came about.)

Feather ticks were a luxury in the West. Out here feathers and down were hard to come by. The ducks, geese and chickens were too few to generate enough soft feathers for a pillow, let alone a mattress. You needed to bring along your own mattress when you came west if you wanted a feather tick.

The five of us boys off the Downey Cruiser didn't even have a cotton sack to put some straw or grass in. No, we didn't have nary a sack to our name, so we slept on whatever we could find that was soft. In the cabin we did have some horsehides, deerskins and some cloth. Being on shipboard we knew how to make a hammock to sleep on with those hides for a mattress. With all my time on a boat I'd learned to sleep quite well on that horsehide swing.

First thing I did when I got the men folks alone was warn them of their foolishness and told them all men in this part of the world were not to be trusted until you knew them. And never first time acquaintances like me. You don't know what my motives are or anything about them or me. This part of the world was full of all kinds of bad men.

The looks I got told me they weren't use to anyone talking to them like that. So I commenced to soothe some ruffled feathers. Old man Firth he didn't cotton to me talking to them like that at all. He had his words with me and I let him rake me over the coals good and proper.

When he was finished reading me the riot act, I related to him what had happened to us and what we saw since we got here. My goal was to just inform him of the dangers of the gold fields. How he took that advice was up to him. When I got through, everything seemed to be okay with what was said.

How those Michigan farm boys ever got those wagons up into the mountains is more than I'll ever understand. There are no roads of any kind coming up here and what deer runways there were, were hard for a horse and rider to navigate in some places. I'm no do-gooder you understand but it looked to me like these folks needed some help. First off they came into the high country at the wrong time of year, it was time to be heading down not up.

It was cold at night and soon winter storms would be hitting them in the butt, with lots and lots of snowballs. It wouldn't be long and winter would be settling into this area and that meant heavy snow and real cold weather. Soon the water would be freezing along the creek banks and one day soon it would be too cold to pan for gold. In fact it was way too cold to play in the water even now. In a matter of seconds your hands and fingers would be numb from the stinging cold water of the streams.

We were luckier than most folks we had knee high boots to keep the water off our feet. Most miners didn't have that luxury and suffered through the cold water all summer long. The water came from the melting snow higher up in the mountains and was freezing cold when it got down to this level.

I took time to get myself acquainted with Mr. Frith, his wife Erma and all his kids Aaron, David, Rusty, Mabel, Mary, Millie, Rodney and Danielle the youngest. Danielle was prob'ly seven. Rusty I heard was nineteen. The two oldest girls I took notice of right away. They were about seventeen or eighteen maybe nineteen and pretty as a picture. Mabel had pretty red hair and Mary's hair was an auburn color. These two caught my eye right away.

I'm sure in the low land men would be buzzing around them like bees around honey. The facts were I felt like doing some buzzing of my own. I was like a moth drawn to the flames. When English looked at them he felt a hunger he'd never felt before. That's when he turned his eyes away from the lovely temptations and talked with the other members of the family.

This ole boy felt a bit awkward in the presence of these exquisite young ladies. They were breathtakingly beautiful and mighty pleasant to look at. Pretty women like these were a rarity in the West. I wondered if I had a hidden agenda in being here. With what I'd seen here what would be my motivation now. They sure got me to thinking about things.

This ole mountain lad didn't let on to the Frith family that we'd found any gold yet. I did tell them of our cabin upstream a ways. They talked to me about everything that was taking place down below in and around Sacramento, the area of their farm. People everywhere were going gold crazy. It seems like everyone down there was catching the gold fever.

Mr. Frith got to calling me English and soon his whole kit-and-caboodle took it up. It was enjoyable to fellowship with this clan. It was the first time in my life that I'd ever talked with ladies without a hostile motive and it was really nice and quite pleasant.

They were a gay bunch and I couldn't get enough of their company. In just a short time Mabel begin to move into my heart and set up residence. Rosemary the younger was different from the two older girls and all had a sweet disposition. The whole family was a treat to be around. They didn't look down their noses at a person and I took comfort in that. In fact the whole family seemed to take a liking to me and talked to me like a human being.

I knew I had no right to be thinking of these girls in this way. This was the very first time in all my life that I'd ever let my guard down and they moved right in without my permission. Unbeknownst to anyone in camp this old boy had them captured in his mind and they were heading for my heart.

For the next five days ole English hung around the Frith camp and helped out when he should have been at the cabin working around the place getting it ready for winter. Earlier Big Mac, JJ and I talked of enlarging the cabin a bit. They wanted me to cut some winter wood and stack it by the cabin. Then cut some poles for the addition.

To tell you the truth ole Mr. Duck hadn't lifted a finger to cut any wood so he got busy and started to cut up some of the downed wood and haul some old logs down to the cabin. Most of the downed wood was well seasoned and ready to burn. As this English duck worked he kept his eyes out for some good poles for a lean-to, onto our shack. Later on I would drag them into the dooryard.

In the evening I'd mosey down their way just to have someone to talk to. In the daytime they were busy looking the valley over. David had been in a mining school back East and knew a whole lot more about this trade than I ever dreamed there was to know. So in a roundabout way I asked him about this mother lode business; what was it really all about.

David Frith sat down and explained it to me in words I could understand. It got me to thinking about this little valley and how the gold in Cabin Creek ended so abruptly and we never found even a little piece any further upstream. I thought to myself, could the mother lode be close by. I kept my thoughts entirely to myself as I worked him for more information.

By the things he said somewhere to the right or left of the stream up on the bank, or under the water there could be a mother lode a waiting for someone to find it. The gold in the stream had somehow through the years came down from the mother lode. They called it the mother lode because it gave birth to all the gold in the streambed.

David wondered out loud, "Why are you so interested in the subject of the mother lode, English?"

Thinking quickly I said, "This ole boy is trying to understand this crazy business and how the gold gets into the streambeds. I'd seen it in our mining book and didn't understand it completely. Although from what you've told me, this mining business is now beginning to get a whole lot clearer. Prior to our talks it was about as clear as mud."

I knew precisely where the gold ran out on Cabin Creek. Soon the boys would be back and we would talk about this. It was too cold to work in the water, so maybe this winter we could work the creek banks to see what might be there, if anything.

David asked about this stream and I told him we had a claim with a cabin on it where we planned to spend the winter and not much else. "David this stream has been worked out and it never produced very much gold anyway. We won that cabin and a worked out claim in a card game early last spring. We just came back here to spend the winter and then get ready to go at it in the spring. I have two friends that are getting supplies over at Buck Shot Creek Mining Camp."

Without bringing up the subject of gold I told of all the scallywags we've had trouble with in this area and about all the good folks that had met their deaths at their hands. Ole English took time to warn the three older Frith boys again about claim jumpers, killers and shysters that were out to get your gold by hook or by crook and maybe one of those sisters of yours. "Gentlemen you need to be on guard at all times."

"I kid you not, David, you and your family need to be on guard every minute. I mean keep a sentry as look out for your family at all times. You know as well as I do that those ladies are mighty precious cargo and nearly priceless. They need to be protected out here in the gold fields at all times. David, do you have some weapons for protection, if you do you better get them out and ready to use?"

"We have five rifles in the wagons that could be used for defense. We brought them along for Indian defense and for deer meat."

"My advice to you is to get them out tonight and get them ready for your protection. Don't leave them where you can't get your hands on them quickly. They need to be primed and ready to shoot just like you did in Indian country." I didn't tell him I knew nothing about Indians and this country or how to fight them, but we had heard plenty from strangers in some of those little mining camps.

David's father had come closer and stood listening to what was said then chimed in at that point. "We want to thank you English for the enlightenment on the area and what is going on up here. But I feel we can make it on our own, we have done it all our lives." I didn't respond to his words although I wanted to.

"English, with David's knowledge and engineering skills, we plan on doing some pick and shovel work yet this winter and try to locate the mother lode of all the crumbs you boys are picking up in the streams. We don't need a helping hand from anyone."

Well I guess that put me in my place. "Sir, I was just trying to help out and be a good neighbor." From now on I needed to watch my mouth, not everyone wants advice. I knew from experience that a person that doesn't want to be counseled couldn't be helped. I had been in the same boat myself before I got on board that wooden tub with Big Mac. I didn't want advice from anyone.

I liked this family to much to take it to heart. The gander had two choices one he could get upset and go home or take it for what it was worth. With Mabel and the rest of the family here, this mallard did the latter I chose not to let him ruffle my feathers.

David's education in a big school back East and with his willingness to talk to me about how to find gold, this ole dude figured he was pretty lucky. In the days to come I tried to pick his mind until this old dude felt he had a general idea of how to go about looking for a mother lode.

He said, "The main vein would not be scattered all over the countryside, like it is in the stream's bed down below. It was usually somewhere up on the bank away from the streams; the yellow stuff just might be covered with dirt or higher up in the rock walls. It could possibly be under the water.

If the mother lode is uphill there will be traces of nuggets in the dirt leading up to it. Most folks will work uphill until they find out where all the gold is coming from. Once they locate the yellow vein, it'll be the origin of all the gold that was found in the creeks below. The mother lode could be a bonanza or nothing.

Ya gotta keep looking in the logical spots up above. English, that's the tricky part for the gold up above may not even be in the stream." This is where David's mining skills would come in handy for them, just knowing where to look and what to look for. This is information this ole boy needed to know. But David and his brothers weren't willing to cough up everything they knew about finding gold. But that's okay I'd found out most of what I wanted to know.

I would watch them when they worked the hillsides and see what they did up there and that would show us a little more of what we needed to know. Up until now we were almost ignorant when it came to uncovering the mother lode.

David wanted to be friendly but he wasn't a fool. He had knowledge he'd never give out to people that were perfect strangers. No matter how much those boys liked me they would only go just so far and I knew it.

Today I'm going to visit with our neighbors down below. When we were together I have trouble keeping my eyes off those pretty young fillies. They always had a quick smile for me and I loved it. I never knew anyone like these two attractive girls before. I loved being near them and listening to them talk.

Maybe I did know some females that were nice and just didn't know it. In all my life I never gave anyone a chance to really know me until Harley, JJ. and the Ames brothers came into my life.

When I got in their camp, the Friths wanted to know where the bear meat came from. They'd heard shooting in the night and wondered if I was having any trouble. In the early morning the older boys started upstream to check you out but saw a good cloud of smoke coming from your chimney and turned back.

So this great white hunter spilled his guts and let them know what all the shooting was about and my late night bear hunt. That Frith family laughed their heads off at the telling of it and I was kidded for the next few days. It was all in fun and I took it that way. There was a time when I'm not sure I could have. Back when I was a kid I didn't do well with people ragging on me.

It was twelve long days before JJ and Harley moseyed on into our little valley. Their packhorses were loaded to the gills and they were glad to see me and were concerned about seeing other folks in our valley

Right away I got the coffee pot and, poured the black stuff and sat down and had a bite to eat with them. Then I took time to explain to them about the grizzly bear and her cub that came for tea and who our new neighbors were and what they were all about.

As we unloaded the horses and stored the supplies in the back corner of the little shack, I told them of the ordeal with the gray horse, the big grizzly bear and the wolves and my experience in the outhouse and the death of the bear. Those two guys laughed out loud at my predicaments and how I barely got through it.

Harley looked me in the eyes and said, "Arthur my boy, you have come a long ways from the streets of London, England. I doubt that you would ever have wrestled a big ole grizzle bear back there. But maybe all those scrapes you had back there got you ready for the wilds of California." Between the two young men they had all kinds of off colored comments and questions for me and my time here alone. We three truly had a good time together laughing and kidding around, yes we were truly good friends.

They were as happy as all get out with all the logs piled around the cabin plus all the wood cut and stacked for winter fuel. I'm glad they were happy with what I'd accomplished in their absence and I was glad they didn't ask any more questions about the wood in our yard.

THE QUESTION

That very day we set about adding onto the log cabin. First we leveled a spot about ten feet by twelve feet and laid the log base. This addition would almost double the size of our little nest and make it a nicer place to hold up for the winter. As seamen we were use to cramped living quarters and this was a mansion in comparison to what we had at sea. By being up off the ground it was warmer.

As we worked I informed them of what I'd learned about finding a mother lode and what my plans were for the winter months ahead. Jared Jenkins asked, "How did you come by all the information Arthur Drake."

"A little bird whispered in my ear. I've had all kinds of experiences since you left for town and I haven't even told you the best part yet."

Talking about the wood piled up around the house, it wasn't the best job I'd ever seen but our addition was coming along just fine. When we got through filling the holes between the logs it would heat fine. The roof had me worried just a bit. We used the dirt that was thawed out and piled the roof high with it and hoped for the best. In the spring the water would probably leak down through the roof soil and make the place a mess.

With the shoe souls of the dead outlaws we hung a door made out of two wide boards. We were now ready to give my mother lode theory a try. Was it a possibility that it was out there somewhere as I thought? The guys were enthusiastic about the possibility of finding gold in large quantities on the banks of Cabin Creek. The Friths were still working the opposite wall and were way, way upstream somewhere. You could see the pocked marked hillside from all the digging they'd done on that side of the canyon. You've got to give it to them, they were hard workers and all the family took their turn throwing dirt.

My guess is if there is a mother lode out there it's on our side of the stream and we made our claim known by our presence there on the site. At the point where the gold ran out we worked our way uphill from the stream with pick and shovel and then parallel to the creek, digging all the way.

We'd uncovered a few small nuggets as we worked. From the point where we found the nuggets we worked our way straight up the hill moving dirt as we went. The afternoon sun felt warm but when it went behind the hill it cooled off really quick. The Friths gave a wave as they drew near and Mabel called out "hello English, what you boys up to? Has the Lord been good to you today?"

My return answer was noncommittal and it seemed to satisfy them as they headed for their wagons below. I watched that splendid looking women until they turned at the bend in the canyon and disappeared from view. Whew was that little lady ever something to look at. I couldn't take my eyes off her until she was clean out of sight.

When I turned around the guys were watching me. JJ said, with a smile on his face, "Do you know that little lady, Arthur?"

Harley got his two cents worth in by saying "I think he has the hots for her JJ. We shouldn't have left him here alone and gone off to town." He smiled at me then made a long sigh. "Look Justin he's all starry eyed and gone ogle eyed for the little lady. JJ, maybe we should lock him up at night before he starts howling at the moon."

This ole gander loved the way these boys made fun of me. It's all in great fun and I loved it. There was a time when I didn't take that kind of kidding from anyone. But this was all in fun. There was no real harassment in their good-natured fun. In England I had my own way of dealing with it and someone would have gotten hurt.

After the sun gave up and started over the horizon it took the daylight with it and it cooled off real fast. In that few moments of twilight it was a beautiful time up here in the mountains. The sky was an awesome sight to see. Gold, red and many other colors mixed and blended to make an awesome sight to see. I'd never seen anything like this in London or at least I'd never notice it.

Most all the time we spent in the California Mountains God showered us with oh so many blessings; for sure we are a blessed people. Below the cabin I could hear the stream flowing downhill on its way to who knows where. The obstructions in the creek bottom only made it talk a little louder.

Yes, I was where I wanted to be. The United States was home to me and I loved it here in these high mountains and to top it off I knew a sweet little lady I was interested in and it seemed like maybe she was a bit interested in me. Will wonders never cease? As I glanced off down the canyon I saw the black smoke of their campfire as it drifted slowly skyward.

The mountain aspens had turned to a pretty yellow color and the leaves were starting to descend to the ground like a boat caught in a whirlpool going down, down and around until they hit the ground. The aspen forests on the mountainside were a bright yellow color wherever you looked. As I looked I wondered to myself could the cold part of the winter be far behind.

I spent some time worrying about the Friths trying to live out the winter in a prairie schooner for a home. I wished they'd stayed down below until warm weather came in the spring. From everything I'd heard the wind could blow up a doozie of a storm in the winter and those covered wagons can be a mighty drafty place.

On the other hand if they hadn't set a course for this Mountain would I have ever met those two sweet girls? I think not. I had mixed feelings about them being up here. The paradox was they should go back down but I wanted them to stay up here.

That family has been so busy looking for gold they weren't thinking of the cold weather that was coming or maybe they didn't know just how cold it could get up here in the Sierra Nevada Mountains or the amount of snow that could descend on them in just a day or so. Tomorrow I would chase them down and try to get them to stop and start thinking about what lays ahead. Those beautiful ladies needed a warm place to lay their lovely heads at night. It is one thing to be cold in the day time and quite another to sleep cold every night.

As if the weather read my mind it turned off bitter cold in the night. The sky was as clear as a bell ringing on Sunday morning and that big ole moon was so close it looked like you could reach out and touch it. As I went outside to use the outhouse my breath hung on the still night air and slowly dissipated into nothing.

My thoughts went immediately to those Frith women and the kids in the wagons below. Well there wasn't anything I could do tonight. Maybe this cold snap would get their minds off the gold and onto some kind of shelter. If they were going to stay up this high for the winter they needed better accommodations then they now had.

This is the first time I've ever worried about someone I hardly knew. It didn't make a lot of sense to me. Must be God is working something in my heart. I was actually concerned about a family I hardly knew, unlike the fellows I'd come to know and trust on board that ship.

I stepped back inside the cabin and the heat from the stove felt good and I backed up to it and warmed my backside. Lifted the lid on the cook stove and chucked in another chunk of wood, this would keep the fire going until morning. We slept in the new part of our little nest where the small door way kept it cooler back there.

Ole English awoke to the rattle of pots and pans as Harley prepared food to start our day out right. Hot flapjacks, bacon and eggs really smelled good and dragged me out of that night swing and on to the floor. Yesterday JJ cooked up some pan bread and that went really good with our morning meal.

The cabin was warm and cozy and I slept great last night. This is the first home I'd ever known. To some folks it wasn't much of a much but to me it gave me a sense of belonging and ownership, which I'd never felt in all my short life.

The great white hunter was having a lot of new and wonderful feelings that he'd never experienced before. It made me satisfied for the first time in my life. As we ate we talked of mining gold and what was the best way to get it out of the ground and if there would be enough in that creek bank to pay to shovel all that dirt that might be hiding that vein of gold from us.

We were out and about and getting ready to shuffle off to the dig when the Frith men folks came up the valley heading for wherever they were going to look for wealth today. Mr. Frith, Aaron, David and Rusty all carried shovels, picks and a rifle or two.

As we walked together along the creek bank David asked "how you men making out, are ya finding any yellow stuff?"

Our pat answer was "not enough to buy a good meal or a cup of coffee but we have high hopes for today. How you making out are you finding anything up above?"

Their answer was as made up as ours, "Today's the day we hit the bonanza and we hope you boys do better today." The real questions were left unsaid. Today everyone seemed to be in high spirits and undaunted by the cold and lack of gold we were finding.

I was reluctant to ask about their wagons and if they slept well. But I was determined right now to ask. "Mr. Frith don't you think you should get your women folks into something with walls where they can keep warm this winter.

"English, that's been a rattling around in my mind for a few days now. We got a couple of places that look like good prospects and we need to check them out first. If they don't pan out we will prob'ly move on to greener pastures."

When he said that my heart sank into my shoes that would mean that those two good looking females would be gone. Somehow that didn't set well with me. I had to admit it to myself I was getting attached to that oldest girl, Mabel, and I thought of her a lot.

Arthur my boy, you are thinking stupid, that girl has never let on that she liked you anymore than just friends. Why are you kicking at the traces? Okay, tonight I'll amble on down to their camp and have a long talk with her and get this thing settled in my mind once and for all.

All day long my mind was on what I would say. What could I say? I hadn't known any of the Friths all that long? Mr. Frith seemed kind of stiff necked about his family. He might not let me talk with her at all. Ouch! If that were the case what would I do then?

The guys guessed that something was bugging me but I tried not to let on to them what I was up to. Harvey and Justin were good men but I knew they would be on me all day if they knew of my plans to talk to Mabel

We moved a lot of gravel and came up with a few nuggets. The last hour we came up with two good size nuggets and we were in high hopes that we were on the right path of the long lost mother lode. JJ knew something was up when I wanted to quit early. Most often I'm the last one to say let's go. From that they started in on me again. Just to be ornery they stayed longer than usual. Those two boys were really great.

On the outside ole English was grumbling at them, on the inside he had to smile a bit for if the tables were turned ole English would be the one holding things up to make them suffer. Man-o-man did I ever like these two guys. Right then Tom and Dick Ames came to mind and my spirit dropped a bit.

It was close to dark when we entered the cabin. They looked kind of queer at me when I started to get slicked up. The catcalls and wise cracks came fast and furious as I put my coat on and fled through the front door. Harvey said as I took flight, "Tell her I love her too, English."

This kid was as nervous as all get out but I was going through with it one way or another. If I got the chance I was going to ask Mabel if she would marry me. I'm wondering if I should ask her father for her hand first or just pop the question. This was ridiculous she didn't really know me at all. I'm sure her folks would think a proposal at this time was bizarre to say the least.

I wasn't much concerned what her folks thought about it, but only what Mabel thought. But this ole Englishman did want their consent. I would somehow have to work it out. Out here in the West pretty women are at a premium and ole English was after the best of the lot.

Arthur Drake must be a little bit nutty for he hadn't even kissed her or held her hand yet and now he was thinking of marriage. I wondered if she thought this English boy was anything but an ignorant ole clodhopper from the old country. She seemed to be educated and I'd never been inside a schoolhouse.

As I neared the Frith's wagons I thought maybe this wasn't such a good idea after all. But a thought kept rolling around in my mind. Someone said, "Happiness is where you find it." Well I'm still looking. This life is a lot better than I had it in London Town or aboard ship that's for sure.

I could see the Frith's wagons up ahead so I stopped to ponder my situation. As the Duck contemplated what to do, over the babblin' of the stream, a voice from the wagons said "hello English, what ya up to, glad to see ya."

I lifted my hand in a long wave and they responded in kind. Now there was no way out I must go on into their camp and at least say hello. This English kid was self conscious of himself. My clothes were thread bare, the corduroy material was starting to wear off and my whole outfit looked a wee bit shabby.

Over all they were the best clothes I had. My long hair was combed as best as I could, the flannel shirt looked fairly good and my boots weren't really scuffed up. I was hoping I was half way presentable as I walked into the firelight. Aaron and David met me at the edge of their camp and welcomed me into their home such as it was. The voices of their family were jovial and they seemed truly glad to see me and they wondered what they owed this visit to.

Ole English mustered up every ounce of courage he had and talked to Mr. Frith. "Mr. Frith I've only known your family for a little over three weeks now. I've studied this out for the last week or so and I like your family a lot. But the real reason I came down here tonight was to ask for your daughter's hand in marriage."

The camp went silent except for the crackling of the fire and every eye was glued on me. For a good long moment all that could be heard was the snap and crackle of the wood in the fire. Finally Mr. Frith cleared his throat and his first words were, "which of these girls are you interested in English?"

I saw the toe of my boot making scuff marks in the dirt so I stopped and cleared my throat. "Sir, all your daughters are very pretty, but Sir, I've taken a fancy to Mabel. I know she is way too good for me. But out here there isn't much time so we need to make our wishes known right off the bat.

Tomorrow you could be up and gone and I'd never get a chance to express my feelings toward her. Sir, I hope Mabel has some feelings for me, if not this will give her a chance to maybe think about us for a bit.

Every time I think about her it's on the up in up. Sir, in my mind I'm cultivating an excellent relationship and a good life for the two of us."

"Are you asking for her hand in marriage, Mr. Drake?"

"Yes sir. I'd like her to share her life with me."

"Aren't you moving just a little too fast young man? The first week you spent a fair amount of time with us and the last couple of weeks she hasn't seen you all that much. Do you call this the correct amount of time for a courtship?"

"Sir, my dilemma is what if you leave this area in the next few days and I never see her or you again. I think Mabel and I can make a marriage grow if she will consent to it"

"I don't know English to me this is too much of a rush job. You set right here on that log and we will talk this over as a family."

The whole family kids and all sashayed away from me, getting out of earshot. They started their own confab and I strained my ears to hear what was said. This went on for about fifteen minutes or so and I couldn't make out heads or tails of what was being discussed.

Finally as a group they moseyed on back to the fire light and I watched Mabel closely and she didn't take her eyes off me. I tried to read something in her long look. I saw maybe, curiosity in that look. I'm guessing that was better than other things I could have seen. Where did that leave me? I guess that would come from her father.

"Well Mr. Drake we talked it over as a family and decided you're rushing this marriage thing just a wee bit. Only because Mabel wanted to try it, we are going to allow you to court her under a supervised situation. There will be no going off alone at any time. Do you understand what I mean?"

"Yes Sir, I do."

"Is that agreeable with you?"

"Yes Sir!"

"I want you to understand that there will be no shenanigans on your part. Everything must be on the up and up and above board."

"Sir, I will be on my best behavior when I'm with your daughter. I will always treat her like a lady and even try to be a gentleman when it's called for."

"Young man this is against my better judgment. I want you to know I was against this right from the beginning but my family thinks it would be good for the both of you. We don't know you at all. Down deep inside ya I see something that looks like a wild streak. I'll tell you right off I'd better never see it come to the surface. Son, My family comes first in my life so you better watch your step."

"Mr. Frith today in my mind I have become a part of your family and if anyone outside of our family messes with the Friths they must reckon with this Englishman. You have my solemn oath on it." You folks are used to handling your own problems, but from now on your problems are my problems,"

At the end of that stern conversation out came the instruments and the singing began. This ole Englishman didn't miss what Mr. Frith said, that Mabel also wanted me to court her along with the family. So as the music started little ole Arthur moved over to where she stood and looked into her face.

It wasn't hard for me to talk to her father. But trying to think of something to say to her was a whole lot harder. After hellos and how are you tonight it all went silent except for the music. I wracked this little pee picking mind to come up with something to say and whatever I thought of fell way short of how I intended it to be. That was probably the best night of my life. The wonderful sound of her laughter was pleasant to my ears. She was more than pleasant to feast my eyes on. The smell of vanilla extract hung in the air and teased my senses. A green and white knitted shawl covered her shoulders and it looked good on her.

We spent the evening sitting on an old horse blanket with our backs against the wagon wheel holding hands. As I was getting ready to leave and head for home she said in my ear "Arthur, will you come again when you can?"

Wow! Would I ever! "Yes Miss. Frith as long as you want me to, I will come a visiting." As we talked I found my eyes riveted on her incredible face and awesome body. She was sure pleasant to look at here in this Rocky Mountain moonlight.

Her hand lightly touched my face and after the touch a sad feeling of loneliness grabbed hold of me that I'd never felt before. How had I ever gotten along without a real woman in my life before this?

"Arthur I'm so glad you came and talked to papa about us."

"So am I, Mabel," right then and there ole Artie decided he was going to love this Mabel with everything he had. Her eyes widened in surprise as I touched her arm with both hands. She glanced over her shoulder to see if her family was watching and listening to what we were up to.

In the semi dark area where we stood she took my hand and held it for a wee bit then let go and said "good night English."

"Good night Miss Mabel, I'll see you tomorrow night if everything goes well."

This ole mountain kid was reluctant to leave but I must go, it was getting late and Harvey and Justin would be looking for my return. My boots reluctantly turned and headed upstream toward the cabin. After a short hike I looked back and my women stood silhouetted in the firelight where I'd left her.

I'll tell ya what, this ole dude felt like clicking my heels together. This was one of the best days of my life. After shooting that ole grizzly bear it seemed like ole English was having a lot of good days. The next couple of days were quite warm for this time of year. Mr. Frith calls this fine weather, Indian summer. Whatever it is it was sure nice. "Lord Jesus, I thank you for what transpired on this mountain this week. You are such a great Savior."

While that lady is this close I'm going to pursue her as best I can. In this mining business the Friths can be here today and gone someplace else tomorrow. JJ often said and it makes a lot of sense to me, 'Ya gotta make hay while the sun shines.' Well that was my intention. I will be tending my Mabel business every day I can.

THE TRIP DOWN

Each day we dug up some yellow metal and every evening found me in the Firth's camp courting my women. What I didn't care for was they were talking about relocating to another valley. They thought the prospect of finding any gold in this canyon was awfully slim and down deep inside I knew they were right.

Two days later they were packing up their things and getting ready to pull on out of here. The Frith boys were anxious to be moving on. Soon the real cold weather would come rolling in and the ground would freeze up solid. If they could, they needed to find some color and get a hole started and fix it so they could work it all winter like we were.

I got into my best bib and tucker, loaded up some of that bear meat and some Belgium moose meat that we had jerked for them to take with them when they high-tailed it out of here. My insides were being torn apart as I said good-bye to the ladies. I didn't care what anyone would say. I took Mabel in my arms and planted a big ole kiss on her sweet lips and held mine there. At first she looked surprised but quickly got with the program and made it a wonderful moment.

You probably wondered why I planted a kiss on her lips; well I wanted that kiss to grow and produce a whole lot more in the future. "Lord, look after her and her family and keep her safe whatever they do." We'd loaned them our extra tent to take with them. I was sure they would need it before spring came and produced some warmer weather.

This kid stood helpless as Mabel climbed aboard that big-wheeled wagon. She blew me a kiss from her seat high up on their Conestoga wagon. This was a bad time for her as I saw a tear slipping and sliding to her chin then drop onto her lap.

This was the only woman I'd ever cared a hill of beans about in all my life and it looked like she would be planted somewhere else. Was this the last time I'd ever see her, was that little woman out of my life forever, Lord, I sure hope not.

Aaron the oldest Frith boy yelled, "up Pat, up May, Mike, Ted" and laid the lines to the horses rumps and the youngest boy cracked the black snake whip over their heads and off the big teams went. They were single minded as they all jumped into action, their muscle pushing flesh into those horse collars and the wheels started to roll and carry my Mabel away from me.

I heard that whip again as I stood there watching them move up and over the little hill and then slipped from view. I climbed that hill and watched until they were clean out of sight. As I gazed after them the morning breezes whispered in the tall trees saying, "she gone Arthur, she's long gone." That wasn't at all what I wanted to hear so I tried to change the tune.

In my mind I thought this family had better locate a good place to dig real soon, for it wouldn't be long and the ground would be frozen solid. Soon those dark ominous clouds up above would be producing a lot of white stuff. This ole dude didn't envy that family one iota. In the next few months that family would have a rough row to hoe.

From what I'd heard these mountains can be a cruel customer in the wintertime. They're a mighty hard place to be, in cold weather. It cared not in the least if you lived or died. It had its own ways and you must conform to them or suffer the consequences. That made me just a little uneasy. But the Firth family were Michiganders and knew cold weather; they weren't stupid so they should be okay if they don't treat this area like the mid-west but as the Wild West.

It wasn't long and I found myself headed up the canyon. Every noise I made echoed off the rock walls and became a lonesome sound as I trudged toward home. The guys were still waiting for me at the cabin with some hot food on the back of the stove. They had some concerns for me as I sat myself down at the table. JJ asked, "are they on their way, Arthur?"

"Ya they left about an hour ago."

"Are you alright English?"

"Well, I should have known they would have to move on one day." But no way did it sit well with me. In the back of my mind I had these plans that just got washed away like so much creek gravel."

The nice breakfast they'd prepared for me tasted bland as I thought of Mabel and my plans for her and myself. Well this unpleasant experience of her leaving was just another bump in the rocky road of life. This ole duck would have to put it all behind him or suffer until we meet again, if ever.

These two friends of mine were the right two to spend the winter with. They were easy to get along with and liked to work and we did a lot of it. Our horses needed a warm place to spend the winter so we took off a couple of days and built a lean-to onto our cabin.

November disappeared and we were well into December. We'd worked hard and were finding nuggets every few feet as we worked our way up that hill. We were about to call it quits for the winter when we hit the mother lode slap dab in a solid rock wall three feet under the California topsoil.

We set up that canvas tent we had, right over that vein and cleared out the loose dirt and went to work on that rock wall. The yellow metal was in a three-inch vein and soon it got bigger. Each night we had all one man wanted to carry. Maybe he wanted to carry more out of there but he couldn't. The yellow metal we were after was mighty heavy.

That bear cub showed up around our cabin at night sniffing that bear hide we had nailed to the outside wall. He made tracks up close to our cabin sniffing out the horses in the lean-to, so I sat up a couple of nights and never saw hide nor hair of him. Justin Jenkins thought the half-grown bear should be hibernating by now but maybe he didn't know how to go about it. Me, I didn't know anything about bears, except they weren't very friendly.

Big Mac and I followed his tracks after the third visit and the tracks seemed to be headed down off the mountain. Well our loss would be someone else's gain. I sure hope they enjoyed him more than we did. After several miles we turned back and got on with our business at hand.

After dividing up the gold each man hid his own share. It took more than one trip for me to get my stash hid. This ole boy was no one's fool, he hid it in several places and the job took more, a whole lot more than one trip out there with a shovel.

On December twenty-third our Christmas surprise was the vein disappeared as quickly as it had appeared. For the rest of the year we worked in vain without an ounce of metal showing up in our pockets. That is when we decided to call it quits for the winter.

We covered our mine with dirt, tore down the tent and carried the whole she-bang back to our cabin. The horses weren't doing so well in the cold so we decided to see if we could find some grass for them to feed on.

The mountain snow was accumulating fast. The horses had trouble finding grass enough to fill their stomachs. Someone would have to take the livestock down off the mountain into the low lands where they could feed on the meadow grass. From where we were at we could see the brown grass way off in the low land.

We took time to hash it out and find a solution to our problem. It was decided that Harley would hang out at the cabin while Justin Jenkins and the Duck would go downhill and find something for our horses to eat. We'd be gone for at least a couple of months or until the weather broke.

We didn't feel all that comfortable with Harley here alone so I pushed hard for him to go along with us. Our gold was buried in the ground and covered with lots of snow so it didn't need a baby sitter. We could take some yellow metal along and enjoy ourselves over on the coast somewhere until spring got a foot hold up here.

Our gold wouldn't buy very much in any of the gold camps plus they didn't have much to offer. I finally got my way and we all got ready to head on out. The horses seemed ready and rarin' to leave so we didn't hold them back.

The unwritten law everywhere says you leave provisions in a cabin in the wilderness if you leave it for any length of time. Just in case someone comes along and is in dire need of some food and shelter. We'd left a note on the table, which said 'you're welcome here'. We really hoped no one would need to stay here or live in our cabin while we were gone.

JJ suggested we leave the gun with the cracked stock just in case our food didn't last them long enough to see them through the cold weather. We also left some powder and lead for the rifle.

The white stuff outside was deep in most places. Up here in the high country, the going was rougher than a corncob. That first afternoon of our trip down we found a bare spot with plenty of grass on the knob of a windswept hilltop. We allowed our horses to graze until they got their fill.

We needed our horses to have lots of stamina for the snow-choked trail ahead of us. The horses worked hard getting us through the deep snow. One of our ole bag-a-bones got stuck in a snow covered hole that had five feet of snow in it and we had to drag that little lady out of there with three other horses.

The going was slow but we must have made close to ten miles that first day and ten the second. On the third day the wind began to blow the snow. By noon we stopped and set up our tent in some pines. It made a wind break for our shaggy beasts. We rustled up some fire wood and hunkered down for a while.

Justin banked the tent high on three sides with snow as Harley set up the little fold up heating stove inside the tent and started a fire. Really quick like the warm fire warmed up the inside and soon you could smell food a-cooking. My job was to alleviate the amount of wind that was pestering our string of horses. There's no feed anywhere for our mounts. They'd have to make do with what they had.

In the night the wind broke and it was quiet out there except for horse sounds and the long lonesome howl of a lone wolf. Soon the moon and stars gave forth their light and it got cold, bad cold. You could hear the horses suffering out there.

The three of us got out of bed and built fires on all three sides of them to help fight off the effects of the chilling cold temperature during the course of the night. The horses had suffered for about twelve hours and now we were trying to ease their discomfort. It took lots of stamina for a horse to fight off the effects of cold weather and our nags didn't have all that much in reserve.

We cut blankets in half and covered the horses. At daylight we went out in three different directions to see if we could find some grass for our jug heads. After a long hour and a half of looking I found nothing so I headed back to our camp.

The horses were gone from their wind brake we'd built for them. The path they'd taken showed plainly in the deep snow. Apparently Harley or JJ had found something and had moved the stock out to feed. While the guys were out with the horses I began to break camp. Once the camp equipment was packed away, I waded through the hip deep snow out to where the small herd was pawing away the snow.

Harley and JJ were helping the horses by removing the ankle deep snow and the horses were mowing away the dead grass. I wondered just how much food value there was in the dead mountain grass. The tops looked like they had seeds on them and that made the difference.

I got in the act and helped kicked snow off the grass and that sped up the process. By noon the horses were not as interested in the feed as they were earlier. It was time to vamoose and get to heck off this mountain.

With their halters still on we led them back to camp and within the hour we were meandering down the mountain. We went through the same process for the next three days until we didn't need to remove any white stuff from the grass.

The snow was a bit below the knees in most places and the grass on the hilltops was clear of all the heavy snow. The sun came out and you could feel it was getting warmer as we descended into the low land.

Something we noticed, there was lots and lots of folks all over the place ready to make the run for the digs as soon as the weather broke. You could see their camps along creeks, and rivers. Some were trying their skills with a pan in the super cold water. What I learned later was that some people were pulling gold from the water and ground in this area.

Many folks had made the journey across the continent and got in here too late to stake out a claim on some creek up higher. In the spring when the weather broke they would be spilling over into the high country like a swarm of locus. These made us take another look at our plans. We must be ready to high tail it up the mountains before the flood of people made their move.

While we were here we would stake a claim on our used up vein of gold just in case the gold was still there somewhere. In the spring first off we would pan above the falls as fast as we could and extract as much of the gold from Falls Creek as we possibly could before the many would be miners descend on us with their equipment.

But for a couple of months we were going to enjoy ourselves and live the life of luxury in some town. In a week we had to look back to see the snow on the mountain. Now all we could see in front of us was sand, rocks, sparse grass and hills with brush on them.

On the second day out of the snow we ran slap dab into seven men who claimed to be about ready to hustle into the gold fields as soon as the mountain snow started to recede. They wanted to know if we had just gotten down from the Sierra Nevada Mountains.

We told them that we'd gotten into this area early last spring and had been up there in the mountains most of last year digging in vain, for the elusive gold. Gentlemen we ain't seen enough yellow stuff to fill your teeth. We were apprehensive about telling them anything for they didn't look just right to us.

The boys were a little on the rough tough side. The problem was every new bunch of these greenhorns we saw had a different look about them. All these new folks out here came from all walks of life seeking the elusive dream of striking it rich.

Harley was bold and asked them where there mining equipment was, for we saw no pans, picks or shovels to move the gravel or the dirt with. Like us these young fellows had a lot of firepower with long guns and revolvers.

Their answer was that their tools were at their base camp over on the next tributary to the north. Harley gave JJ and me the high sign and we said our goodbyes and moved our horses on out of there. We didn't need any company tagging along with us.

From the backside of a low hill with just our heads looking over the top we watched through bushes for a spell as they gestured and pointed in the direction we had taken. This didn't look all that good to me. Did these men have the same mind set as the outlaws we faced last summer up in the Sierra Nevada Mountain Range?

After much talk one man got straddle his mount and slipped on out of there, moving on our tracks. This ole English lad was anxious to put a whole lot of tracks on the ground and do it in a hurry, but not in too much of a hurry. The horses we rode made a dust cloud a blind man could follow. We left the small stream and headed for the open desert. With this move if the men followed us we would know for sure what their intentions were. We were pretty sure they were after our outfits and any gold we might have.

We took some time and rested our mounts for they needed it. Off a ways behind another small hill I watched a black buzzard circling high above looking for a lunch. Then coming around a far off hill I saw their whole crew moving our way. They were careful not to make anymore dust than they had to.

As we rode we made plans, to be doubly sure that they were truly on our tracks. After fifteen miles we separated. Harley and the duck circled to the south and came up on a hill that overlooked our horse tracks. As we hunkered down in the dirt we laid out our weapons and got ready to stick it to them when they got a little closer. We both had three long rifles each. That would be six shots and we hoped six dead pursuers, if not six dead men, at least enough to discourage them from pursuing us any further.

We saw their dust long before they came into view. As I lay waiting I watched a small spider making a web in a mesquite bush. The riders were coming at a snail's pace. Would they wait until after dark to hit us? Puffy white clouds meandered slowly across the evening sky and slowly but surely the clouds turned a pretty red, gold with a touch of pink thrown in.

The evening shadows were getting long on the ground and the twilight sun was dragging the daylight over the horizon. For some reason our newfound friends stopped a good half mile away and built a small smokeless fire. It looked like they were making coffee and preparing an evening meal.

Had they given up or were they planning to hit us after dark. After eating their evening meal, a lone horseman picked up our trail and came on. The rest were breaking camp and within a few minutes the six other horsemen were following him.

Big Mac and I decided to play the waiting game and see if the main group of riders would follow us and try to do us in. When they came by at the foot of this hill the two of us would do as much damage to them as we possibly could.

The point man was a good two hundred yards ahead of his cronies. When the larger group came even with us we opened up on them. Right off the bat two riders caught a deadly chunk of lead in their brisket and tumbled from leather.

For an instant turmoil rained down on the group and that's when spurs dug deep into flesh and horses moved in every direction. Killing was inevitable at this place and time, as men and riders raced away I fired and a rider sagged in the saddle, leaned to the left and slowly tumbled from leather.

Big Mac did a number on another rider and he was holding on for dear life. The two that were still upright were pouring lead at us as they rode heck bent for leather trying to get clear of our deadly fire. They also carried extra weapons and were now throwing hot lead our way and some shots were coming close. They were pretty good at judging the Kentucky wind-age on a bounding horse.

One ole codger was pretty darn good with his revolver and we kept our heads down. In the near dark, off to the south I could see their point man a-coming in a flat out run. The horse and rider rode as one, as he virtually flew across the desert floor. It looked like he wanted to lend a helping hand to his comrades. There were four of them upright and riding hard, so we decided to vacate this little hill as quickly as we could.

Three of the seven had bit the dust and one dude looked quite bad off as they came together just out of rifle range. As we left the hill we could see the last three men, untouched by lead, follow their wounded comrade out into the desert. I sure hope we've seen the last of them scallywags.

Justin was mighty glad to see we were alive and well when we caught up to him. That night no fire was seen in our camp and we posted a guard. I vowed not to be caught off guard tonight or anytime soon.

Those boys were fit to be tied and as riled up as a nest of hornets with a stick run plum through their nest. Revenge for those that died and the rewards of lots of money can sometimes be a big incentive to pursue us when they know they shouldn't.

The one thing we had going for us was they didn't have any idea how much gold we had or if we had any gold at all, but if they could get our horses and our equipment that would bring a pretty good price up in the mining camps. I'm telling you that there is no way they will get our things without a good battle.

We stayed the night out on the desert and the next day we made a large circle back toward the stream and found a place with plenty of green grass to feed our stock. After three days of being on our guard we mounted up and headed west.

With our horses rested and well fed we made good time on into town. Sacramento is half way between the Sierra Nevada Mountain range and the ocean and was a much bigger town than any we'd seen anywhere in California since coming ashore or when we were on our way inland.

Small gold field camps were springing up everywhere in the mountains. The city of Sacramento was a young and growing town.

The village of Santa Cruz on the coast where we landed last spring was way south of us. Every village we'd seen in California was a whole lot smaller than this place. At this time the gold rush was making the city of Sacramento a growing town, way out here in California. It was growing and one day it would be the capital of this vast area.

I was from London Town back in England and houses back there were built right close together. In the last few years I hadn't seen a town like this and I didn't feel comfortable out in the streets. But I made up my mind that I would try to cope with it.

This place is still a mining town and things were chaotic. Pack horses and mule trains arrived most every day from a place on the coast called both Yerba Buena and San Francisco. Frisco was eighty-five long miles away.

Flat boats made their way up the Sacramento River almost daily. So supplies were quite plentiful in this two-horse town. The prices here in Sacramento were a whole lot more in line with prices elsewhere in the world. The prices in the mining camps were way out of line but miners had to pay the price or go without.

The first thing we did after selling our unwanted horses and taking care of the others was to get a hotel room and order up a good hot bath. In all my born days this is the first hot bath I've ever had and I took advantage of it by having more hot water brought in and put in the tub. Wow was this living or what? I'd taken many a baths in that icy cold water in the mountains and that's all right but it doesn't compare to hot water in a tub and time to enjoy it. Up there it was get in and scrub yourself as fast as you could and get out before you froze to death. It was the nicest bath I'd ever had. It made me relax, feel comfortable and at ease. Man-oh-man did it ever feel good.

As ole English sat there his thoughts turned to Mabel Frith. I wondered where she was today and if she was all right. I knew in my mind that I'd probably not see her again. She was more than likely frozen to death up in those hills, if she wasn't she must be cold up there. This desolate country has a way of swallowing up people if you don't keep your eyes on them. The Friths were gone and so were the Ames Boys and I had to resign myself to that even if I didn't like it one bit.

In my mind I still remember Mabel's lighthearted laughter that came from her, on those nights we spent together, that lady was as pretty as any painted picture I ever saw. Her long red hair was a sight to see and I wish I could see it now.

Well that's one wish that I'm pretty sure won't come to pass. But if they are still alive she's more than likely up there with her family in that deep snow digging around for the allusive gold. I hope they have found what they were after and feel comfort in what they have. Thinking like that gave me a heavy heart.

Gold is where you find it, that much I've learned. (Back in 1842 near Los Angeles the first authenticated gold mine was worked.) Back then this area called California belonged to the Mexican government. I heard the United States purchased this and some other lands in the treaty of Guadalupe, which included the whole southwestern part of the country.

Sacramento, California was a growing mining town; in fact this is where it all really began. Captain Sutter who owned eleven squares leagues of land here and close to thirteen thousand head of beef, was looking for a sight to build a mill. In the process one of his men found some nuggets in the millrace and from that discovery the word got out and this peaceful country became what it is now.

You wouldn't think it but those few pieces of gold changed everything and everyone. Captain John Augustus Sutter, a former European army officer, employed several hundred men at the time. Fort Sutter had prospered and became famous. Before all this happened it was the greatest trading post in the entire West.

But once that yellow hunk of metal was found everything in California changed for the worse. His hired help deserted him to seek out the yellow metal. They thought that gold was everywhere around the American and Sacramento rivers of California.

Once Captain John Sutter lost his hired help, new people came flocking in and were stealing him blind. His cattle and his lands were soon gone. (Later in life Captain John Sutter died a poor man back East.) Right now he was fighting to save what he had.

Now this was a mining town and everywhere you looked you could see men digging and panning for gold. Some folks looked like they had no idea how to work the gold out of the ground and rivers. They were kind of like we were when we first came into this area. We were as green as grass or should I say we were ignorant about finding gold.

Like I said the prices were pretty good down here but don't get me wrong the prices here weren't reasonable by any means, but a whole lot better than the mining camps like Buck Shot Creek where an egg might cost you a buck each and a hot meal ten bucks or more.

This area down here was farmland and Mr. Sutter raises wheat and where he could get water on the soil he could grow almost anything. The problem was he couldn't get it harvested and folks stole everything that was in the fields. I wonder what it is like to be a dirt farmer, to turn the soil then set back and watch food sprout, then grow to produce a crop and build a home and raise a family with a good wife and kids.

Poor ole John Sutter must have had some pride in his accomplishments here; before this area turned topsy turvy and his holdings started to slip through his fingers. Somewhere out there the Frith family owns some farmland. Land they planned to live on some day.

That would be the downside of owning a piece of land like this, to build it up into something good and then have riff raff come along and snake it away from you a piece at a time, especially after all the time, money and hard work you put into it.

As I thought on it I decided to buy a good chunk of that farmland out there for my very own to live on and some day raise a family. All kinds of people were speculating with land in this area and city; lots all over town. Business lots would be for sale after the first of the year, in the city of Sacramento.

We decided to buy up a dozen city lots just as an investment. I wondered if we would make a dime on them. The six commercial lots were on the main drag and would be for small businesses. Plus we put some money down on half a dozen residential lots just in case we wanted to settle down here some day.

Mabel Frith and my time with her got me to thinking along the lines of settling down. I won't always be grubbing around in the water and dirt for gold. One day that will all be behind us and someday the gold will run out here in California and we must be prepared for life after gold mining. I wondered where all the folks out here would go when people couldn't find any more yellow stuff.

The weather down here in the low lands in the wintertime was quite respectable. But up there in the Sierra Nevada Mountains a fellow could freeze his tail feathers off real quick and never be seen again.

As we moseyed around town that second night we took time to stop in at the assayer's office to see what people were getting for their precious metal. As we watched folks being paid, it looked like we had a bonanza stashed away up there in those dirt banks. I hoped it would stay safe, up there in those hills. Someday we needed to get the gold down here and turn it into cold hard cash.

The very next day we turned some of our yellow metal into hard cash. By the looks of things the gold we'd brought down from the mountains was going to be a bonanza for us. Once we saw this we decided to buy up more than a dozen city lots here in Sacramento. Once we got started buying we didn't know when to stop.

We looked for and found a shack here in town to rent for a couple of months. The outlandish price made me wince but for two or three months I felt we could handle it. We walked up and down the streets and all around the town and took in all the city sights. Everywhere there were things to see so we went hog wild.

THE AMES

On the fourth day in town we ran slap dab into the Ames Brothers and we invited them to come and stay with us until they could find a place of their own or whatever. I truly wanted them to get back with us on a permanent basis. A man can never have more friends then he needs and I was no exception.

The Ames boys, Tom and Dick, had struck a good pocket and drew enough gold out of it to make them rich. They'd buried most but before they had it all hid a gang of claim jumpers moved in and robbed them of nearly all that they hadn't buried. It's lucky they were still alive. They thought they still had a pretty good stake to see them through whatever was ahead in life. I'm sure glad that they made the big strike. I often worried about them and I was glad they made it off the mountain alive.

We were around the kitchen table shooting the bull about everything that happened to come up. Tom in his travels met a nice young lady that he's taken a shine to and she'd told him about the land back East and how the grass grew thick and lush to a horse's belly. The land should make beef grow strong and fat and further east there was a market for them.

Right away I got interested in the girl that he had met. Tom said "her name is Mary Ellen, We found her and her family snow bound up there on the mountain. That gal is something else; she's as pretty as any picture I ever saw. Mary Ellen has a sister that will make your eyes pop out."

"Is her sister's name Mabel Frith and does she live with a big family in a couple of praire schooner wagons?"

"You got it my friend, how'd you know about them? Did you meet them somewhere? Wait a minute are you the guy Mabel is always dreaming about? No way, are you that nice. No it must be someone else. If it's you where did you meet her, English?"

"They pulled their wagons up at the mouth of Cabin Creek last fall and checked that canyon out for gold. That David Frith really knows mining. He makes us look like a bunch of ignorant bums out there grubbing around in the water."

"Ya, I heard. That boy is sure tight lipped about what he knows about mining. But I don't blame him a whole lot. They aim to find a mother lode for themselves first. I'm rooting for them to strike it big. Well anyway Dick and I helped pull them off the mountain and got them down to the low land. Somehow they had two wagons up there. With all the horses, theirs and ours we rescued one wagon and the family. Early next spring we must help them get back up there and retrieve their stuff before someone else does."

"Where are they at now Tom?"

"Art, they got a place northeast of here with a house on it. When we pulled into their dooryard about eight claim jumpers occupied their house. Dick and I didn't feel like it was our business, especially since the Friths were going to try to evict them by legal means. But I didn't see any law in this jerk water town to speak of, so what recourse did they really have? Not very much is my guess."

"Tom do you know where are they staying now?" In my mind I thought man-oh-man was I glad that Mabel was close by,

"English they have a tent pitched and their wagon is parked just west of town on the river."

As his words died away I was on my feet and headed for the door. I was gonna go see my girl before she found someone else to think about. As this ole gander started to waddle up Main Street he thought, I wonder how far out of town their camp is.

From the edge of town I looked north and saw nothing that looked like their outfit. That's when I decided to go get my horse. Their camp was about a mile outside of town on the river and as I arrived I could smell coffee and saw Mabel bending down tending the fire.

While I was still a good ways off I dismounted and in a strong voice I said "hello the camp."

Mabel stood up with a start, looked my way and with a squeal of delight gave out with a "hello English."

With her apron in hand she made a mad dash my way. Before she got to me I could see a black smudge on her nose and cheek, but what I was looking for was the wonderful smile she always had for me.

She slowed then stopped and a big smile captured her face "hello English, I'm sure glad to see you again."

I said, "I've missed you Mabel."

At those words she came into my arms, "Oh Arthur, I've missed you so." At first I didn't know where to put my hands so I didn't touch her with them. I change my mind as she hung on tight and didn't let go. When I looked down at her beautiful face those luscious lips came up to meet mine and held on tight. Wow was this ever a wonderful reunion.

This was something wonderful to savor. Heaven must be nice but can it ever be any better than this? "Lord Jesus, I thank you for this women that seems to want me, need me and somehow she loves this ole boy from England." The Duck didn't hesitate, he told her right off, "I love you girl." Wow! I didn't think she could hold me any tighter but she did.

This ole gander listened real close to Mabel's words, as she said "Honey, I've missed you so very much. I wasn't sure I'd ever see you again once we left your valley. Once the deep snow and cold weather came I wasn't sure we'd make it out of the mountains alive. I know now that those mountains get plenty of deep snow in the winter time and we were lucky we got some help." She hugged me tight and said "Oh Arthur, I'm so glad to see you again." I hadn't missed the words 'honey I've missed you so.' That is my sentiments exactly.

We talked for a long moment about how we missed each other and kissed a lot more. No matter how many people were watching us we were by ourselves. Then hand in hand we ambled on back to the fire and the Frith family that had gathered to watch.

Mr. Frith had hard eyes for me at first but softened a smidgen when Erma his wife slipped her arm into his and said something into his ear. Aaron the oldest son, trying to ease the moment, asked, "Is the coffee ready yet? If it is I'll take some in a cup, hot and black."

Mabel still holding my hand said "would you like some fresh coffee, Arthur?"

"You bet your bottom dollar I would my sweet lady."
With a big ole smile just for me she let loose of my hand.
Put on her apron, then picked up the hot pot with the corner
of her apron plus a tin cup and filled it to the brim. Then
she went around the campfire filling every cup from the big
coffee pot. I watched her every move as she went about her
business. Wow what a lovely woman!

When she'd finished she came back to me and snuggled
up close. Her show of warm emotions was a big surprise to
me. This English lad glanced at her folks across the fire to
see if everything was okay with them. They were talking and
didn't seem to notice.

I must admit I liked what I saw; this young lady was all
women. Her long red hair was soft and silky and came below
her shoulders. She was quite a sight to see as she moved
around the fire. That lovely lady of mine watched me and
smiled her big smile just for me.

"Arthur, my folks and I have come to an understanding
and now agree that I'm old enough to make the decision on
who I want courting me. They will all watch out for me. My
whole family will point out any faults they see in a man."

I felt that warm body up close to mine and I began to
sweat like a leaky wooden pail before the water swells it
up tight. I had no idea I would get this kind of a reception
when I saw Mabel again. I thanked my God for small favors.
"You know Lord I really don't know very much about this
marvelous vivacious little woman and I'm already thinking
of my life with her in some small house somewhere. I realized
that small houses are all I ever lived in.

The outward things I can see like she's energetic,
cheerful, spirited, effervescent and just full of life. But this

ole gander doesn't know her likes and dislikes or her moods. I'm a-guessing we need to spend a whole lot more time with each other. I just love being around her and this closeness is fantastic." With that said I pulled her a smidgen closer to me, just enough so that only Mabel and I knew it.

For the first time in my life I felt pride and a whole lot of admiration for this little lady. Somehow she had worked it out with her parents and they now accept me as a man to be trusted with their lovely daughter. Now I've got to live up to their expectations and prove I'm worthy of their trust.

In the next couple of weeks Tom and I spent more time with the Friths than we did with Big Mac, Dick Ames or Justin Jenkins. This was a pleasant time for me and I got to watch Mabel in good times and in bad. I was beginning to know her like no other woman I had ever met, which didn't include very many women.

She was more than a friend to me; she was fast becoming a woman to love and I did love her. But was our time together to short to court good women for marriage? Any other place in the world I'd say yes but out here to many things can change in a short time. Without marriage once we leave Sacramento things could change completely and I might never see her again.

I must make my move now before we leave or possibly I could live my life without her. I made up my mind to talk to her folks again very soon. I felt Mabel wanted me or I'd not say a word to anyone. All I had to do was work up the courage to ask Mr. Frith for this red-headed beauty's hand in marriage.

Tom Ames had eyes for Mabel's sister Mary Ellen and it looked like a good match. Some folks would think seventeen was a bit young and maybe it is, but out here women often were married a lot younger. I watched them and they looked good together and I knew Tom was very much in love with Mary.

Tom had a good stake and would treat her well. He was a good man, the better of the two brothers. Yah, it was a good match but I can't speak for her folks. They seemed to hold a tight rein on their women where men are concerned.

Did Mr. Frith want to marry his girls off, absolutely not? He seemed to be holding on to them for dear life and I guess I don't blame him one bit. What would English do if he were the head of that clan? Her older brothers were okay with me for some reason, but with others they were as protective as all get out. I'd be mighty hard on any strangers chasing after my daughters if my girls were as desirable as these young ladies were. Their brothers did run off some suitors. I'm betting these two red-headed ladies have a hot temper if pushed too far and not allowed to let off steam once and a while.

I'd only seen the good side of Mabel and I'm not sure there is a red-hot side of her. I'd seen her in some spots where she could have lost her temper but that stern loving disposition always prevailed. Mabel seemed to have a level head on her shoulders and she wasn't afraid of hard work.

You could see the helpmate in her. She was a pleaser and more than willing to do her fair share and seemed to be quite secure in who she was. These were things I noticed in her as I observed her in her daily routine. All these things only made me want her more. Yes, I loved her enough to make a commitment for life.

As I looked at life with her and without her, I chose life with her every time. If I thought about life without her I'd get a sinking feeling inside, kind of like when they shanghaied me aboard the Downey Cruiser three years back and was thrown in that dark hole. That my friend is an occurrence I never want to experience again.

She told me that she'd been a schoolteacher back up in Michigan for two years. She gave it up to come out west and be with her family. She loved kids and wanted a passel of them. Mabel opened up to me and revealed herself. It was quite an eye opener.

I was impressed that she would open her life to me like this. She told me many wonderful things and I loved every minute of it. She told me things I thought were really outstanding in a women or anyone for that matter. After she'd rattled on for awhile she turned to face me and asked, "Tell me about your life as a child, English."

"Honey you don't want to hear about what I've done in the past. There ain't any of it good. I was merciless and cruel, not ever caring a wit about anyone. That was the old man before Jesus made me as I am now. Mabel honey, I hate to think back on some of the things I did as a kid, but that's all under the blood of Jesus and he has thrown it into His Sea of forgetfulness. Never to be remembered again."

She didn't give up altogether but said, "Okay you can tell me later."

Everyone around knew they were mighty handsome ladies. The time I spent with her made me want her even more. This love affair was all I could think of. I must make her my wife before we return to the Sierra Nevada Mountains and that's only a couple months away.

Saturday was the day I planned to approached Mr. and Mrs. Frith and ask for Mabel's hand in marriage once again. What would I do if they said no? Well this ole dude wasn't gonna let them say no or stall me this time. This Englishman was determined to take this lady for better or worse. I knew she would make my life a whole lot better once we tied the knot.

They'd gone to the new town marshal and were getting nowhere fast in displacing the squatters on their home place. So we talked about going out there in force and see if that might make them want to leave on their own accord. Mr. Frith was a farmer at heart and wanted to get some fieldwork in and plant some crops. He felt there would be a great demand for fresh vegetables and such like in the mining camps next spring and I think he's right.

Aaron, David and Rusty told me earlier that they were pushing to have their family stay on the farm when they moved back into the mountains in the spring and ole English agreed with them whole-heartedly.

Thursday early in the morning, Mr. Frith, his three older sons, Tom and Dick Ames and we three started for the Frith homestead twenty miles to the northeast on the American River. As we traveled we carried pots and pans and extra food in our saddle bags and on a pack horse, a tent and all we would need in case it took a little longer than we thought to pry them loose from the Frith's house.

It was about two in the afternoon when we saw the homestead off in the distance. We hoped a show of force would do the trick and get them to leave the place on their own. We were ready to carry it to them and do what was needed to be done to get the Firths back on their home place.

We three were pretty sure they wouldn't be moved on their own so Harvey and I prepared the men on how to approach this eviction. In my little pea picking mind I thought anyone that takes over someone else's place and moves right in and then won't move out when the owners return home aren't going to just up and leave without a lot of prying.

I'm a-thinking this bunch of hard noses will have to be made to leave. To tell you the truth I don't really know what that will cost them or us. This helping the Friths get their home back is not my cup of tea. I'd learned as a little boy, don't borrow trouble and here I am getting into a peck of trouble and it ain't even mine. If it weren't for that wonderful gal of mine I'd be back in town ordering up another hot bath at the hotel about now. That would be a whole lot more enjoyable than getting shot at by a bunch of hooligans.

If they wouldn't leave the premises the only other avenue was to bring gunplay into the equation. This ole boy was trying to live above that kind of life, if at all possible. America is proving to be a really wild and woolly place out here in California and way short of law and order. Without any law to speak of in this area men thought they could do as they darn well pleased and in many places they did without any hindrance from the law or anyone. Mr. Frith and I would ride up to the front door; the others would hang back. We would dismount and put our horses between the interlopers and us and ask them if they would please leave the premises. Let them know that Mr. Frith needed to get his family back into his home and show the intruders that he had ownership papers.

The others would hang back and use their horses for a shield and keep their rifles at hand and ready for war if it came to it. Our hope was that a show of force and common sense would prevail here today.

Tom Ames said "English, don't you take any chances. The house isn't worth one life good or bad. If we have to we can burn it down to get them out and just build another one, English."

"Ya, I hear ya Tom." I thought to myself he's right it isn't worth the life of any of my friends. At a hundred and fifty feet, six of my friends stopped, dismounted and prepared to wage war. We moseyed into the dooryard dismounted and put our horses between the house and us. When we were ready Mr. Frith hailed the house.

A big man opened the front door and looked out. He hesitated for a bit then stepped out on to the porch and said, "Good afternoon gentlemen." Another man followed and I knew him from our ordeal when we came down off the mountain. This fellow tried to ambush us on our way into town, the guys we led out into the desert.

The very instant I recognized him he recognized me and got as jumpy as a toad on a cook stove then went for his revolver. I'd never drawn on a man before but it was time to be down and dirty. The young man was an eager beaver and pretty fast but somehow my revolver cleared leather first. Then I felt the buck of it in my hand and a red spot appeared on his chest and his knees gave way.

His red and black-checkered flannel shirt ended up with a little round hole in its pocket. The forty-four slug flung him backwards into the house. The big bear of a man dove back inside right behind him but I think someone put lead into him for I heard someone in there yell in pain as the door was flung shut and latched.

Gunfire erupted from the house and down went my mount. He was thrashing around on the ground so with my revolver I finished him off. A slug from the house traveled through my new shirt, the bullet jerked me sideways and took some flesh from under my left arm. The crease wasn't deep but it sure did hurt as blood quickly showed up on the cloth.

I could hear gunfire from behind me and from the house so this ole boy kept his head down. The Hawkins rifle was leaning against the barrel of the dead horse and my revolver started punching forty-four caliber holes in the house near the windows.

Mr. Firth's horse was down and I could see he had a wound in his leg. Blood was dripping down his leg into the dust. The man didn't give up, he was active with his shotgun and I heard it spiting double 0 buckshot into his house.

The next time I looked his way he'd pulled off his red neckerchief and was about to bandage his left leg. His teeth were clenched tight together as he fought the pain. He was a tough ole codger that's for sure.

The duck had one slug left in his pistol so he decided to save it until he saw someone to shoot at. I quickly pulled out the cylinder and pushed powder down in each hole. And shoved a chunk of lead on top of the black powder seated them and started to replace the percussion caps onto the nipples.

I realized the gunfire had slowed then stopped all together. I figured the men were reloading, when that happened the door of the house popped opened and two gents made a mad dash at my position firing all the way. I had three caps replaced by this time so that made four chambers ready to fire. Quickly I put the pistol back together and got ready for trouble.

As they hot footed it my way hot lead hit the first man in the stomach and that look on his face was imprinted on my mind. He lost his revolver and skidded in the dust and moaned and groaned not ten feet away. Let me tell you something that episode gave me the willies and hurt me down deep inside. But I didn't have time to dwell on it, for death was stalking me on two legs.

The second man had his revolver lined up on me when someone from behind me took him off his feet. Whoever did that may have saved my life for my shot probably would have been just a smidgen too late. My reactions allowed another slug to bury itself in him. The man was stopped dead in his tracks and then thrown backwards to the ground.

I saw red and gray stuff escape from the back of his head and splattered into the dooryard. A third man almost made it around the corner of the house before JJ's weapon made its presence known in this little war. Somehow ole Jenkins had dodged every bullet fired his way. This man must be light on his feet.

From that point on all I could hear from the house were moans of pain. Justin Jenkins' horse was still on his feet. JJ was moving toward the front door as fast as he could go and I was hot on his heels.

We both busted through the front door at the same time. There was no real resistance from the outlaws inside the house. All resistance had flown the coop along with the last three trespassers. Every intruder in the house was down and bleeding on the floor or deader than a mackerel.

As we were removing the weapons from the house a rifle roared from outside. As I moved through the doorway, out in the yard the guys were all looking to their right and Big Mac was lowering his rifle. My eyes quickly picked up what they were looking at. A man was on his knees by the outhouse, with his head down looking at the blood spot on his chest. The guy was a young man probably not twenty years old yet.

This kid had English thinking of his life as a kid back in England, ouch that could have been me with a hole in my chest, living on the wrong side of the law. That could be me over there sucking the sod just like he is now. Once I found Jesus, He took away the will to do evil and exchanged it for a will to do what was right and help others.

Everything in my life now revolves around loving and doing good for other people. That's why it hurts so much to see men spend their lives so cheaply. Back in the house a man swore and was cussing a blue streak, he was dying and wanted to know if his boy was all right.

"Sir, is your boy about eighteen?"

"Ya, he was out to the john taking a crap…., will ya look after him for me…., He didn't want to be on the owl hoot trail with us…, I forced him to come with me…., Please help him get back home to his ma…."

He sank back to the floor and just looked at me; the talking had sucked all his strength out of him. I watched him as blood was being pumped from his body. In a matter of moments he breathed his last. His last breath came out in one long exhale.

I couldn't see any reason to tell him his son had paid the ultimate price for riding with men on the owl hoot trail. Why should I burden him anymore than he already was? I was feeling a smidgen dizzy myself so I sat down on the floor and leaned against the wall. All of a sudden this English kid was worn plum out and a little sleepy.

"JJ asked, are you alright English?"

"I'm not sure, maybe. I feel a little woozy when I try to move around. Maybe I should stay close to the bed if I can."

Just then the guys came in. Mr. Frith came hobbling in with them. They started dragging the dead bodies out into the dooryard. The blood was soaking into the board floor and the ladies wouldn't be too happy about that. I'm hoping they didn't haul me outside. Right now I didn't feel up to it. Along with all the talk English heard horses' hooves in the dooryard, so he hollered who is that? Guns appeared all over the place and men headed for the door.

I heard Mabel's voice out in the dooryard. But ole English didn't feel up to moving, so he stayed right where he was and just listened to the guys talk. David Frith said "what you girls doing out here? I thought we agreed you would stay at the wagon until we came and got you?"

Without answering him Mabel said for all to hear, "Where's Arthur? He better not be dead? Where is he?"

"Calm down girl he's in the house. The boy's been wounded." Justin said later with a big oh smile on his face. David told her, "I think he still alive" and that boy got a dirty look.

That girl didn't waste any time getting off her horse and finding me. Boy-oh-boy did it feel good that she was so protective of me. I think they would have been in a whole slew of trouble if I'd died in here. That's the woman I've got promised to me and she is quite a gal. There ain't no way I'm gonna let her slip through my fingers. She had unlocked the door to my heart with all this love, care and concern for me. This sweet little lady of mine looked me square in the eyes and said "how you doing honey?"

"OK, I'm sure glad you came."

She pulled my shirttail out of my pants and gazed at the wound and then called for someone to get a clean pail of water. She looked for and found a clean granite pan and drew some warm water from the reservoir on the back of the cook stove and put the pan with the water in it on the stove to heat.

No one was in the house but us. The first thing this ole dude knew her lips were on mine and she began to smooch with me. Man-oh-man did Art ever love those velvet hands all over his face and neck. This foxy lady was as pretty as a wild flower in full bloom. Her hand got close to the wounded area and I stiffened up like a board.

She said "oh honey did I hurt you?"

"Not too bad, the duck hollered before he got hurt." I didn't say it but the wound hurts like billy blazes all the time.

She held a clean rag on the wound as she waited for the water to boil on the wood cook stove then added cold water and began to cleanse the wound of all foreign material. I watched her face to see how bad it was and from the looks it wasn't all that good. The blood had never stopped trickling down my side.

When she was done with the cleaning she went about bandaging it up. The dressing was tight and should stop the bleeding after a bit. Mabel had done a good job. Next she got her father inside and repeated the job on him. We were laid on the beds that were moved from the bedrooms and made to stay in them.

I tried to get up off the cot and almost fell on my face. The loss of blood made me weak as a newborn kitten. That is when her red hair started to show her true colors. Needless to say this ole dude got a good tongue lashing for not asking for help when he wanted to get up. But after she made her point she settled down immediately and my rewards were phenomenal. I was treated even better than her father.

This kid dozed off for a moment and awoke to find it was dark outside. I said "hello" to no one in particular and straight away Mabel was at my side. "Honey, where is everyone?"

"My brother David is here and your friend Harley MacDonald. They will stay until they get our family moved out here. There were more bedrolls laid out then there were men in the house. The men aren't sure that all the gang was at the house today when the shooting took place. So they're hid out a ways from the house and were keeping the three of us safe. The family will all be here tomorrow before dark sometime.

Arthur, do you want something to eat or drink, the outlaws left us some victuals to eat and we have some yummy chow sitting on the back of the stove."

With that said she gave me a big ole smile. "Mabel, when your father has something to eat I'll have a bite to eat with him, you don't need to fix a meal special for me, I'm not the King of England."

She bowed low and said "your highness, King Arthur, it's warm and ready to munch on anytime you want some."

She laughed and I had to smile at what she had to say, this lady had a wonderful sense of humor and it only made me love her more, if that was possible. This ole hardheaded Englishman could hardly wait for Sunday to come around and have this awesome woman become my wonderful wife. Oh how I love this little lady and oh the oodles and oodles of love I want to bestow on her.

Everyone knows about this incredibly, sweet, charming and beautiful redhead. God was really shining His love down on me. As this hard headed Englishman thought on this she came and sat on the edge of the bed and we talked of our life together.

"Honey babe, what do you want out of life?" She smiled and we talked about everything from soup to nuts. Mr. Frith was in his bedroom snoring up a storm as we talked. His snoring might not have been a thunder storm but it sure sounded like a grumbler to me."

We got acquainted with our likes and dislikes and we had a lot of the same things in common. She wanted a large family and I'm not so sure about that. I kind of liked the idea but I've never had a family around except Harley, JJ, and the Ames brothers, Tom and Dick and those boys aren't little kids. Little kids are something different they look like they might break in to real easy. No I'm not all that sure about little kids.

She said, "Just you wait, once you get a hold of one of those little buggers that belong to you it'll change your mind. Babies are the greatest thing that ever was. If you want to stay neutral you don't ever want to hold them in your arms and say sweet things to them. If you do you'll love them to pieces."

Just that statement alone made me want this gorgeous gal. She had a deeper insight into life than I'd ever dreamed anyone could have. Yes, babies are a subject that I'd never put much thought into. My thoughts were mostly on what was best for Arthur Drake and how to survive in this rough ole world. All my life I'd fought against authority of every kind, until I ran head first into the love of Jesus.

I see a lot of wisdom in what she had to say. You better bet she is going to make this man a wonderful wife and a marvelous mother for my kids. She must have been an awesome teacher to have all this love for the people and hand it out to all that she came in contact with. Man-a-live this lady was really something.

Her life hasn't been any better than most anyone you see out here, but it hasn't done anything to turn her sour and that's a wonder to me. Yes she knows Jesus, if she didn't I couldn't possibly make her my wife. Without Him in her life we would be in two different worlds. My Lord is who I really see when I look onto that lovely face of hers.

"Lord, please don't let me ever take Mabel Frith for granted and help me treat her as the lady she is." I see it all too often how women seem to become like slaves to their men folks. God's word tells us that women are our helpmates not a doormat to walk on. We talked for a little longer and my eyes wanted to close so I lay back and she stopped talking and it wasn't long and the duck was off to nodsville.

I woke with a start; Mabel's hand was on my forehead and when my eyes opened she put on that big ole smile just for me. "How do you feel English?"

"I've felt better in my life. I'm gonna get up and move around a bit if I can. This ole boy didn't get shot in the foot or the leg like your dad did. How is your paw anyway?"

"You both have a low grade fever but we'll know more about it in a day or two. If it doesn't get any worse than it is right now, it'll be a breeze for both of you."

I was in the living room and he was in a first floor bedroom. Mabel's family hadn't gotten here yet and David Frith was in a dither about it. Mabel told me "if they weren't here by night fall, David was going to look them up first thing in the morning."

I had little fear for their safety with the Ames boys, JJ and the rest of the Firth clan riding escort. My biggest worry that I didn't tell anyone about was, are all the gang members dead and buried or would some of them come waltzing in here and cause us some more trouble?"

I needed to get up and move around in case it came to a confrontation with someone. I wondered if I could be counted on to hold up my end of the deal. When I got up everything began to swim and this duck sat back down to rest. After a minute or so King Arthur tried it again and got the same results. I'm a guessing it's time to sleep again.

Unbeknownst to me five men rode in just before dark, looking for their friends and Harley sent them off to Sacramento to find them. At first they were a little hesitant about going but Big Mac spun them a story as to why they left. Soon they were straddling their mounts again and headed southwest toward Sacramento.

Later there would be more people here to defend the place. Mac said, "Mabel was out there with a shotgun ready to do her part. English, I'm not sure you're good enough for her. That little lady is quite a prize. I'm telling you right now, sonny boy, you'd better treat that woman right or you'll have to deal with me and I ain't planning on being gentle with ya."

He was smiling but I knew he wasn't funning with me. He was serious and the gander caught that little message. He didn't need to worry I had the best intentions in the world for this exceptional little lady.

What he said about her I already knew she had it in her. She had an inner strength that said whatever I need to do I can. Anything she did wouldn't surprise me one iota.

It must have been around eight o'clock when the Frith wagons rolled into the dooryard. It was dark out there. They had trouble on the trail and needed to put the steel rim back on the wheel and soak it in the American River for an hour or so until it was tighter on the wood spokes. That's the reason for the long delay. Just sitting around out in the sun, the wood dried up and shrunk.

They were sure they'd seen the five riders that had stopped here looking for their friends. The boys were a long ways off moving toward Sacramento. They would soon find out that they're old friends were not in town. Once they found that out what would they do about it?

The Family had a pair of crutches for Mr. Frith and he picked them up right away and started to use them. He had no broken bones only a flesh wound. We were both mighty lucky in that respect.

After a week the outlaws hadn't shown up so Dick Ames, JJ, and Harley MacDonald started off for town and a good bed to sleep in. Tom Ames was interested in Mary Ellen Frith so he stayed on and made his bed in a shed. It was probably as good, if not better than our shack up on Cabin Creek.

Our wedding didn't come off as we planed because of things that had happened but the following Sunday was the projected day. And come H-E-double toothpicks or high water it would happen or I'd know the reason why. On Saturday morning early Tom and I headed for town. I got the smoothest riding horse on the place. He was a friendly ole fur ball and that ole boy was smooth at any speed. I got into town without breaking open the wound and I felt relatively good.

The Friths would leave real early in the morning for town and we would all meet at the Methodist Church for Sunday school at nine-thirty. The wedding would take place at two in the afternoon. The preacher man was informed and the congregation was invited to celebrate with us. Everyone would bring a dish to pass and we'd have dinner on the grounds.

Many towns' people were getting ready to head for the mountains. Many men had worked the American and the Sacramento Rivers looking for the elusive gold and had worked in vain for it. There were a few working mines scattered throughout the valleys, along the rivers and streams.

Before long folks would be flocking into the hills. As soon as the weather warmed up a bit they'd be on their way. Some had jumped the gun and started into the mountains during the warm spell, then had to come back when the deep snow stopped them cold.

Others came prepared with snowshoes and got the jump on the rest making it to the high country. All the mountains and valleys were filled with snow and they couldn't do very much but would be up there when they could. Their thinking was they would get the jump on everyone else in finding the gold. When everyone else was still down below wishing they could get started they would already be up there.

The snow was bad enough when we left the mountains and they had gotten a lot more of the white stuff since we left. We weren't much worried about the gold we'd buried last fall. With all that snow up there no one could ever find it but us and that wouldn't be easy. The guys were kind of anxious to get back to work. But this ole boy had other things on his mind.

I had trouble getting to sleep, my thoughts were on Mabel Frith, our life together and our wedding tomorrow. I had no doubts about her; she is the one I wanted to spend my life with. While convalescing we talked often of what we would like to see happen in our lives.

She had no idea we had all that gold stashed away up there and that we were moderately rich. To tell you the truth we were so green we didn't have idea one how much gold we had stashed away. If we were careful it should set us up in a good business and see us through some hard times, if we got away from the high prices that were found in the gold fields.

WEDDING BELLS

We were up early and busy around the house getting ready for the day ahead. The guys were excited for me and kidded me all morning long. It was going to be a good day. I could hardly wait for my bride to be, to show up. The church was a little Methodist Church on the corner over on the main street of Sacramento.

It had a bell tower, a front porch and was relatively new from top to bottom. The preacher had gotten out here last fall and right away they put the thing up. By nine-thirty the Friths weren't here yet so the five of us ambled on inside and took a seat near the back so when they did come they could be seated with us without disturbing the service.

They ended up being about fifteen minutes late and for that quarter of an hour this ole duck conjured up all kinds of bad things happening to them. Big Mac put his hand on my shoulder and said "don't worry they'll be along in a bit." The big man tried to settle me down as best he could. So I made an effort to relax and it help a bit.

The real reason that I conquered the nervousness so well, was no more than twenty seconds went by and that lovely lady slid in beside me and give me one if those wonderful smiles and said "did you miss me, honey?"

I couldn't lie to her so the duck said in her ear "ya, I was a bit worried that you might be having some troubles getting here."

"Honey, everyone came in for the wedding, even Pa insisted we bring him and I'm pleased that he wanted to go through all this hassle to see us tied up tightly together. Paw has come around in the last month or so and I'm happy about it. I wanted him in favor of our union and not wishing it hadn't happened."

The Sunday school message was on a woman that touched the hem of Jesus' coat and was healed and why it happened. I'd never looked at it that way before. The worship service was really good and the lunch was great. The wedding took place at two-thirty. Holy cow was Mabel ever beautiful. Oh how lucky yours truly was that God saved this little lady for me.

We spent two days in the hotel enjoying every luxury they had, hot baths and all. Mrs. Drake was game for anything and it was a magnificent time for us. We left the hotel only twice and that was to go to the restaurant to eat, the rest of the meals we took in our room.

Until the gold fields opened up in the spring we would alternate our time staying at our little house and out at the farm. We talked about staying in the gold fields this summer and in that time we would decided where we would spend our lives. At this time we had no idea what we would do after we were done digging for gold.

We talked it over and purchased the small house in town that we'd rented. Even if we left this area the Friths could use it when they came to town to sell their products or buy supplies for the farm. Thirty miles was too far to go home after selling all day. It would be after midnight before they got home.

We clued Mabel in on the fact that we'd taken some gold out of the ground up there in the Sierra Nevada Mountains. We didn't tell her how much only that it was a fair amount. More than enough to get a business started.

My little confession surprised her. She thought all along that we were just making it and were still looking for the big strike. What really took her by surprise was when I told her of the small vein we took out of Cabin Creek Canyon. David was sure that there wasn't any gold to speak of in that Canyon. "We thought you guys were just wasting your time digging up there.

"Honey, that stream was used up. We'd taken some gold out of it and we knew right where the gold ran out so we had an idea where to look. David gave us enough information to find it and we watched your family dig holes and copied what your family did and hit a vein in rock that yielded up a fair amount of the yellow stuff. Don't ask me how much we have Honey, because I'm not sure.

We'd decided to divide our gold, share and share alike with the Ames boys. We would put it all together and divide the money evenly, that way they could get a good start. Or start one huge business and all work in it. We don't have it all worked out as you can see."

Mabel asked, so I went on to tell her how we come to end up in America. This ole London bad boy left out who I was as a kid and picked it up when I left London Town and paid passage on that tub bound for New York and was kidnapped by the captain. I related to her how we five escaped and won the mine and the little cabin in a card game and I haven't played a hand of poker since.

"Honey, I'm not sure God wants me fooling around at the card table anymore and I'm not sure He ever did. Back then the duck had nothing to lose but now he has everything to lose. An old man in London Town once told me a fool and his money are soon parted and I ain't—haven't forgotten it.

It was the last of February that we saw three men from the wooden tub that we'd escaped from. They said "they'd gotten free shortly after we did." Was that the honest to God truth or a bald face lie, to throw us off guard? These were the captain's men so we didn't know if we could trust them or not. We set a watch on them. For two long days we kept an eye on them and they left and went down river.

Mutiny was a capital crime and none of us wanted to swing from the end of a rope so we all packed our things and got ready to move out of town. We stayed at the Firth's farm for a week and finally said our goodbyes to the family. That sounded strange to me 'the family.'

It was the first of March and we saw the rivers in this area starting to crowd their banks then overflow them. We were on our way east, the whole gang of us, toward the mountains, the three older Frith boys, the Ames brothers, Big Mac, JJ, plus my honey and me.

In the distance we could see that the mountains had plenty of snow yet and if it was like it was last year they would have snow until mid-summer. Last summer the Sierra Nevada Mountains really never gave up all the snow. In the shaded areas and places high up, it kept its hold on some of the white stuff until snow came again.

The Frith brothers knew exactly where they wanted to go. First they picked up their stranded wagon and then headed north away from us.

The snow was deep in places but we made it into Cabin Creek Canyon. From a distance we saw dark smoke drifting lazily skyward. It was a quaint sight with the snow covering the landscape and that ole cabin setting on that knoll above the creek. The bright sun, the creek, the cabin with dark smoke drifting skyward, the dark green pines and high mountains peak all worked together to make this a beautiful scene.

Not a thing moved except the smoke, clouds and the babbling brook. The hut like house looked toy like in the distance and a man stood like a tiny tin soldier, on guard, under the eaves, watching our slow progress.

Up the mountain a shadow broke over the hills and followed a cloud across our canyon floor then up and over the next hill and out of sight. A slight breeze gusted and moved the pine tree next to me and I heard it whispered "hello Arthur." Off in the distance we heard the forlorn wail of a lone coyote seeking its mate. As we moved in this country the crystal clean snow crunched under foot.

We rode into the canyon, up the creek and eased up to the cabin. First thing I noticed was that the bearskin that we nailed on the side of the cabin was missing and the woodpile was a lot smaller then when we left. They had a tiny little mutt that yapped all the time. I wonder if he is the reason they knew we were coming from so far away. From what I can see there isn't going to be anyone sneaking up on them.

The small cabin was occupied by two men and that dog. They had come up on snowshoes last winter to get a head start and almost froze to death in one of those winter mountain blizzards. The men wanted to thank us for all we'd done for them and they did thank us over and over again for the shelter food, fuel and that big warm bear hide that kept them so warm on those long cold nights.

The two men told us that it wasn't all that easy to sleep in a hammock so they put all the hides on the floor and slept on them like a real bed. They asked, "did you take any gold out of the stream in this canyon?"

We weren't all that sure we wanted to answer that question so we told them "we were up here all last summer, but never found enough gold in this stream to make it pay. We were finding some yellow stuff just before we went down, but that ran out on us also. We filed on that spot while we were down in Sacramento, but we aren't sure there was any gold still left in the ground or the water in this valley. Over the winter we decided to give it one more try and see if there was any gold left in the ground. We're going to try digging a few days and see what we come up with. We wouldn't even do that except we have a warm place to sleep on these cold nights. If we don't hit pay dirt pretty darn quick we will be leaving this valley and looking for greener pastures.

We added onto this cabin last fall so we could stay the winter. But if we had stayed, we'd have lost our horses to starvation so when the snow got real deep we high tailed it down to Sacramento and are we glad we did."

From that encounter with those two I could see I needed to keep an eye on folks for these guys couldn't keep their eyes off Mabel. No way could I blame them for she was something special to look at. The duck has a prize much better than gold and he must look out for her at all times.

Do you men have a tent or something to stay in; we do need our cabin back. They gathered their stuff together and set their tent up a quarter of a mile downstream and played around in the water a little for two days hitting the high spots in the creek and then pulled out for greener pasture.

We got settled in and the guys let Mabel and I have the back room all to ourselves. Except for all the food and supplies they piled in here. We had a bed instead of a hammock to sleep in. It was nice to have a warm woman to lie next to on these cold nights.

We set our biggest tent up over that mineshaft again and the five of us went to work and moved a lot of rock without finding that vein again. We'd all but given up on finding any more yellow stuff in this dry hole.

The third day Mabel came up to visit. As we stood there talking she knelt down and picked up a bit of rock and asked, "What is that in there English?" She handed it to me and by golly she found a rock with a sewing thread size piece of gold running through it.

I guess you know we took our time and inspected the mineshaft a little more closely and found where it took an almost 90 degree turn to the left. The size of the vein was so small that we had missed it in our eagerness to extract the gold from the ground. If the vein didn't get larger soon it would take a larger operation than we had to harvest what little gold there was in the ground here. Our hope was that in a foot or two the thread size vein would get a whole lot bigger.

After pounding our way through solid rock for another eight feet we gave it up as a lost cause. The mine had just petered out. We filled in the hole, tore down the tent and took a week off to rest and relax.

We always kept an eye peeled for two-legged trouble. We'd seen six miners enter Cabin Creek Canyon in one day. They went way upstream to pan for gold. We took time to explain to them that there wasn't any more gold in this valley. They weren't convinced and headed upstream. I guess I understand their reluctance to believe strangers.

The next day four more men came in. The day after that eleven more made it into our valley. Tom Ames and Justin got a chance to talk with one man and he said "the reason we came up here was, two claims had been filed in this valley already and they assumed there was gold up here waiting to be scooped up off the ground."

"Sir, folks have scoured this valley and there ain't been enough gold found in here to feed a flock of chickens fer a day."

The way folks were streaming into this valley we figured it was high time we lit a shuck out of here and head for a place that would produce for us before someone else moved in and set up camp.

On Tuesday we loaded our mining equipment, food, clothes and everything we would needed on our horses and lit out for Falls Creek Canyon and the operation we'd started there. The weather had turned off really nice. The snow was melting fast and the water was pushing out of their banks and rampaging downstream on its way to the American River.

The Ames boys had never been in this valley this high up. It was an all-new experience for them. As we climbed higher and higher they were surprised that there was a falls up here and how tall it was. We worked our way up and around it and pulled into our former camping area by the stream.

They were surprised at the unusual color of the almost orange metal that we took from the cold water. The water didn't run with a rush like it did down below. The weather up here wasn't all that warm. The three warm days we had was making lots of water. It was starting to crowd its banks with all the new melting snow.

The higher up you were the slower the snow became water and so less of a rush to the sea. When the higher up water mixed with the melted snow further down it would become a flood and fight with its banks in its rush to find warmer weather.

It took a week for us to see our first gold seeker and after that there was a couple each day that wandered into our area.

Mabel wanted to help so we strung out along the creek to protect what we had found. One man stopped and got right in between Big Mac and Tom Ames and there was almost a fight. He didn't want to leave but finally he took his stuff and headed upstream and started working the creek up there.

We each staked out about twenty yards of Falls Creek and guarded it like it was a matter of life or death. Our tents were set up right on our claims. We had a guard on the tents that over looked our claims at all times. Even my sweet wife took her turn with a shotgun in her hands.

To tell you the truth I didn't get much done those days trying to dig gold and protect my sweet wife without her thinking I was.

The Ames boys took time and went over into Miners' Creek Canyon and tore down that sluice and brought it up to our mining camp where we assembled it and dug up the creek bottom and shoveled it into the sluice. In a month's time we'd taken every ounce of gold out of our claims.

The four guys JJ, Harley, Tom and Dick, hop-skipped and jumped around the miners that were working upstream from us to see if there was any gold further up the canyon. The last few miners they checked weren't finding any so we gave up on that idea.

For a week the four of us hit only the spots that looked good further upstream. We worked the stream for about a mile and a half from our camp and found nothing. We would return to our tents every night.

Not to give up this early in the season the five of us carried that monstrosity we called a sluice, downstream to the head of the falls. That water logged thing of ours weighted a ton and we had to float it when we could. All in fun everyone blamed me for riding and not carrying my share of the load.

Once we got it down to the head of the falls where we started so many months ago, from there we worked hard to work ourselves back upstream away from the falls. We shoveled every bit of that creek bottom into that sluice as we worked our way upstream back toward our claims. We had already worked this area with pans so we took very little gold from down here.

I watched the other miners from the hillside and made a mental note of who was finding gold and who wasn't. I could see where the gold ran out. Later if we needed to we could check here to see if there was a mother lode in this area.

I must admit this time spent up here with my wife was a special time for the two of us. She had taught me many things and was it ever fun learning from a good woman like her. This ole dude was a mighty good student and he didn't want the lessons to stop and she didn't want to stop teaching.

Mabel had eyes that said many things like "I love you"; on the other hand they could cut right through ya. You know what; I liked her sweet loving side a whole lot better. This sweet gal was game for about anything. Whatever I suggested she was ready to do it. I could have looked a million years and never found another one as good as her. Yes this is a fabulous female and she made a mighty wonderful wife.

MABEL

What was in store for the six of us? As much as we enjoyed this digging around in the dirt for gold we felt it was time to move on. The men felt we had enough gold stashed away to see us into a good business somewhere.

No one could think of a business that we all wanted to do. The one thing the guys didn't want to do again was break up the group. These young men had come through a lot of good times and they wanted to stay together.

I held back from expressing my view for a day or two then one night I presented my idea. They all thought it sounded like a pretty good idea even if it did come from me. I suggested we form a company and find a small town that looked like it would grow and each man find a business that he wanted to spend the rest of his life doing and start it in that place. If we work together we can make some small town grow and prosper. Everyone took hold of that idea and ran with it. If the truth were known the guys all loved the ideas and started making their own plans for what they wanted to do. If two wanted to do the same thing then we could work that out together.

I wondered why the guys brought so many extra horses up into the mountains. We had the six good ones we rode and eight big pack animals that had only light loads on them. Once we started picking up the heavy gold they had stashed all over the place, I begin to understand why. The yellow metal that they'd stashed away was mighty heavy and it didn't take much to load a horse down. In the process of collecting the gold we headquartered at the small log cabin on Cabin Creek.

When they came from the stash where the mother lode was hidden, in the ground, two horses couldn't carry it all. How could these men have found all this gold without an education in mining? They were sure closed mouth about what they'd collected last year. This ole girl had no idea these boys were so rich. English tried to prepare me for it, but I couldn't comprehend all he said about it.

They had talked about finding gold but I thought it was gonna be just a meager amount like most miners had found up here. They'd hidden everything they'd found up here in dirt banks all over the area. Back down below in Sacramento they let me see the small flecks they had in their leather pokes, but it wasn't all that impressive. That's all behind me now. Now I'm in awe of their stash.

I'm not only impressed but worried that thieves might find out we have all this gold and try to take it away from us. I sure wish my brothers Aaron, David, and Rusty were here to help guard all this treasure as we transport it down to the flat land.

It's been four months since Arthur made me Mrs. Mabel Drake. Arthur has proved to be a good man, a man worthy of a woman's love. From the first day I met English, up here, I think I've wanted him and God had brought it about. In his Word, Jesus says 'He'll give us the desire of our hearts.'

We are trying not to get me pregnant until we get off this mountain. We are using the rhythm system to keep it from happening. All farmers know about this and teach it to their kids early in life. English is open to all my suggestions on this subject, for he had no idea what to do.

The men keep asking about the mid-west and what it's like and if I thought it would be a good place to start a new life. This ole gal would tell them about it but it didn't make me happy. All I could think about was my family here in California and us moving back East, but a woman needed to follow her man.

We all knew these good men had jumped ship and come ashore southwest of here and the shipping company might still be looking for them in California. Arthur said, "He saw some of the crew from the Downey Cruiser when we were in Sacramento the last time and it worried him." I had mixed feelings wanting to stay in this area where my folks were and feeling a need to go with my husband so he could be safe. He needed to get far away from the seacoast to be safe and build our future.

English told me, "He really didn't know if the crew members were still loyal to the ship owners, the captain or like they said, they were on leave from the Downey Cruiser. He was pretty sure those boys would turn us in for any reward. I wondered if they were on leave looking the gold fields over or what." I'm surprised more crew members haven't jumped ship but maybe they don't have the chance.

We had so much gold at the cabin that only two men now went out to pick up the buried treasurer. The guys felt they needed more men to guard the cabin and the gold, we'd already gathered, and not so many out pulling it out of the ground. Justin Jenkins, Harley MacDonald and Arthur had to trade off making trips out to the mining area. They had buried their own stash secretly from each other. So if someone tortured them they couldn't give it all up.

Dick Ames left out of here like a big bird in a windstorm, looking for my brothers. The guys wanted more people to help move this load down out of the mountains. There were way too many places to ambush our party along the way. Once we were out on leveler ground it would be easier to be in control.

The gold was all in and we were talking about going down off this mountain to see my folks and stock up on supplies before we started east. That night Tom Ames came and sat down by me to talk. "Mrs. Drake you know Mary Ellen as well as anyone, do you think she'll say yes if I ask your Pa for her hand in marriage? She seems to like me and we get along just fine when we're together. But is she in love with me?"

"How do you feel about her Tom?"

"Miss Mabel, I love her a lot but it's hard to express it. I've worked hard to just work up enough courage to talk with you about her."

"Well Tom make it simple on yourself and just ask her, say Mary should I ask your pa if I can marry you and then see how that goes. Maybe you should first tell her that you love her and see how she reacts. That my friend is a way to see if you're the one."

I watched that good boy wrestle with what I'd said to the point that sweat broke out on his forehead and ran down his face and dropped off onto his flannel shirt. I liked this kindly gentleman a lot and Mary Ellen couldn't do much better. He respected people and lifted women folks up on a pedestal.

Besides, that young man was really good looking. He was a hard worker and had a good head on his shoulders. He was the more stable of the two Ames brothers, Dick was the older of the two and Tom let him have his way in some of their disputes. It was because the man had respect for his brother and you can't down grade that.

The guys kept two guards out all night long. The surprising thing was these men trusted each other with everything they had. Arthur said, "If we can't trust each other after all we've gone through, who can we trust? We've been through a lot together and I've trusted these men with my life many, many times.

Without them I'd be dead today. They saved my life even before they knew anything about me. I'm here and if they stole every ounce of gold we have I'd still be ahead of where I'd be if I'd never met them. This gold is going to make a difference in all our lives and I thank God for that. My hope is we can do some good with it."

Dick, Rusty and David rode in an hour or so before dark to help us. Aaron the oldest stayed on the claim they had staked out. I was glad to see two of my older brothers before we left for the East.

Those two brothers of mine brought in a goodly amount of the yellow stuff for only a couple of months of work, while they were in the low lands. They wanted to turn it into hard cash and put it in the bank so ma and pa could draw off it.

Art told Rusty, "You probably shouldn't put it all in the bank. What if something happened to the bank and you lost it all. No matter where you put it in this wild country there's some risk."

The next morning by daylight we were up and around and long before the sun poked its light rays down into Cabin Creek Canyon we were moving out of it on our way back to civilization. I watched Arthur take some time and look back just one last time. Even Mrs. Duck wanted to imprint that scene in her mind. The crooked trail we traveled led us downhill toward Sacramento. The small cabin and the valley soon faded from our view.

The mountain stream made a soothing sound as it flowed over the rocks. We rode parallel to it for over an hour. The creek was still trying to bust over its banks from the melting snow up higher. Cabin Creek Canyon had passed from view and our lives. It was good to be on the move again. I was enjoying this trip down off the mountain. The sun was warm on my back as we traveled westward down the mountain. Was I becoming a vagabond with all this travel? If not I'm at least becoming an ole gad about.

As we rode I watched butterflies dart in and around the mountain flowers, even the honeybees were busy. The magnificent colors gave added beauty to the mountainside. The white puffy clouds were moving east pushed by a gentle breeze.

High up the mountain it was a white world yet. Glancing back all I could see behind me was God's wild and wonderful world. It was oh so beautiful and so rugged looking. As we slowly traveled downhill they grew smaller and smaller as distance gobbled them up.

From the rocky ground along the hillside the sound of our horses moving downhill bounced off the rocks and returned to us a smidgen louder. Up ahead of us were the Sierra Nevada Foot Hills and way beyond that you could see the Great Sacramento Basin, way out there in the distance. High above us you could see a giant bird of some kind making circles on the wind.

My family was out there not having any idea we were coming home or that we weren't going to stay in California. I knew my mother was going to be heart sick when she found out we were headed east in a week or so. She wasn't the only one for I had a burden placed on me because of our decision to go east.

No way would I let my man know how I felt at this time. He had enough troubles riding on his shoulders. You could see that these men looked up to Arthur for leadership. Anyone could see he was the man to lead this outfit. He was a natural born leader.

He said once that as a boy back in England he had a bunch of young folks that looked up to him for leadership and he let most of them down. That didn't seem like him at all.

He let on that he would be glad to get out of that roll and gave it up for good; he tried to shake loose of it when he came to America. The early part of his life was a mystery to me. When I'd ask he'd say that all those things were passed away when he found Jesus aboard ship. That man of mine was still young so how bad could it be. He assured me that one day he would confess to me his sordid past.

My thoughts returned to the now as the squeaks of saddle leather and clank of the bit chains came to my ears. This steel gray horse I rode was a big strong animal and a good one. I feel he was a runner although I'd never opened him up to see.

All but one of the ten packhorses were loaded down with just gold and we all carried some yellow stuff in our saddle packs behind our saddles and in saddlebags. One of the smaller packhorses carried nothing but tents, food, dishes and camp supplies as we made our way down off this mountain. My brothers had some gold stashed away on one of their horses.

This area had a multitude of miners working every stream, brook and hillside in the country. Later they would spread out and cover the land. I wonder if half these greenhorns know how to find gold if it was right under their noses. I really felt sorry for those who sold everything they had back East to come way out here in California to strike it rich.

With our little army of eight soldiers we made good time with no trouble at all. Arthur had out riders in the daytime and two sentries out every night. The sixth day we rode onto flat land and a day or so later we were in my parent's dooryard.

ARTHUR

Mr. Frith had oats growing in the field north of the house and a small field of corn northeast of the buildings. He was growing melons, cucumbers, squash and all kind of things in a big family garden. I don't think I ever saw a larger garden anywhere in all my life.

This garden was weed less; not even the gardens in England that I stole from were this big or this clean. This good family really knew how to work and they kept the whole she-bang in tiptop shape. They had repaired the house of all the bullet holes that were put in it last winter and it looked good.

The dooryard was raked and had no road apples or cow plops anywhere. They'd been picked up and thrown on the garden for fertilizer. Mabel's pa was a worker and was teaching his family to work.

He said last spring he was gonna supply food for the mining camps and it looked like he had a good start on it. Some of the fruit of his labor were about ready to be sent off to market. These crops would go good up in the hills or right here in Sacramento.

Mr. Frith had his own way of making money. Everyone out here was looking to make a buck one way or another. The nine of them were building something out here and soon Aaron, David and Rusty would be home from the

Sierra Nevada Mountains to lend a helping hand. They talked about picking up some more land with the gold they had already brought home from the mountains.

When we rode into the dooryard the family came from everywhere to greet us and Mabel was mobbed and hugged good and proper. The gander got his share of hugs from the females of the house and lots of back pounding from the males.

We unloaded the horses onto the porch. The amount of gold was impressive and Mr. Frith was happy for us, but warned us, "Be careful, people everywhere were looking to get a quick buck anyway they can get it."

I already knew that but I thanked him for the good advice anyway.

As our cavalcade rode into town we noticed that two buildings had been erected on two of our lots up on Main Street. What was that all about? We rode on to our small house and unloaded our things inside. We had purchased this small dwelling before we left for the Sierra Nevada Mountains and had a local builder put a lean-to on the backside for Mabel and me. We needed to have some room of our own for privacy. The place needed a good cleaning and we got right to it.

Bright and early in the morning we ambled on down to the land office to check out the ownership on our lots and see if something had gone amiss while we were gone. The property was still in our names and the clerk didn't have any idea why someone had built on it without first getting ownership.

Harley, JJ and I hustled down on Main Street to have a talk with whoever had moved in on us. The three of us hadn't neglected to start out well healed. We all had revolvers strapped on our hips to be used in close quarters. I carried a shotgun and the two guys had long rifles under their arms.

The two businesses were both of good size. One place of business was the Blue Bell Hotel and the other was the Bull Dog Saloon. The same person owned both establishments somebody named Floyd Williams Jr.

As we pushed through the front door we saw that the place was done up really nice. A red carpet covered the hotel floor, wall paper covered the walls and head mounts of deer, elk, prong horn antelope, bear and buffalo lined the walls high up. A wide carpeted stairway with a banister ran to the second floor.

A clerk was dusting some picture on the wall and when he spied us he returned to the counter. "May I help you gentlemen this morning?"

"Well sir, are you the owner of this establishment?"

"No sir, that would be Mr. Floyd Williams."

"Is he in?"

"No sir he's out at the moment."

"It is quite important that we see him as soon as possible."

He walked down a hall and opened a door to the outside and hollered out back, "You whooo, Tim would you come in here for a moment." In ten seconds a boy about thirteen came inside. "Tim would you run and find Mr. Williams for me, these men want to see him. Tell him that these gentlemen have important business to talk to him about."

Tim asked, "Do you have an idea where he's at?"

Not for sure Tim, he could be anywhere. Check his house first and then the food palace but stay at it until you find him."

"I got ya, seek until I find."

The boy left at a trot and we found a seat along the wall and sat in silence. Ten minutes passed by and we told the clerk that we would take a seat out front.

"Good, I will inform Mr. Williams when he comes in."

The overstuffed furniture outside was quite comfortable and the warm sun felt good on my body. We spent a good twenty minutes waiting there when we saw a man coming our way with Timmy. We assumed it was Mr. Williams.

Tim veered off and the man with him ascended the steps and pushed on into the hotel lobby with us hot on his heels. Mr. Williams was cordial at first as we talked of pleasantries but it turned a little cold as we talked about the property.

As we spoke to him his anger right off the bat showed through his hard smile. He told us that this was his property and no way could we get it away from him. The fact that it was on our land didn't seem to matter to him.

That is when the stuff hit the fan and he lost it. He yelled "I purchased this land from good reputable people and had it registered by men from the land office. In fact they came right to the property at the time of the sale and did their work. The deed has an official seal on it and it is legal so go take your crap and spread it somewhere else."

Our parting words were calm and to the point "Mr. Floyd Williams, you need to go to the land office and check it out for yourself." We were not out of the hotel more than ten seconds when the door flew opened and out he came on his way to the land office.

I felt that the man had been swindled so when we got back to our small house we sat around the table talking about what we could do to get this thing settled. Based on the evidence we had so far we decided that we would let him have it at our cost, just what we'd paid for it. In our next meeting we found out that it wasn't to be. Floyd Williams decided not to pay us one red cent and would buck us all the way.

The sheriff wasn't an overly ambitious man and hem-and-hawed. So we went to the judge trying to get some satisfaction. He had the clerk take some eviction papers to the sheriff office. If Williams wasn't out in thirty days he must come and show cause why he wasn't.

A well-dressed man in a suit met us on the street. He was interested in purchasing a couple of lots in town and was looking for a lot up town and a residential lot. The residential property must be away from all the hustle and bustles of Main Street. Our business lots were right in the heart of all the business, some of the very best lots, for they were right in the heart of town.

Our thoughts had changed on Williams and we would now go all the way to extract money from him for the lots.

About a week later as we ambled up Main, on our way to breakfast, a shot rang out and the slug clipped the top of my shoulder and put me to the ground on my back. Harley and Tom saw the black smoke and took off on the dead run heading for an uncompleted two story building up the street. By the time they arrived at the half completed building there was no one in sight. They heard nothing and saw nobody.

The girls hauled me off the street into a harness shop with my help, then pulled off my shirt and held a hanky tight to the wound. The storeowner brought a large white rag and Mabel cleaned the wound and put it over the bloody spot and bound it up tight. Then she asked," Honey, why is everyone shooting at you?"

It wasn't long and the guys returned and helped me back to the cabin. I could have done it by myself but Mabel wouldn't let me walk on my own. It was silly but I loved her for it.

The guys made a trip to see Floyd Williams but the man said, "I know nothing I've been here in the Bad Dog Saloon all day long. I was here with a drink in my hand when the bartender and I heard the gun shot. Ask him if you don't believe me."

Waiting for the court to move on the case of eviction Mabel and I got a buggy and headed for her folk's farm, Tom went along to drive the buggy horses. I loved the trip out there with my wife beside me. It was getting harder and harder for me to get any time alone with my wife, so I treasured every minute I got with her and no one else.

In the morning after a good breakfast I eased outside and sat with Tom Ames on the front porch. We sat for a spell and then he moved off to feed and water our buggy horses. Mabel and Mary Ellen had their heads together and were talking out by the windmill and they both took a long look at Tom Ames by the corral.

Now what was that all about? Were those two women hatching up something between themselves? I think poor ole Tom was in for some trouble and he didn't even know it. I guess whatever they were hatching up would all come out in the wash later on. I'll just keep my eyes open and wait and see. We talked it over with the Frith brothers and asked if they knew what the girls were hatching up for poor ole Tom Ames.

Soon we found out that Tom and Mary Ellen had made some kind of a commitment to each other and Tom was going to talk to her father. I was there when Tom Ames stumbled through his little speech to Mr. Frith and got his permission to marry that little redheaded girl.

From that point on they were always together and the big quacker must admit they were a good-looking couple. Mabel was more than happy for them. That Mary was always poised and pretty as a picture. As young as she was she seemed quite mature. I've come to understand that a man without a good woman is only half a man.

In the two weeks we were there at the farm. I took some time and told Rusty and David about the thread size vein of gold in the rocks on the hillside and revealed the location to them up in Cabin Creek Canyon.

I gave them the history of the vein and gave them the claim to the mine and our cabin; we were leaving the area anyway. David could later analyze it and explore the possibility of it producing any more yellow stuff. When they got time later on those boys could evaluate and investigate the possibility of the mine ever producing anything and then act accordingly. I've heard how a vein like that in another foot or so can open up and produce a bonanza of gold and also peter out to nothing. We left that up to the Frith boys to figure it out.

Erma Frith told us about eight distinguished looking gentlemen that came here three days ago looking for you young men. They said they needed to talk to you about something. They wanted us to write to them if we saw you again or knew where you might be.

They gave her the name and an address to write to. It was the name of the company that owned the ship we sailed on. The name was Live-a-More Lines out of Liverpool, England and the address they gave Mrs. Frith was Abby Lane, Liverpool England. It didn't look like the shipping line had given up on us, not in the least.

We knew they would never give up looking for us. It was just a matter of how bad they really wanted us and at how much expense they were willing to incur looking for us. If they caught us we would surely swing from the yardarm back in England and you can bet your bottom dollar it wouldn't be a front porch swing either.

After two weeks we found ourselves back in Sacramento. The wound was coming back together nicely and had a good scab on it. No one in town had any idea who could have taken the shot that put me down. No shots had been spent on the other guys as they went about their business.

Mr. Floyd Williams would not talk to the fellows about making a settlement on the price so I'm guessing it will go to trial. I for one couldn't understand his reasoning unless he was looking for sympathy from the town's people. If he were a scaly-wag he would need all the good people of Sacramento to feel sorry for him, to stay in business.

The following Sunday saw Tom Ames and Marry Ellen Frith standing before the minister hearing the words love, honor, obey, cherish, until death do we part being spoken to them. We gave them a couple of days to get their lives together and started off on the right foot. I think that those two will make a go of it. They really gave the impression that they loved each other a lot and they both seemed to have a stick-to-itiveness to get them through any tough spots in the future.

The trial with Mr. Floyd Williams went about as I expected it to. The judge asked Mr. Williams if he would meet the price that we had offered him or was he ready to vacate the premises. The amount we ask for was now double what we had asked for earlier. The man raised a ruckus but in the end he paid us the amount we ask plus the court cost.

After that was settled we lit a shuck for the Frith place. We gave Mr. Frith permission to sell the remaining lots in town. And use the small house or sell it and keep the money. We said our goodbyes for we were going to head back east in a couple of days. Most of our loose ends were tied up and we were now anxious to be out of here before the Downey Cruiser came back to port and the crew came to find us again.

They'd seemed to be locating all the people that we knew and were asking all kinds of questions about us. Before they pinpointed us we wanted to be clear of this area. Back East it would be harder to locate us for we intended to settle at least a thousand miles from the east coast that would keep them off our backs.

One week from the day that we drifted onto the Firth's homestead we packed up bag and baggage. This meant keepsakes, gold and everything we wanted. The three wagons were loaded in no time flat and set in the dooryard until we got back from town. Once we were in town to lighten the loads on the horses we exchanged gold for greenbacks and we were getting a whole lot more money than we ever expected to.

Harley tried to hire a couple of respectable men to go along with us but they were eager to hit the gold fields as soon as they could and try their luck up in the mountains looking for gold. Sacramento was a hard place to hire men to do anything; most had their sights set on finding the heavy metal.

We had it planned out and would start out in the middle of the night, not wanting anyone to know we were moving gold out of the area. We'd had our fill of bad men when we first hit the gold fields over a year ago. Those episodes last year made us extra careful. We had what we came for and were not willing to just hand it over to anyone.

About half of the greenbacks are all we could stash away in our eight carpetbags and large saddlebags and tote bags we had made up special for hauling the United States currency back east. It was July 2th, 1850 and we had to hurry to get somewhere back east before cold weather set in.

The state of California gave us an IOU for a large amount of our gold to be redeemed at any large federal bank back East. We didn't want to take the currency and gold with us for we didn't know how far we would get before winter set in. The gold we saved out was the funny colored gold we discovered above the falls.

The assayer told us that Jewelers back East just might give you more money than we are allowed to give for your gold. "The gold you have there is an unusual color and it assays out really well. I've never seen anything as pretty as those nugget you showed me. I think you men have a gold mine so hold out for a good price for I think you will get it."

Not counting the unusual colored gold we were hauling back east; we were toting nine hundred and fifty thousand dollars in U.S. notes and greenbacks. The wagon for the gold was built extra strong. We would take two prairie schooners to live out of and haul our belongings in plus an extra heavy duty wagon for the gold.

I went into orbit every time I thought of all that could happen to us on our trip back east. When worry set in ole English got as nervous as a fox inside a hen house with the chickens squawking their heads off.

It cost us a bundle of money but we finally hired three disillusioned men to go with us back east. There were now nine of us counting the ladies and we all carried side arms, shot guns and all kinds of long rifles were in the wagons. Each man had two rifles that he carried, one in his scabbard on his horse and one in his hands. We hoped we were ready for anything anyone could throw at us. If there were any loose ends we couldn't think of them.

We heard in Sacramento that California was now a state of the United States of America. Just three years ago these lands belong to Mexico. The treaty of Guadeloupe gave California and a lot more land to the U.S. A place called Texas was admitted a few years back. This new country was growing by leaps and bounds and people were filling up the land.

Mabel and Mary Ellen had cut the apron strings with their family and were now tied to our group of men. We picked up a map in Sacramento, of the trail back to the east. My sweetie had a good sense of direction and remembered most of the route through the mountains and many of those that they'd traveled coming out here two years ago.

This down to earth lady of mine was a willing helpmate in everything I wanted and needed to do. This ole dude tried to keep it fresh in his mind that she was going to be separated from her family and that was hard on her. Sometimes at night this lady of mine would get in that melancholy mood and big ole tears would come rolling down her cheeks and all I could do was kiss them and wipe them away.

That's when I'd take her in my arms and hold her and try to kiss the tears and fears away. Being without a family for my growing up years gave me an idea how she was feeling being separated from her family. I'd have those same feelings if I were to lose her and the guys. I wonder if I would do as good as she is.

When the Ames boys struck out on their own looking for gold, I was having trouble enough coping with that at the time. These were the only people in the whole wide world that I had any feelings for, maybe a little for the Frith family.

Perhaps it's like when the Ames boys wouldn't leave Dead Miners' Creek and come with us into Falls Creek. During that time this ole boy did have Harley and Justin to ease the pain. I'm thanking my God that Mary was coming along on this trip to help ease some of Mabel's pain. Without Mary along, Mabel might suffer a whole lot more. Throughout their lives these two ladies spent a lot of time together and this would help them both considerably just being together.

This trip was being planned out to the last little detail; it was hard to work out all the details for we'd never been across the continent before and this was all new to us. Mabel and Mary were our sounding board as to what we would need to take east with us and when they didn't have the answers we went to her father to get his advice. Mr. Frith had led his family and two wagons across all those long miles not that many months ago and the man was quite knowledgeable of the trail and what it took to make that journey. We got what we needed to know from him to make the long trip to the east coast.

We had four tents so Tom and Mary had one of their own, as did Mabel and yours truly. The six single guys would bunk on cots under the wagons or set up the third tent. One of the tents we would use for storage of our harnesses and riding gear and such. We had purchased one of dad's Conestoga Wagons to take with us back East.

This all seemed to work out pretty darn good or at least it looked like it would. Everyone in the party would be sleeping up off the ground in the wagons. Hammocks were not made for a love affair. It hindered the smooching quite a lot.

The path we would use going east on, was the main road out of the state of California. It didn't look like a road anywhere along its route. But it was called the California Trail by everyone. Folks were still pouring into this country by this route. I'm sure that many were as honest as the day is long but how does a person know the heart of his fellow man whether it is good or evil. Were folks genuine or do they have a bent to do evil. I guess only God knows the hearts of man so we'll steer clear of everyone we see along the way.

From the map we worked over we saw it was nigh onto two hundred miles to Reno, Nevada. This trip was over two hundred long hard miles of mountainous travel, with the possibility of trouble at every turn. The first leg of our trip would keep us on our toes.

The main part of our plan before we left Sacramento was to let no one in town suspect we were going anywhere or that we were loaded down with gold and cash. Tonight after midnight we would start the first leg of our trip back East.

OCEAN VOYAGE

Out here in gold country trouble was always nearby and gave you no warning before it landed on top of ya. Harvey MacDonald, Mabel and I left the Sacramento Café' and headed for the wagons. We would be leaving in a couple of hours for the East. As we stood on the restaurant porch four men rushed out of the darkness and I felt blows to my face and head before I went down. The last blow felt like someone clobbered me on the head with a club of some kind.

That's all I knew for the lights went out in my head and I awoke with a headache to end all headaches. One eye was closed tighter than a metal rim on a wood wheel and the other was but a slit to peek through. Both of my hands were tied tightly behind me and I had been thrown into a wagon of some kind and was bouncing all over the place as the team that pulled it was moving on down the road at a pretty good clip.

Where was my sweet wife? What had happened to her? In low tones I said "Mabel." Then just a little bit louder I said "Honey, are you here? Mabel!" There was no answer so I said it again a little louder, "Mabel, sweetie."

The voice that came to my ears was not that of my wife. The voice I heard had a stern quality to it. "Your woman is still back there in Sacramento right where we found you my fine-feathered friend. Right now, Mr. Arthur Drake, you are on the first long leg of a trip back to England and a hangman's noose for your neck. You have your friend Harley MacDonald to keep you company on your long trip home. That ole boy wasn't any more willing than you were to take an ocean voyage and it is all expenses paid all the way to England. Just so you know we couldn't fine the three Americans that jumped ship with ya.

This part of the United States has people from every part of the world and we couldn't locate them so they could enjoy this trip with ya. But you two guys with your unmistakable foreign dialect, stood out like a sore thumb in every crowd."

With that said the guy asked his first question, "Are them three other Yankee boys living in this vicinity?" I didn't say a thing and received a swift kick in the ribs for my silence and one to my head for good measure. The excruciating pain did a number on me and I passed out cold as a stone.

Lying on the boards in their wagon bed and bouncing all over the place made my body hurt and it ached all over. The next day in late afternoon, I found myself in a dark place and the ropes were off my hands. Trying to move I found out a couple of things, first I had a splitting headache, I hurt all over my body and there were chains on my leg fastened to some kind of a post or something in this dark area.

This ole-bruised banana from England was really missing his wife and he wondered if he would ever see her again, probably not in this lifetime, my woman was gone but surely not forgotten. Mabel was made for this young country and fit in oh so well. Me, I was an outsider trying to fit in. I was getting a handle on it and starting to mold into the West, but that's all ended now.

As I think back it is a wonder of wonders how I found her and her family in those high up mountains of California. We both came from many, many miles away and both ended up on that mountain at the same time. I worked on that slow moving boat and she came across country on a slow moving prairie schooner.

The timing back then was just right and we both ended up at Cabin Creek at the same time. Jesus, oh what a miracle worker you are. Oh the joy we had for a few months. I found more joy in that short period time than I did in all the rest of my life. Being kidnapped in Sacramento put an end to that. Leaving England is when I got the ball rolling and in time I ended up there on Cabin Creek at just the right moment. How do ya figure a thing like that if God isn't in it?

I missed that soft womanly body of hers close to mine. Plus I missed all those romantic moments we spent together up in the Sierra Nevada Mountains. I wouldn't trade that for all the gold in all of California. She was gone from me now and those moments were now just a memory in my mind.

At that moment a long low groan broke the silence and brought me back to the dark cell. It was Big Mac's voice that said, "Are you alright English?"

"No Mac, I got some bad hurt all over the place. I'm hurtin' from the top of my head to my feet. I'm hurting quite bad, Harley. How long we been here? Do you know where we are?"

"Ya, we're in the hole of the Downey Cruiser. Can't you feel the slight motion of this little tub when it is docked? You should have known by now with all the hours you've spent down here in the past. You should know the feeling by now. English, my boy, can't you feel that slight roll of the ship?"

"This place does feel familiar. I've been here often enough in the past I should have known it right off the bat, but I didn't. I guess my mind was clouded with all the pain and what I'm missing by being here."

I checked myself out in the pitch darkness of our prison to see just how bad this banana really was. I got to feeling all over my body for the bad bruises that I'd collected in the little scuffle in Sacramento and that ride into San Francisco. There was a big goose egg on my head and sore spots all over the place.

In the process of feeling around in the dark I found my high top miner boots and still in the knife pocket on the side of my boots I found my fold up jack knife. The ole girl was a real nice piece of work; some Mexican craftsman had put a lot of work into it.

In the pitch-black darkness of our prison I found Harley's arm and slid the little knife into his big hand. With a start he said, "What's that?" Then the realization of what it was caused his mouth to clam up. After a moment he handed it back. All he said was "interesting."

Big Mac said, "They didn't find the other three guys, let's see one was that JJ kid and them two brothers. These sailors don't realize those three boys went back home a long time ago. They're back on the east coast somewhere helping their families.

English, the sailors kept a watch on you, Mabel and me for two days and never saw those dudes, so they made up their minds to grab the two of us and get us back to the ship and here we are in our glamorous state room, waiting for room service. First Mate McNeil said they only found us by our accents. Me, I didn't think I had an accent to give me away." The duck had to smile at that. Harley's thick tongue was a dead giveaway and told everyone that he hadn't been born and raised in America.

"Mr. McNeil said that this tub was going to set sail tomorrow on the afternoon tide and was going to hit every major port on the East and West coasts of the Americas and then take us home to swing from the yardarm. It looks to me like we will be in for a long dark sea voyage. Do you think you're up to it mate? If not I'll try to get in touch with Captain Nelson Rodgers and see if he'll put us off at the first port we sail into."

"If I said I don't feel up to it, do you think they'll put me off at the next port?" That brought a chuckle from Mac. "Did you see Mabel? Did she get hurt in the scuffle? Is she OK?"

"She wasn't hurt they just pushed her out of the way. She did hit the porch floor but she was up in a flash trying to talk some sense into the crew. One man held her by the arm like a gentleman as she scolded them good and proper. But the Downey crew had their orders and they couldn't give us up even if they wanted to."

We couldn't see a thing so we couldn't be sure if someone was in here with us or not so our conversation was limited to just idle chit chat. No way would we put our friends in danger with loose tongues or reveal that we had a knife in our possession.

Most of the time the only sounds we heard were the soft moan and groans of the ship as the seawater moved it to and fro. Somewhere in this black hole we could hear a cricket making its mating noise and it got me to thinking of Mabel again.

spirit

We had intended to leave California by land for the eastern parts of America the very night that we were captured. Well that won't be happening at least not for Harley MacDonald or the Duck. I had to smile at that, Mabel loved the word game we played with that last name of mine and she became Mrs. Duck and I was Daddy Duck. (Drake)

Mabel crept into my thoughts often; she was what I was missing the most. She wasn't sure but she thought she might be pregnant. We both wanted to wait until we got back East but once we found out we might become parents we were excited about it.

I'm not sure I want her in the motherly way now with me on my way to uncertainty and probably the gallows. At least she has her parents and the money to fall back on. She also has Tom Ames and JJ that will stick by her through thick and thin. Dick is questionable. He has a mind of his own and will make it up any way he wants to regardless of what others think.

Bread and water was slid under the door, but not much of either although we knew from long experience we must eat every ounce of it, for we needed every scrap of it to stay alive. The grub we received tasted like it had mold on it although we saw nothing in the darkness.

From sun up until dark it was pitch black in here, we were pretty sure we wouldn't see the light of day for a long while yet. Off and on we heard the clang of the ship's bell or a whistle to alert the crew to the time.

Water for washing would be nonexistent, as would everything else except our daily ration of bread and water. We assumed the chains would be our constant companion for the remainder of the trip that is if we made it all the way back to England.

If for some reason Captain Nelson took us off this bread and water diet and gave us a chance to get into some sunlight, we couldn't afford to take any lashes from the first mate that would doom us. Four days later we got to see the sun for a little bit as they loaded cargo into the hole. We were chained to a post all that time but we did get some rays from the sun. The crewmembers complained the hole was getting way to ripe, prior to lowering the lid down over the hole and fastening it up tight.

Some good Samaritan dropped a hand full of food down to us. I knew the man by sight but couldn't remember his name. He was a part of the crew way back when. I knew his face fairly well and if we ever shook loose of this ship again, he would be rewarded for his kindness.

We horded what he gave us and made it last for about five days. This is only a guess for it was black as pitch in here and we didn't know night from day. We still received bread and water and that helped some. The men that worked down here on the next stop began to gag as they entered the hole. We had no sanitary place to put our waist so it was a foul smelling hole for those that didn't stay down here all the time and weren't use to the smell.

Our Good Samaritan this time left half a coconut, a lime and some fat off some meat. This was a life saver and helped our diet immensely. With his help maybe we would make it back to England alive. If he were caught helping us he would be in the same boat we were in at least for a few days.

The crew let the captain know that something had to be done. It took a couple of days, but while we were in the next port we got a chance to get some sunlight while we took our time and cleaned out this stinking hole we lived in. Overhead we saw a clear blue sky and sea gulls looking for a hand out.

The smell lingered down in the hole and made the men want to vomit. The crew that worked down below in ports still had trouble loading and unloading cargo. So the Captain broke down and gave us a pail to do our business in and each day we got to dump it over the side. That might not seem like much to you but for an hour each day we got a chance to clean up that stinking hole and sunlight came shining in.

This new job afforded us the opportunity to work in the sunlight and for that we received extra food each day. From our duties aboard ship we picked up the names, stinking swabbies as we mopped out our living quarters.

Now we could count the days just by the fact that we cleaned up the hole each day and kept it so the men could stand to work down there. This may not seem like very much to you but to us this was a great opportunity. With the extra work we did aboard ship Captain Nelson increased our food supply a little tiny bit. With the extra food, just maybe we might make it back to merry ole England. That is if the Captain didn't get something crosswise in his craw and take it all away from us.

We tried hard not to rock the boat in anyway even though we knew we were going to hang in England once we got there. But ole Harley kept harping on this one adage 'where there is life there is hope,' sometimes he'd add 'son keep your chin up and think positive.'

Several of the crew members were silently on our side and several worked to help ease our discomfort. There wasn't much that they could do without the rest of the crew finding out and bringing the wrath of Captain Rodgers down on their heads.

It seemed like a good month of travel and we were rounding Cape Horn. This was an adventure in itself. It felt like we were a cork as we bounced up and down and all around. The water was really choppy. The waves were very high and Big Mac and the Duck got as sick as a dog down in our little dungeon. In this type of weather we were not allowed to venture up on deck or to see the light of day.

No one was let out on the deck unless they had a good reason to be out there. With the high waves and fierce howling wind that came at us with a gale force, the motions kept us sick as a dog. The wind pushed and pulled on the water and the waves rolled across the deck and tossed us about like a fishing cork.

Salt water was knee deep down here in the hole, we shivered uncontrollably and we prayed a lot for we knew if the ship went down so would we. The Captain had no love for us or what we'd done and said so to everyone aboard ship. The men in the crew that were faithful to Captain Nelson Rodgers agreed. But most aboard the Downey Cruiser saw it quite differently than they did.

In England the law was the law and the penalty for this terrible crime was death by hanging. Being it was an English ship and flying an English flag we were subject to English law. And it looked like we would swing from the yard arm before this thing was over.

Tom, Mary Ellen, Dick Ames and Justin Jenkins at this point were not mixed up in this and were far away from all our troubles. My hope is that the guys would use their money to get safely away and settled into a business somewhere. Mabel was my only real worry. She would miss me like I was missing her. Yes, we had a magnificent love affair that was wonderful for me and mighty amazing.

Mabel Drake took her love and unlocked my heart and made a man of me. How long would she suffer not knowing my love? My wife was a sweet lady with a super build and she had an inner strength that not many knew about. Down deep inside she was strong and would get through this time.

She could be whatever she wanted to be; she had a fortune in cash and gold to make life easier for her. Tom and JJ would look after her until she got on her feet. That part the duck didn't worry about for Mabel was tough and could cope with whatever life threw at her. The bad part was yours truly missed her more than anything. Before this stinking swabbie got captured he felt like he was her man and loving her was his plan, but my plan had gone bust. In fact there was no plan at all. I'm sorry to say on this trip ole English was just along for the ride.

The travel speed in this ole tub was mighty slow, it seemed like we were going nowhere fast. While going around the cape they lost one seaman to the angry waves that pounded us for three long days. The sea lost much of her orneriness on the other side and we were busy pumping water by hand, out of our sleeping quarters.

Down here in this dark smelly hole it would be easy to let your thoughts run away with you. You could let your mind wander and imagine we weren't going to make it and it could give you the screaming memes if you let it. Everyone knew what was waiting for Mac and me if we did make it all the way to England.

When you put it in that perspective it made life on board ship easier to cope with. It all came down to live or die, sink or swim, none of it mattered more than a hill of beans. In the end we were going to die. It was just a matter of how or when. Of course I wanted to live and see my sweet wife again and feel her in my arms.

When we came out the other side the water was as calm as a lap dog. The first time I rounded the southern tip of South America it didn't seem this rough. But on the other hand I've heard that it gets a whole lot worse than this. The stiffness and soreness had dissipated from my body. As dark as it was down here, it was easy to take a header and end up kissing the floor.

Something had a ripe smell to it, our big ole slop pail was full and running over before we got the chance to see the great outdoors and dump that smelly stuff into the Atlantic Ocean. Then it was back to cleaning up the hole again and the nasty mess down there.

Up north it was getting on to winter but on the other hand down south spring was in the air and it would be getting warmer almost every day. I wasn't sure how long we were going to be able to enjoy our scenic cruise with our luxurious accommodations. "Ha, Ha, Ha."

A good fellow, an able bodied seaman told us "you have about forty days under your belt so far and the captain figured another thirty days and we would head east toward England and your trial for forsaking the Downey Cruiser. English law didn't care one iota that we had been forced to serve on this floating bathtub after being shanghaied. The Downey Cruiser flew the English flag and we were subject to English law.

In our long journey along the coast there were times when I felt like knuckling under and giving up. Oh English decided that wouldn't do. I've got to get hold of myself and buckle up and take it like a man. In times past it seemed like I was like a cat no matter what happened to me I always landed on my feet, but this time around it looked rather doubtful.

What really got to me is when I thought of Mabel and not having her near me. In the few months of being together we were as close as any two people can get and this ugly ole dude needed her. She is what kept me dreaming and planning for our future. Then there's that little question that keeps popping up, is Mabel in a motherly way or was it just a false alarm. I'm on the fence as to whether I want her pregnant now or not.

If she gets married again she doesn't need to be dragging a little one along. I wish for her the best in this life. I sure wish I was going to be a part of it, but I ain't. Well I had six wonderful months with her up in the Sierra Nevada Mountains and I have dreams of the most wonderful woman in the whole wide world. A person really feels it when a good woman is gone, it's like part of his life has just washed overboard.

In this dark hole I think of her all the time except when Harley MacDonald has me engaged in conversation. There are two things we don't talk about unless we are absolutely sure we are alone and out of earshot of everyone. One is JJ, Tom and Dick. If we feel we must we act like we are talking about Mary Ellen? The other subject is the gold we dug up in California in the last year or so.

Here I am a rich man and living like a hermit in a dark hole. That made me smile for a bit, just how can you have a hole to live in way out here in the Atlantic Ocean when water seeks its own level. We were now let up on deck for about three hours a day, if the weather was good, but they always had us on the end of a mop or working on something on deck.

They were still short handed so we were doing the work of crewmembers; it was usually the worst job. The days the wind blew hard or it rained we were kept in the hole in the bowels of the ship.

Harley and I had both lost weight from our poor diets. The Captain did increase our food allotment sense we were working as part of the crew. The two of us always kept our eyes open for a chance to go overboard. We looked for any chance at all even if it was slim. We could swing, starve or die trying to escape, it didn't matter, dead is dead no matter how it comes about.

Then Captain Nelson Rodgers allowed us to have a hammock to lie on and a couple blankets to cover up with, this was a big improvement over the wood planks we slept on in the bottom of the ship. The first part of the trip we had nothing. Our furnishings were up to two swinging beds, coverings and a wooden pail. We were now close to being in hog heaven.

The food had come up to the same standards that the crew ate at every meal and our ribs didn't stick out like they did a couple of weeks ago. I'm not insinuating that the food we received was all that good, just more of it. I guess enough is as good as a feast.

One of the mates came into feed us one day and spent some time just talking. He seemed to want to help. He said he could get us off the boat on the eastern coast of the

Americas for a little cash so we got to talking about the deal. The problem was we had no money with us and he wasn't willing to incur a necktie party to help us on just a faith promise.

The men on shore needed a little cash in hand before they would lift a finger to help out. So the whole deal all went up in smoke. We had no connections on the east coast or any place else for that matter so that deal was a bust. The man left us without a commitment of any kind.

It seemed like everyone wanted to get into our pockets and fish out what they could. They must think we'd struck it rich in California and they wanted in on the cash flow. Gold and family are subjects we never discussed with anyone.

My friends, the gold and my wife were gone from me, gone like a drop of water on the top of a hot stove now only something to remember. It disappeared from view but it's not forgotten. Like that drop of water they're out there somewhere we just can't see them.

It's a dirty rotten shame that in the beginning every one of us five were shanghaied and had no say in whether we wanted to be sailors or not. Once we were on board we had no right to abandon the crew or the ship for any reason. If you do, it's a capital offence and the penalty is death by hanging.

In our travels we stopped in about every port, it seemed like. We were always picking up small loads here and there and distributing things along the way. It seemed like we were going nowhere fast on our trip north. But Harley and I weren't in any big hurry to reach merry ole England. Life is precious and we wanted to hold onto it as long as possible.

In my youth this swabbie did things, that if he'd been caught he would have been thrown in the clink. But the circumstances were a lot different. Back then I was a vile person with a nasty, mean, wild streak with a cruel and uncontrollable temper. I had no respect for anyone or their property and waged war on everyone that got in my way.

Hatred had poisoned my mind as a youth. The Good Book says that what-so-ever a man sowth that shall he also reap and God's Word can't be broken. My miserable life has come down to reaping what I've sown in my younger days and the crop is overwhelming me.

I did so many mean and hateful things in my youth that the seeds I sowed back then are now coming home to roost. It is truly catching up with me with a mighty bad crop. It started with that man turning me into the Bobbies in London and then being shanghaied aboard ship.

Ole English thought he was through the harvest until those men rushed him in front of that café in Sacramento. Now it's hitting home with a clout that leaves me devastated. But why is Harley all mixed up in this, he has lived a quiet life from birth until now. Harley is a mighty good man and doesn't deserve all this.

To me Harley has always been a model citizen since I've known him. I guess that's the penalty he must pay for hanging around with a guy like me. I wonder if I'll live long enough to get through the harvest that I've prepared for myself. Big Mac led me to God and in my mind that changed everything. Hatred and loathing had no place in my heart any more. But English law didn't care one iota how this stinking swabbie was now. To them that wasn't important or relevant. Nothing the gander could say was relative to the fact that we had skipped out on Captain Rodgers and the crew.

In a port in Brazil two men abandon ship and got into the city. We spent two weeks in chains while they took time to look for them. After two weeks of scouring the city and not finding them we pulled out of port and made our way north.

Captain Nelson Rodgers was having all kinds of trouble trying to keep men aboard the Downey Cruiser. They did get one American to sign up to sail as a crewman from that port. He was looking for a way home to Maine. I hope Rodgers lets the new man off when we get to New York City.

The little ship was already shorthanded before the two seamen jumped ship. That put Captain Nelson Rodgers in a surly mood for the next few days and everyone felt the brunt of his anger. Harley and I were back to bread and water and our chains, twenty-four hours a day.

After four or five days he ordered us up on deck to help with the duties of the crew and that kept us busy aboard ship. We thought about doing nothing but then thought better of it. We remembered what the penalty for disobeying a direct order was. I guess we were now thought of as full-fledged crewmembers except we had different living quarters.

Every night we got reacquainted with the chains as we slept in the hole. The only thing about this that was better was we were on deck most of the daylight hours and had better food. Of course in port we were down in the hole working and not on deck. The two of us were always vigilant and very much aware of all that transpired around us every moment. Escaping our captivity was always on our mind.

Harley and I were getting lost in the daily routine of the ship. My past wild life didn't come to mind all that often, everything on my mind was on the back burner, except the short time I treasured being with my sweet wife. The amount of time this ole duck spent with Mabel in the mountains was the best part of his life.

That sweet magnificent little lady was unforgettable and in so many ways a desirable delightful and beautiful jewel to treasure and prize all my life. It didn't look like all my life was for very long. This ole boy always wanted to handle and caress a thing of beauty like her. That my friend is all I ever dream about. Oh Lord how I needed to hold her close again. At night I would think of her until this ole swabbie dropped off to sleep. "Dear Lord Jesus be with her and wrap your arms around her and love her for me, please."

The weather was getting colder after we crossed the equator and one morning we had a coat of ice on the rigging and sugar snow pelted the deck as we floated into New York Harbor. This was our last American port before we sailed toward England and whatever that place held in store for MacDonald and me. I'd been in the New York harbor more than once and I haven't ever seen its shoreline or the cruddy gunky stuff that floated on the water in the harbor.

Once the Downey Cruiser left the seacoast of North America we hit choppy water, which was the normal way of it. In that ocean voyage across the Atlantic the weather was cold and windy and we made only fair time. This ole swab didn't really want to be on this ole tub but for some reason he was. I had no desire to get to a place that wanted to string me up and put an end to my life, but it looks like that's where I'm headed.

This ole coot thought of my wife a whole lot on this part of the trip, this man would give his eyeteeth to see her again and a whole lot more to put my arms around her and hold her close. "Lord Jesus, please comfort Mabel and send your mighty angels to watch over my women and protect her. Lord, give that lady of mine good council in whatever she does in life.

I didn't want to think of it but please send her a good man to fill up her life. I only want the best for her Lord. That sweet woman you sent my way is a prize. I just don't understand why you sent her my way when you knew that we wouldn't be together all that long. Don't get me wrong; I'm glad you did for she is the one bright spot in my life. I'm thankful for that marvelous time you gave us.

Lord, as I spend some time thinking of Justin, Harley and Tom and Dick Ames, I think of how dedicated we all were to each other. Lord, our time together is nothing to sneeze at. The Friths left a lasting impression on me. But with this desertion charge hanging over our heads, we are bucking a stacked deck."

All of those folks that I call friends are people you could trust and depend on with your life at stake. Those four men I call friends from the boat are men to ride the trails with. They have proved themselves over and over again in the past.

A few years ago I had no one to lean on but look at what I have now. Some men are lucky if they have one close friend but look at me I have loving people all around that love me and care about me. Harley would cut off his arm to save me and I would do the same for him and he knows it.

Is my life short? I can't see it any other way. Since this ole dude met Jesus I've lived my life, as He would want me to. How do I know that, well it's that verse in His Word that says 'Do what you know to be right and don't do what you know to be wrong.' If you do that and love the Lord your God with all your heart and read His Word so you will know what is right in His eyes then you will be okay.

I've done many things that outsiders might say isn't right but my heart knows the truth. For instance killing those robbers and killers, would I kill those murders if I had it to do over again? That is right I sure would? But not if they would repent and not ever do it again but then I'd have to take them in and let the law deal with them.

When they repent that squares it with God but what about the people they killed? Those folks haven't forgiven them and can't. That my friend is why murder is so serious. My loving Savior is a forgiving God if you're sorry for what you've done and not just because you got caught.

When the little tub we were in hit some rough sea the timbers would creak and moan Mabel's name. It seems like that sweet altruistic lady was always on my mind. This kid down in this hole heard her name in every noise that the ship made. Was I going nuts in my loneliness? I had Harley and without him here I'd have been off my rocker a long time ago.

When you traveling toward what we faced it's hard to get on top of this feeling of being alone and done for. For the remainder of the trip we were on we tried to boost each other's morale but it was a mighty tough job when we were both down in the dumps about our situation. We often talked about the good times in our past. It helped a little but soon after our talk we'd slide right back into that pit we'd just climbed out of.

I've heard people talk about wealth and how it will solve everything in their lives. Me, I'm wealthy and I'd give it all way to shake free of this mess I'm in but that isn't possible. The law will decide everything. Whether it is life or death and from all I hear it will be death.

We heard from high up in the crow's nest, "land hooo." just before they slammed the lid down over the hole we were in. That meant there wasn't any escape for us here in the harbor. Where we did get a chance to see the light of day, they came down into that hole with shackles and hog tied us.

One thing I'm grateful for is we didn't have to walk to down town London that was way too far. They had a two-wheeled cart there to haul us off to old London Town. Many of the streets and roads we traveled on along the way were familiar to me as we rode the cart toward the Tower of London. I looked but saw no one that I knew. Were they all in the gray bar hotel for their misdeeds or possibly dead?

The streets were lined with brick and stone houses. This part of town was a lot different than Sacramento, California. Back there everything was put together in a hurry, while the homes here had come together over a long period of time. Don't get me wrong; there are a lot of slums all over London. This swab knew because he'd spent a good share of my life living in them.

I watched a Road Island Red Rooster as he flew atop a split rail fence and before we were fifty meters down the road he cocked his head and began to crow, that my friend was music to my ears and I thank God for small favors.

My one wish for my old friends here in London is that they have at least one chance to hear the gospel of Jesus before the death angel takes them home. But that didn't seem like much of a probability down here in the slums. If you don't know anything different then what you have everyday it's mighty hard to escape your circumstances.

The old lamp lighter had started to do his job as the day was coming to a close. Shortly after seeing him our rig pulled up to the prison gates. Two months of being on the Downey Cruiser didn't prepare me for the shock of being in the Tower of London. The Tower of London housed much of the scum of all England. This was to be our home until we came to court.

I thank God that Harley and I shared the same dungeon for we had the same interest and could trust each other. The smells were really bad; we'd never got a whiff of anything like this before. This place had an aroma of its own and it wasn't good.

Our only light was a torch that spilled its light through a small window in the door. It was enough so we could make out things in our cell. The cubicle was quite small. The cell was about three meters square and two meters high. Harvey would bump his head on the ceiling every once in a while if he wasn't careful.

A man came and brought us some clean prison garb. Harley laid them out before me and said, "welcome to your palace King Arthur is there anything else that I can get you before you retire for the evening?" The laughs were strained but it did break the mood of the moment.

Getting shuck of this bad feeling of depression for very long was like trying to sink the Downey Cruiser with a slingshot. It isn't going to go away and stay gone for very long.

The terrible conditions inside the prison were atrocious. But as appalling as the cell was the food was even worse. The one thing that was better than the Downey Cruiser was the small amount of light that crept into our small cell, plus the inmates came by each day and emptied the thunder mug for us. That doesn't sound like much but it was to us.

The next morning the jailer came by to say hello. Through the small cell window he smiled a big ole smile and showed us his brown rotting teeth. At least the ones that were still in his mouth. It seems like every jailer in this place was missing some teeth, was there a reason?

As time dragged on Harley and yours truly would often get lost in our own thoughts. In the last few months we had talked about everything under the sun and about everything we'd ever done and his home life up in Scotland. Frequently our conversation would drop off to silence.

Harley felt real bad that his family didn't have any idea where he was and it hurt him to know he'd never get a chance to see them ever again. He wrote letters but we found out later that they never left the prison.

In the lonely silence, that's the time my thoughts would head directly for Mabel and our time together. I'd think of what she might be doing in California and what we might be doing if we were together. Often times this old gander thought about that trail east we would have taken if this whole thing hadn't happened and I often wondered where we might have settled and what kind of business we might have gotten into.

This was all just wishful thinking on my part, but what else did I have to think about. I didn't want to dwell on the negative for that was so depressing and would make our stay in this luxury hotel even worse. Many times I'd find myself staring off into space for long periods of time and seeing nothing. Sometimes I'd even compare this place with hell. Was it better or worse than that place down there? I already knew the answer to that question for I'd read in the Good Book about the discomforts of that place.

Mr. Firth said to me once "if you don't know what is in the Bible then you don't know anything. The Bible has all the answers to every question in life. My mind could still conger up the place where he stood when he'd said it and the cabin in Cabin Creek Canyon. Those were my good old days.

Before this all came about, I was kind of like a cat no matter what happened in life I'd somehow end up on my feet but not this time. This time there was no way to come out of this alive. This time I couldn't shake free from this strangle hold that threatened to end it all. No matter what I did my mind couldn't conceive of a way of escaping the noose and the scaffold.

Oh how I'd love to see the white puffy clouds race across the California sky once more or see the lightning fall from the heavens and hear the thunder echo down one of those canyons and watch the rain slip in and soak me to the bone. Or see the water roaring down one of those creeks and run its course toward the sea. I'd love to see the simple things like the sun fading from view over the western horizon; these were things we all take for granted until they aren't there to see any more. Of course I'd want to see it with my wife Mabel.

This kind of thinking would leave me in a state where I'd want to swear out loud but I'd stifle myself and keep it inside. This kid was only feeling sorry for myself and having a pity party to go along with it. Poor ole King Arthur just can't command his subjects to obey him in this old castle.

What is Harley MacDonald going through? It's the same thing I'm facing and I haven't heard a single bitter or harsh word of any kind from his lips. With all the things I knew about this good friend, ole English was getting a new respect. His gentleness was beyond description.

I rummaged around in my mind for a time that I'd seen him mad at anyone. Even when the killers were working us over back up in those hills he didn't lose his cool. Don't get me wrong Harley was no softy. Harley was a deep man but affectionate to them that knew him.

He is what I'd call a man's man and did he ever love to brawl. That man could really hold his own. Since we were captured in California it has been a long arduous journey, but soon it would be all over and done with. Our trial would be in a couple of weeks or so.

This time in prison was taking the wind out of our sails and it looked like we were going nowhere. We were overcome by the daily wear and tear of prison life. Did this jail bird fear the gallows that lay ahead? I heard someplace that if you fear nothing then maybe you love nothing.

Well I have a love affair that won't quit so it must be true. In my mind death was stalking us and was hot on our tails. One morning before the cock crowed the jailer appeared out of the semidarkness. Four men came and dragged us out of that square cubicle and hauled us off to a room that was cleaner and had a lot more light to see by.

The bright light at first hurt our eyes and we had to stop and let them get reacquainted with the sunlight. This cell had a barred window to the outside that looked down into a courtyard and the sunlight was flooding into our cell. This small room was larger and we received better food and more of it.

The bed bugs in the other cell were huge and those big buggers were about to eat us alive. Harley and I wondered what being here meant so we started asking questions

Right off the bat the jailer said, "You fellows will soon be going to court so they want you to be more presentable in the court room. This new cell will be your home for a little while. It's a whole lot better than where you came from."

Sir, "will we have a lawyer to represent us? Or do we go it on our own?"

"Yes sir, you'll have someone to represent you in fact you have a great lawyer, you have one of the best legal minds in all of London to handle your case. So get yourself cleaned up for you'll be getting visitors in the next couple days"

"What is this all about? Who in the world would do that for us? Who is the visitor? Is it the lawyer? Did the court system have a hand in fixing this up for us? Sir, I'm not so naive to think we have the best lawyer in town."

"Mr. Drake, from what I glean from the grapevine some rich lady in London has taken a special interest in your case and has put forth the money to get you the very best lawyer money can buy."

"Who would do that for us?" I'm just a little bit leery of what he was saying. Who would do that for a couple of strangers? No it can't be true the jailer is just playing with our minds. If yours truly had his druthers I'd rather not be here at all but back home with Mabel. But that's not an option for us.

"This ole jail bird didn't know about that but this he knew the food here is a lot better then back in the dungeons. Just that much should be a picker upper." The heavy steel door to our cell clanged shut as he left us and all was silent except for the heels of his boots, as it struck the stone floor. You could hear him as he hurried down the passageway.

We tried to enjoy the small comforts of the diminutive space of our new home. What were two law abiding fellows like us doing here anyway? I truly intended to be a good citizen when I got to the United States of America.

Well that's all water under the bridge or over the dam now. We had no illusions about what we faced in the next month or so. The gallows in the courtyard below told us that. They were ever present and kept a hold of us and wanted us to come out and swing. That is one invitation we didn't want to accept or even hear.

That high-fluting lawyer and his expensive duds came by the next day and we had a long talk about our situation. He informed us that our trial was to be in thirteen days and yes some rich lady who didn't want anyone to know her name was paying for our defense.

C3　C3　C3

The boys and I had just gotten up from a good meal and Arthur and I were going to take in the sights of Sacramento. Later on tonight we would be eastward bound, but before we left Arthur and I would go window shopping in Sacramento. This newly formed mining town was a pretty bad place for a lady to walk alone after dark. Although most men were honest and had respect for a women, the thing that kept the low-grade men at bay was the honest hard working men of Sacramento, they wouldn't put up with any kind of shenanigans from roughnecks.

More than fifty percent of Sacramento was set up to be a mining town and had all the things that a single man wanted. I needn't explain all that that statement involves. The miner's part of town didn't display much in the way of women things. Arthur would enjoy himself just looking at the new and different things in the stores. I enjoyed his presence and just being with him was great for me.

This little ole girl would hold his strong arm and we would stroll up and down the main drag or sit on a bench and watch the people do their Saturday night thing. Being together was all we needed to be happy.

As we left the chow hall there was a commotion on the front porch as four men started fighting with Art and Harley and I saw a club come down on my man's head. He staggered a bit, and it looked like he would fight on. Then from behind him he was whacked again and down he went like a stone and hit his head on the wooden porch floor.

This ole gal tried to reach his side but got shoved to the porch floor herself, for my trouble. I tried to reach his side on hands and knees as he laid either dead or out cold. A man blocked the aisle to him with a knife. Miss, you stay away from him. He's going with us back to England. He's got to answer for his crimes. The man turned around and checked to see if Arthur was still breathing and he said to me "ma'am, he's still alive. Ma'am, I'm mighty sorry but we got orders to bring him back to the ship one way or another. We got no say so in this. If we disobey the direct order the Captain gave us we'd be in the same boat the English kid is in."

He held my arm and pushed me a little further away from the commotion. Harley was putting up a real struggle and four men were all over him trying to wrestle him to the floor. I watched one man as he went flying off the porch and into the dust of Main Street. They were working Harley over with a club of some kind.

This huge hulk of a man and those oversized pair of paws of his were making them pay right through the teeth for any victory they achieved over him. He was like a bull in a china shop just lashing out at everyone he could reach. One fellow with a club connected with Harley's head and down he went to one knee. He struggled to rise and that same club connected again on top of his head, down he went like a sack of potatoes and he went out like a light. His body language told me he was out cold.

The man that held on to me whispered for my ears only, "Ma'am, I'll look out for your man if I can. I won't be able to do much but I'll try to get him to England in one piece. I always liked this boy and I feel he got a raw deal." Unseen by no one else I handed him some currency I said for no one else to hear, "Thank you, sir, I'll appreciate anything you can do for him and if Arthur and MacDonald are alive in England I'll make it right with you." He let go of my arm and followed the other men toward the wagon parked on Main Street.

I followed him as they moved toward the wagon. Before they left I got a chance to hold Arthur's head for a moment. Then the big man on the seat cracked the whip over the horse's ears and yelled hee-yah to the team and away they went up Main Street in a cloud of dust.

I saw the sheriff coming down the street as I looked up Main. I knew the lazy lubber wouldn't do much if anything, but I did fill him in on what had happened here on the streets of his fair city. Right off the bat the man started making excuses of why he couldn't do anything and that they were now out of his jurisdiction.

Oh my God what am I going to do without my man? "Oh Jesus, you know I love him so please go with him and watch over him?" This ole girl felt helpless as she watched Arthur being thrown into the wagon bed. So far he hadn't moved a muscle. The horses were pushing hard into their collars as I watched that team move that ore wagon down the street and on out of town.

I was mad and at the edge of tears and wanted to hit someone as I watched them move clear out of sight. People stood around the porch and looked at me in wonderment at what had happened here. One man asked me, "What was that all about, lady?"

"They took my husband sir, they've shanghaied him?"

His profound answer was "Oh." Then he turned and walked on up the street. Justin Jenkins and Tom Ames were in town somewhere. I needed to find them real quick so I headed down the street. It took awhile but I found them. They were both inside the saloon and sure enough they were singing up a storm to the music of the piano. Jared Jenkins was light on his feet and dancing a little jig.

The two of them saw me coming and headed my way. "What's up Mabel? Where's Arthur? Mabel, someone needs to be with you when you walk the streets after dark."

"They took Arthur."

"Who took him?"

"Some men from the Downey Cruiser shanghaied him and took both Harley and Arthur off in a wagon not more than fifteen minutes ago. They were headed toward San Francisco the last I saw of them. I'm going after them wherever they go. I'm going to follow and somehow get my man back. Guys this could be really risky but will you help me?"

"Darn it all to heck, on the eve of our departure, what bad luck."

"Hey guys we've got to get my man back. It could be real dangerous if you decide to get involved. If they catch you, you could be in one heck of a fix. The consequences could be devastating and maybe end your lives."

"We understand all too well just how ticklish this situation can be for us, Mabel. But before we go gallivanting off to England, we need to get some money out at your folk's place. Money is the only thing that will set him free. We could cry until dooms day and it wouldn't make a bit of difference. Money is the only leverage that will pry him loose from English law."

"Tom, we need to take some time and figure out what we need to do to set Harley and English free and plan how to go about liberating them, for the law doesn't give a hoot who ya are if they think you're guilty." We found Mary Ellen at the small house at the edge of town getting ready to leave for the East. We picked up four good horses to ride out to paw and ma's place. Mary and I took time to put on our riding clothes for the trip.

When we got there we informed the folks of our dilemma while the guys loaded up every bit of cash money we had into our wagon and most of the gold that we had gotten ready for our trip back East later on tonight. Now we needed to grab all the money we could lay our hands on. It was all loaded into six large carpetbags and buckled up with heavy belts around them to help support the load. We picked up a dozen big bags of gold and were they ever heavy. One bag was all two men could handle.

We needed one of our big wagons to carry the load to San Francisco. I got lots and lots of kisses from the family before we left. Ma broke down and cried up a storm and pa was having trouble keeping his eyes from filling up with water. Pa warned us that we were playing a dangerous game. You kids are headed right into the lion's den. He helped harnessed the horses and said he was going to Frisco with us.

I'm glad we got a chance to say good bye to the family it would be awful for us to just up and disappear and them never knowing what happened to us. As we went west we told paw of our plan, as we knew it at this point. At some eastern seaport we'll send you a letter explaining everything that we were going to do in England once we had a better picture of the situation.

We never got a chance to inform Dick Ames before we left. Tom left him a note at the house saying good-bye. We would turn all the gold we had with us into gold coins in Frisco for we didn't know what we would need once we got to England. This was going to add a lot of weight to our already heavy load.

It was close to mid-night when we hit the limits of Sacramento right there we camped for the night and slept until six o'clock in the morning. Then loaded up and high tailed it for San Francisco. Within two hours time we were clear of town and pushing the four-horse team for all they were worth toward the coast.

The horses and wagons were raising dust toward our destination which was the San Francisco Bay area. We must hurry as fast as we can until we catch a ship out of Frisco. We hoped we might have a chance to spring Harley and Arthur loose here in California. We knew it was a slim chance but it was a chance we needed to take.

In the ride west we all made up names and took them for our own. People could still be looking for Justin Jenkins, Tom and Dick Ames. It would do no good to spring Arthur and Harley loose and have these two locked up and maybe hung.

We must make plans and follow them as best we can. It was a hectic ride all the way to Frisco and while we rode we hashed it over and came up with a skeleton of a plan and then as we worked on it we started to put some meat on those bones. We knew we would have to play it by ear much of the time and maybe change our plans at a moment's notice.

There were so many variables to this plan of ours and we had to tuck in all the loose ends if we could. There were so many ifs, ands and buts in our plans that needed to be ironed out as we went along. Without becoming aware of it we might have to change our plans and come up with something altogether different at a moment's notice. Such are the circumstances we find ourselves in.

If we can spring Harley and English free here in Frisco we will grab our wagon and head on out of here in a hurry. Get our stuff at the house and head east as soon as possible.

If the Downey Cruiser has left port and set sail we must make some adjustments and take up the chase by ship. If that happened we were going to hop a fast moving ship over to England, a ship that was faster than that old tub the Downey Cruiser and see what could be done over in the old country.

Could we get them free? We had no idea what we were up against or going to be facing if and when we got to England? But as my dad would say, "nothing ventured, nothing gained."

This ole country girl was starting off on quite an adventure. I'd never even seen the ocean or been on a boat larger than a rowboat, except for those ferries that took our wagons across the Mississippi River.

No two ways about it, in the last two years since we left the farm back in Michigan things were moving way too fast for me. Arthur was the only solid rock I could lean on in a world that kept changing on me and now Captain Nelson Rodgers was taking my man away.

Getting those two men out of the pickle they were in is one thing I had to do, no matter how long it took. Tom and Justin informed me that I must do all the negotiating for they might be found out and slammed into jail for they were still wanted men.

It took nearly twenty-four hours of pushing our horses for all they were worth to get to San Francisco. It was very early in the morning when we spied the coal oil streetlights of town winking and blinking in the distance. Once in town we rented two rooms at the hotel with our made up names. Mary and I slept in one room while the men slept in another. By eight o'clock in the morning we were on the waterfront down by the docks looking for a swift running ship out of here.

We found out very quickly that the Downey Cruiser had already left the harbor docks and set sail for England I suppose. We could still see her white sail as she sailed up San Francisco Bay. Slowly but surely they moved on out of sight. Could they beat us back to England on that old tub? Fat chance! We could swim faster than that!

Tom said, "We needed to catch a fast moving clipper ship, out of here. The clipper ships are slender and fast in the water. The swift running clipper ships would catch that ole tub in no time flat and get us to England way before the Downey Cruiser. These babies could really move on the open seas. They looked gorgeous under full sail.

The clipper ships were the new kids on the block and were quickly replacing the older wider ships. There were three trim Clipper Ships in port two from the East coast of the US and one from England. The slim and sleek clipper ships were beautiful even when docked. This English ship traveled from England to San Francisco by way of New York City picking up cargo where they could. The captain and his crew then returned to merry ole England. This English ship only stops at the larger ports for short stays. They pick up cargo in the major ports as they traveled back and forth.

The four of us ferreted out the Captain of the ship, a William Bradford of the East Indian Company ship line and booked passage to England. The ship was a trim sleek beauty that could really move through the water once under full sail.

Dad parked the wagon in front of the bank and we got most of our gold turned into gold coins. The weight was more than any six men could carry so we all got in there and carried the loot back out to the wagon. Once the gold coins were loaded on board ship, we saw dad head off for home and we got the rest of our money and belongings aboard ship.

Once we got settled in Justin and I left the Clipper ship and went out to find some high fluting duds to go along with our everyday things. Tom and Mary Ellen did the same when we got back on board ship. We needed to protect our cash for we would probably need every bit of it before this trip was over. I didn't show it but my nerves were a jangled mess because of the delay. We took the time to pick up what we needed to take along with us. We really needed some high-class duds so we could start learning to put on the dog. For we would be talking to people of substance once we got to merry ole England.

We were all from small farms back East and didn't really know how to put on the dog for anyone. We had to make English citizens think we were people of money. So we got a book of etiquette (A Book of Etiquette for Those That Need It) so we could all brush up on our manners and become proper young men and women.

I was being affected by the delays and I grew nervous and was chomping at the bit to be moving. Arthur was always on my mind and I needed his loving arms around me again. So I took hold of myself and tried to settle me down somewhat and get control of my nervousness.

As I stood on deck with Marry Ellen and Tom the breeze off the water was cool on my face. This was late September and soon the cold north wind would be keeping us inside our cabins until we headed south. To while away the long hours of the trip we picked up some table games. (Cards, checkers, chess and several others) In bad weather these little games would help keep us occupied on those long days and my mind off my man, I hope.

Our plan on this end of the trip had come together without any bad hitches. All seemed to be working out right and we were ready to hit the salt water for England. In our spare time at night we got together and brain stormed on how to get Harley MacDonald and English loose.

We didn't stop with one plan but kept revising the older ones. Evenings we spent a lot of time getting all our ducks in a row and going in the same directions. Our plan was not to run around willy-nilly when we got there. Everything we had planned revolved around those suitcases of paper money and gold coins in our trunks.

Finally on the third day the ship shoved off from the Frisco docks and we were on our way up the bay and out into the Pacific Ocean. When Captain Bradford and crew saw us in our finery, we were treated like royalty. The first part of our con game was working out great and we worked hard to keep up the deception.

Captain Bradford wanted to know about our old clothes and why we wore them when we first came aboard. Tom explained, "The West was not conducive to our present line of clothes. Could you picture my wife laboring in Sacramento in that lovely gown she was now wearing? I don't think so sir."

After a rain the streets have knee-deep mud and an inch of dust when it doesn't. Commerce can't go on with the local yokels when they think we are lording it over them. So we dress much like the people that live there."

Then we dropped the bomb by saying, "to further develop our business here in San Francisco we are looking for a ship to buy to speed up shipments and cut down the cost. On our way out here from the East it seemed like we stopped in every little port along the way.

We need a vessel to cut down on our cost of shipping merchandise around the horn. We want to eliminate the middlemen if we can. We're on our way to England to do just that. We're hoping to find a cheap ship of some kind to purchase. It needn't be all that large just sturdy. Our impression is that California is going to grow and we plan to grow with it and England seems to be the place that has older ships, which might be for sale, reasonably."

Captain Bill Bradford agreed and promised to lend us a hand once we got to England. He said the older wider ships are not as profitable and there might be some good buys in some of the shipyards. The faster sleeker Clippers ships are the vessels of the future. You might want to look into one of them and check out the cost. If there is some way to lend you folks a hand with your purchase just let me know.

"Sir, we will make it worth your while if your help leads to a purchase of an adequate vessel."

From a short distance I listened to Tom Ames weave his web. Up until now I'd not dreamed he could talk with such elegance. He was going to be a real asset in our quest to get Arthur and Big Mac free.

I'd gone to an advanced training school back East for six month to get myself ready to teach school and now all that time spent in school was coming into play as we all brushed up on our English, reading and mathematics.

All we did was just an illusion, we hoped it would give us the appearance of wealth and breeding and make things go a lot easier in all our dealings and divert attention away from JJ and Tom. Right now everything seemed like a long stretch, but those two men were like a dog after a bone that another dog has. Once they got a hold of it they wouldn't let go.

As I found out Tom didn't have all that much formal education, his mother had taught him to read and worked with him until he was sick of it and went down to New York City and got himself shanghaied onto the Downey Cruiser.

When the Night Hawk Hit the open sea Captain Bradford hoisted all sails and the riggings creaked and moaned as the northwest wind filled each sail to capacity and the Night Hawk knifed through the waves and skimmed over the water heading south.

The cool breeze of the ocean felt good blowing through my hair as we often times stood in the bow of the ship and watched the waves roll on by. Up ahead was a big ole bird, bigger than any I'd ever seen before coming out here. The huge bird soared high up in the sky. Someone on board called it a condor, a California condor. Well I learned something new today. Those big black ugly birds we watched are condors.

Before the end of the second day, off in the distance we saw tiny sails that turned out to be the Downey Cruiser in the distance. It was dark out when we sailed on by her. It was good to know that we'd passed them by and we would more than likely be in England long before they left New York, City.

We had lots of work to do before we saw my man again. I just hoped we four hadn't bit off more than we could chew. Mary and I would do most of the legal work once we reached England. Tom and Justin were wanted men by the authorities there. Would men deal with us? That was yet to be seen. But money was a big incentive anywhere you go.

Captain Bradford, Tom and Justin warned Mary and me about the cape of South America that the seas would be rougher than a corn cob but they didn't come near to revealing the true nature of that rough water. At the cape we were tossed every which way but loose.

We found out what the correct meaning of what seasick truly meant. Mary and this ole Michigan landlubber were sick all the way through that miserable stretch of water. When we finally reached the other side of those mile high waves all I could think of was, we had to come back this way when we returned.

They told us when you've gone through that caldron of wild water then you've become a true sailor. Well from the beginning of our adventure I was never interested in becoming a sailor on the high seas or any place else for that matter and now there are no doubts that I'm a dyed in the wool landlubber.

The further north we went the cooler the weather became and as we went further north it cooled off some more. We stopped in South Carolina and that was a beautiful city. Little did we know that in less than fifteen years a Great War would destroy this town and this whole area.

Justin Jenkins and Tom went ashore and in their travels they picked up a funny looking pistol. It was a revolver that had two barrels. One was a standard barrel. The odd part was that the other barrel was about two foot long, kind of like a rifle barrel. It made this weapon a six shot revolver or rifle. They looked all over the place but that was the only one that they found for sale. They had an idea that they just might need it if things went bad for them in England. I hope it never comes to that.

The weapon needed repair but JJ saw right off what the problem was. The guys tried to dicker on the price but the man wouldn't budge an inch. When they got it back to the ship it wasn't fifteen minutes and Justin had it together and working.

Every day we two girls took time to pray for our mission, that all would go according to our plans. My hope is to do everything by peaceful means if we could. If it went sour the guys would have little chance to escape back to the United States. So these two red headed girls prayed hard for help from on high.

We stayed three days in New York City and took in the town, three of us at a time. One of us always stayed with the money for safekeeping. That new weapon Tom picked up, only a week ago, made us feel secure when the men were off the ship.

The guys started to grow beards to kind of hide their faces and we girls took time to form the hair so it didn't look scruffy. I must admit the guys looked rather nice with beards. I was excited and nervous at the same time as we left the New York Harbor. Straight ahead of us a ways laid the coast of England and all the hard tedious work we had to accomplish in the next couple months or so. I just hoped we weren't making a bad mistake and weren't in over our heads.

The coast of England was a welcome sight and the harbor as bad as it was, was a welcome relief from the many days we'd spent aboard ship. True to his word Captain William Bradford gave us a list of names of several shipping lines and the Live-A-More lines plus the West Indies Line were on the long list of shipping lines. He suggested that if we had any troubles finding any of the shipping companies or in any other way, that he would be docked here and be on board for nigh on to a month. Just drop in any time and he would help us out if he could.

I would have to gear myself up for a fight because it wasn't in me to cause trouble of any kind. But my man's fate was in the balance and that meant I would go to any length and do the unthinkable to spring him from the grasp of those that held him captive.

JJ and Tom weren't going to let anyone jerk me around and try to run a scam on our plan, or us. Those boys were up to the task and ready to get at it.

A large carriage from a hotel pulled up to the docks and two men loaded our things on board. The drivers whisked us away to a nice hotel not too far from the harbor. Before we moved bag and baggage into London Town, we needed to put our crafted plan into motion.

C3   C3   C3

This new jail cell that we'd moved into was oh so much better than the one we left behind us two weeks ago. Our high monkey monk lawyer has been to see us several times in that two week period that we'd been in here. I was glad he was on the case for he tried to keep us abreast on the developments on our case.

In that time we found out that the rich lady that hired him was my wife. She had somehow gotten to England and was trying to put up the best defense with the best lawyer that money could buy. I hoped she wasn't here alone.

The lawyer was working hard to give us the best defense he could. The problem was there wasn't much ground to stand on and wiggle around in. He said, "You, Arthur, have a better chance of beating the gallows because you were a paying passenger and most lines didn't want it to get out that a paying passenger could be shanghaied into service."

The action that Captain Nelson took with you, Mr. Drake, could make folks going abroad think twice about paying passage on that freight line. His actions could cost the big lines a lot of money over time. Would the rich folks going abroad take the chance of paying their money and end up as a crewmember? I don't think so."

The owners of the Downey Cruiser are getting a lot of flak from other shipping lines after our lawyer let it be known that he had the case and would let all England know of what they'd done to me. The prosecuting lawyers would try to keep that part out of the court records if he could. I think his chances were slim for our lawyer man was crafty, but did I want to spend the rest of my life in this hellhole?

The Downey Cruisers' lawyers argued that I was no more than riffraff but our lawyer didn't let it faze him in the least. He told me, "Mr. Drake, in the long run it probably wouldn't make any difference, but you never know. The real bug-a-boo in this case is you did jump ship and that is against the law. But there are justifiable circumstances in this case. You were abducted and held for a long period of time against your will.

Captain Nelson Rodgers might lose his ship for the move he made. But we aren't interested in his case, we've troubles enough of our own."

On the day of our court case we were moved to the courtroom in leg irons and under guard. A wagon dropped us off at the back doors and we shuffled inside. We had been gotten up early and forced to shave and bathe. Ha, Ha! Then they had to force us out of the warm water for it was magnificent. Baths in this place were as scarce as hen's teeth.

I wondered who was with Mabel. I guess I'd find that out when they came into the courtroom. The lawyer thought it might be an open and shut case for the ship owners were going all out to blow us out of the water. I don't want you men giving up yet for I've had tougher cases than this and won.

The lawyer said "the two women and their men have been working like beavers on something apart from the court procedures, on their own. They won't tell me what it is and I didn't ask any questions."

Harley and this ole Englishman were seated in our box when Justin, Tom, Mary and Mabel came ambling in. Oh what a sight my Mabel was. She wasn't with child after all; I don't know how that makes me feel. She was an amazing woman and was dressed fit to kill.

It was just for me and was she ever beautiful and oh so easy on the eyes. That lady and the way she was dressed she could pass for upper crust. I'd seen plenty in my time and she would fit right in if that was her desire. This jail bird couldn't take his eyes off that amazing lady; they were riveted fast to her and every move she made.

Her eyes were fixed on me and my Adams Apple got stuck in my throat and I swallowed hard and tried to match her awesome smile. I felt the smile fell far short of what I intended it to be. My face felt like it was a wax manikin and the whole thing felt fake to me.

The circumstances I was in didn't seem to affect her for she gave a wave of acknowledgement and that made my day. The crew of four from California seemed cheerful and I wondered where Dick was. Mmmm! What I saw didn't seem to fit what the lawyer told us yesterday, unless the guys wanted us to swing and that wasn't in their nature.

Harley poked me in the ribs with his elbow and said," something is going on here English." The lawyers were running around like a bunch of chickens with their heads cut off. The Judge on his high seat pounded his gavel and then invited the prosecuting attorneys to the stand. They got their heads together to talk for a spell.

I glanced back at the guys and they all looked somber and sad all except Justin. He had a tiny smile on his face that disappeared in a quick hurry. What was going on here? What did my friends know that Harley and I didn't? As I watched Mabel closely her left eyelid came down and right back up again. She winked at me! That lady of mine knew something we didn't. What could it be? It was more than her saying she loved me, for I already knew that and she knew I knew it.

Now our defense lawyer put his two cents worth into the mix and a mild argument broke out in the front of the courtroom. The judge took control and calmed them down a bit. The two lawyers were led into the Judge's chambers for some reason.

Where were Captain Nelson Rodgers and his men that would testify against us? Those boys weren't anywhere to be seen. Were they off in another room waiting for the courtroom to get organized and start the session? The judge postponed the trial until tomorrow at noon.

As they were removing us from the courtroom, Tom Ames gave us the, don't worry signal and that everything was all clear. These were the signals we used to communicate up in the Sierra Nevada Mountains but what did it mean here in this courtroom?

Harley got the signal also and asked, "What's going on here English, what did he mean by it's all clear?" I've never been in court before but this doesn't seem right to me. The witnesses against us didn't show up. Is that what all the hubbub is about? Is that why they were going at it hammer and tongs?

I'm thinking Big Mac hit the nail right on the head. Our lawyer came by and said, "They couldn't locate the crew of the Downey Cruiser. Those boys knew about the court date and should have been here. If they never show up that might be a good sign for us. They were subpoenaed so they should have been here."

As we were maneuvered through the back door I blew a kiss toward Mabel. It wasn't very long and we were back in our cell. Still wondering what had happened to the Downey crew, were they thinking about the wrong date. The lawyer's last statement was "I'll see you men in court tomorrow afternoon."

Seeing my wife stirred up some old feelings I'd buried down deep inside of me and all those romantic moments back when we were together. The duck was missing that magnificent women a lot tonight. People often said we were quite a pair and I agreed. As she entered the courtroom today her movement was something to see. Now those beards on Tom and JJ were something else again.

Her refined walk and perfect posture stirred me a lot. She wore a light blue dress, with a wide white collar and her long red hair was down on her back. Mabel and Mary were captivating and many an eye followed them as they moved to a seat.

Harley asked, "What's the matter with you Arthur?"

"Seeing Mabel today excited me, man-oh-man is that girl ever something special to me. I know I may never see that lovely lady again. Gee-will-a-curs am I ever in love with that wonderful woman. That my good friend is what is a matter with me. Did you see my foxy lady, Harley? The lady is exquisite." Big Mac didn't answer but I knew he knew.

I thought I was tough enough to stand about anything people threw at me but seeing her leaving the courtroom today that my good friend just about did me in. Everything drained out of me when she turned to leave, my knees got as weak as a new born kitten's and I was glad the guard had a good hold of me or I would have gone down and I didn't want my gorgeous gal to see me fall to pieces in front of her.

ɔ৪ ɔ৪ ɔ৪

Speaking passionately to our little group I said. "Fellows, we have to get Art and Big Mac out of there. When I first walked into the courtroom and looked around I didn't realized that it was Arthur that sat in that box. Arthur and Harley looked just awful. Guys, I don't know about you but I didn't recognize them at first and when I did I wanted to cry. But no way, could I let Arthur see me break down in there. I owed my man that and much more. Those guys made it all the way from Sacramento to London living like dogs. I'm betting they felt that no one in the whole wide world cared a hill of beans about them except maybe us; guys, outside of us who would miss Art and Harley if they cashed in their chips, here in London Town?" My voice trailed off to a whisper and then died out all together and all was silent in the room.

Arthur is my very best friend and I feel safe and secure when he's around. How am I going to live without him? God has written this man on my heart and I can't seem to get him off my mind.

I think of Justin Jenkins' family along with Tom and Dick Ames and their family plus Harley MacDonald's families. I've taken on a heavy load, for their families don't have an idea one of what happened to them. I feel down deep in my heart a heavy weight for their mothers and how they must be still worrying about their sons after all these years.

I've done what I can to spring the boys free so I've got to make sure I don't get all screwed out of shape for what I might not have allowed for. We had worked it all out in our minds a thousand times and we can't see where there is anything else we haven't covered. I pray to God that some unforeseen thing doesn't pop up, unexpectedly, at the last moment and have the loose ends jump up and choke us.

This trip to Europe has cost us all a pretty penny. It's like Art often says, "seemed like everyone was trying to get their hands deep into our pockets." But that's the price you pay for putting on the dog and doing everything in a hurry. People have you over the barrel at a time like this and can squeeze a good price out of you. Whatever we spend here in England will be well worth it if the guys get free of this thing that hangs over them.

The next morning bright and early we were up and around and getting ready for our court date. At one o'clock we were seated but the judge was nowhere to be seen. Our lawyer was in the courtroom and so were Arthur and Big Mac.

The prosecuting attorneys were absent also and that put a smile on my face. Looking at Art his continence seemed to brighten up as he watched us so I gave him a bigger smile and a wink. That seemed to make a difference and a smile captured his face. Harley MacDonald had a funny look on his face with a big question mark written all over it.

These two men of ours were in the dark as to what we've been up to in the past three months, since we last saw them in Sacramento, California. For sure it has been a busy time for us and a nearly hopeless time for them with no future at all. They've gone through Hell in that amount of time. Our dear Jesus only knows how bad it has been for them.

It was almost two o'clock before the judge and the prosecuting attorneys entered the courtroom. The judge asked if the prosecuting attorneys were ready to present their case. They asked if they might approach the bench and those arguments that commenced yesterday started all over again with our mouthpiece right in the middle of it.

In ten minutes the judge made his decision. There are no witnesses in the case against one Harley B. MacDonald and Arthur C. Drake the case is dismissed and down came the gavel.

That is when I left my seat and headed for the accused box. My man was still in irons and was limited to what he could do but not me; this ole girl wrapped her arms around him and nearly smothered him with kisses. He had trouble catching his breath and he couldn't talk. The man sounded like he was going to die from lack of oxygen

That didn't slow me down for I couldn't get enough of him. I was breathing hard and was all over him. I felt Mary's hand on my back and I stepped back a step but Arthur hung on tight to me. She said Mabel, honey; give the man time to catch his breath.

The guard finally came and released him from his chains and I felt his body snuggle up close to me and those wonderful lips captured my two and held on tight. His right hand grabbed some hair behind my head, his left arm was around my waist and he drew me closer than I'd ever been before. Wow this was heaven for me!

My knees got weak and I couldn't stand on my own two feet. I'm glad he had a hold on me or I would have hit the floor. In his grip he hoisted me and smothered me with his wonderfully sweet lips. "Thank you Jesus for what you have done for us here today. Oh Lord I thank you."

Our lawyer was there and suggested we vacate the premises before the Downey Cruiser crew happens to come in to testify. That got my attention right away and I said, "Let's get out of here before Arthur sucks the life out of me and I can't walk at all." They all agreed and off we went. We set a course for our hotel room.

Harley and Arthur both needed a good hot bath and to soak for a week to get that prison stink off them. You know what? I wanted and needed to be a part of all my Englishman did and I bathed him. I needed to pamper him and keep my hands all over him. It was good to have my man with me again. If the tub had been bigger I would have been in there with him.

Arthur and Mac had all kinds of questions for us and we told them later when we get settled down, then we can talk. At that time we would be glad to answer any questions you have for us." As soon as we got settled into our rooms and after the long bath the questions came fast and furious.

"Mabel, you know I love you."

"Yes, I know Darling."

"Sugar Pie, while I was in that pig pen that old saying kept rattling around in my mind and the thought goes all the way back to my youth here in London, 'be careful of the trouble you stir up today you may have to drink it down before your through'.

Mabel, honey, a week ago this ole English kid didn't think he had a snowball's chance in the hot place of you getting us free of all the trouble. You know, I'm not even sure now of what happened. I'm not even sure I'm out here free as a bird, but how did it happen? All I know is that Captain Nelson Rodgers and the men from the Downey Cruiser, for some strange reason never showed up for the trial. You know that's a mystery to me. Captain Rodgers went through all the trouble of looking us up and hauling our ornery hides all the way back to England and then not show up for the trial. It doesn't make a lick of sense to me. What do you make of it sweetie?"

229

"Well Arthur sometimes the best laid plans of mice and men often go astray. Their well-laid plans didn't come to fruition for one reason or other. No two ways about it their best planning just fizzled out."

"To tell you the truth, honey babe, I thought I was headed for the marble orchard on the other side of town. You know the place where the folks go when they get their necks stretched good and properly by the hangman. To tell you the truth, sweet thing, I'm glad to be free from that necktie party they had planned for the two of us."

Before bedtime we all got together and we told Arthur and Harley of all that had transpired since we left San Francisco. Of the quick trip around the cape and our speedy trip to England; we told how we purchased the Downey Cruiser from the home company and with all rights and obligations to go with it. Our lawyer in Liverpool wasn't sure that the purchases of the Downey Cruiser would relieve you of all your criminal obligations in the past so we took another step to save you men.

The Captain of the Night Hawk, William Bradford, gave us some help there. He suggested we hire an understanding captain. So we hired his young Executive Officer to be our ship captain. We had gotten to know him in our long sea voyage to England. Tucker Meredith knew the shipping business as well as anyone.

We took him into our confidence on some things and set up a table on the dock by the gangplank and hired all the men that wanted to serve with an increase in pay. The man that got food to you guys on your return trip to England was hired on as first mate and all that had helped you out got a significant signing bonus.

We signed all of Captain Rodgers men that wanted to sign on. The ones that were loyal to him we didn't sign. We got all but a few of Captain Nelson Rodgers men to sign up with us for the trip home. Those few that wouldn't sign on, we had another plan for them and we put our plan into operation right away.

The ones that missed their court appearance were out to sea in the bottom of the Downey Cruiser locked in the hole. We had the captain and all his henchmen all shanghaied that very night and locked in the bottom of the ship. During the trial they were out to sea on a shake down cruise against their will. Arthur, honey, we are going to treat them just as they treated you and the boys when you were on board ship.

We've loaded up on all kinds of supplies for the long trip home. With the burden lifted off our shoulders the guys think it would be good to settle down in California and grow a business there. The possibilities for growth in and around both San Francisco and Sacramento could be pretty darn good. Honey, we have four carpenters signed up for one year to help us get a good start back home. Without Captain Rodgers chasing after you our time in Sacramento could be pleasant. Arthur, what do you think?"

"Honey, I think you're just wonderful, the four of you have done well. It was planned out well, what do you think Harley, my good friend?"

"From all I hear the plan sounded sweet to my ears. But there is one thing that I'm troubled with."

"What's that Harley?"

"Well it has been several years since I've been home to Scotland to see my family and friends. I haven't seen the folks in too long a time and while we're here in England I need to spend some time with them. Is there any chance that we might go up there before we set sail east for America?"

"Harley with all that's been going on since we left California I barely had time to think of how you must be feeling about your family up in Scotland. I'm sure that Arthur and everyone here would be more than happy to get you home to see your folks.

If it was me I would scream bloody murder if I couldn't get to go home while I'm here. You my dear sweet friend have been away from home a lot longer than I have and I miss my folks more than you can imagine. This boat is partly yours and we can make a small detour for you if you want to go home, for a visit."

Arthur came and put his arm around Big Mac and said, "It's settled then, Scotland and your home are on our itinerary." The guys talked and hashed things out until late into the night. It was good to hear my man take charge again. Our first night back together was a night to remember and I did for a mighty long time. With Arthur being with me it made everything seem right again.

Right after breakfast Justin rented a nice horse and headed for the seaport to see if the Downey Cruiser was there. As he talked with some sailors on the docks they saw the top of the sail right there just over the horizon. He waited to talk with Captain Tucker Meredith and then hurried off to collect the rest of us.

That night we were all aboard ship. Captain Meredith had loaded lumber aboard ship that day. The lumber would be used to fix up the living quarters for the crew and passengers as we sailed for home. There is one thing we had to do as ship owners, which we didn't like. The rules were, as ship owners we had to furnish booze for the crewmembers, to get around that we offered cash instead. Many didn't drink so that was a good deal for them. In the months to come we had less trouble.

By daylight we were under sail and headed north for Scotland and a rendezvous with Harley's family. We'd never seen that man that nervous before. Arthur and JJ engaged him in conversation and I saw him settle down a bit.

THE DUCK

After my imprisonment I was glad to be standing here on the deck of the Downey Cruiser once more, but on this occasion the whole situation has changed. At this moment I wasn't a slave to Captain Nelson Rodgers. For the first time ever I was happy to be on board ship and headed for home.

I was informed by a couple of the crew members that my old friend Captain Nelson Rodgers was on board ship. They laughed as they pointed down below. I hoped he knew how we felt when we stayed down there.

Harley was a happy camper for he was going to see his family for the first time in several long years. I envied him for he had a mother, father and some siblings. I wish that I had a family to miss and go home to. I don't know what I would give for loving relatives to go and see. Well there ain't, so no sense crying over spilled milk. Love, sweet love, ain't it wonderful. I know because of Mabel and the guys. I'm lucky in a sense for I have them as my family unit.

When I was back there in the jail cell I thought, could things get any worse? That was the worst of times and I'm glad to put them behind me. What's done is done and no way does this ole coon dog want those days back.

In the course of time the Downey Cruiser came to rest in a Scotland harbor not far from Harley's home place. We were all moving to slow to suit him. He did his best to control himself when we were around but many, many times he wanted to throw up his hands and leave and go on without us. But ole Harley let his patience rule him and he managed to put up with us and our short comings in our travel.

He led the way as our group stretched out for a hundred yards along the road to evade the dust from the horses and buggies. When we pulled into the yard Harley lightened leather and strolled toward the house. A female came from a chicken coop out back; then she stopped to have a look at who was filling the dooryard

When it became clear, who the lead man, in our procession, was she squealed out his name "Harley", dropped her egg basket and came on the dead run hitting him at full speed repeating Harley's name over and over. The impact almost took that big man off his feet. Those big strong arms hung on to her like a precious pearl and held her close. Her tears splashed onto his shoulder as big Mac held her close.

No sooner did I see that, than the door flew open and an older man came through the doorway and took his turn at hugging my friend. I heard a scream inside the house then out came his mother with flour on her face and an apron tied around her waist. I watched as father and daughter stepped back as mom took her turn in Harvly's arms.

I found my wife's hand and took her in my arms and held her tight. Here was my family right here in my arms and no way was I going to forget it. Mabel looked deep into my eyes and puckered up, that was all I needed to search out her lips and plant mine on them. I've seen the worst of times and now I expected to see some good times from now on. Across the way Tom and Mary held hands and took it all in.

The greetings went well and we all poured into the kitchen to have some cookies, coffee and good fellowship. Mr. Harry MacDonald looked at my friends, my wife and me and then said "your feet are welcome under my table anytime." Man-oh-man was the grub ever good. After all the swill we have eaten in the last few months this was wonderful.

The MacDonald family had no idea what had happened to their oldest son and had given him up for dead long ago. In the course of time we found out that Harley's family hadn't been doing all that well and were glad he was home to help. Their jaws dropped a foot when he said he would be leaving in a few days.

It took him all afternoon to fill them in on all that he'd gone through since leaving home so long ago. He revealed to them that he was rich beyond his wildest dreams and wanted them to come to America and live close by him.

At first it was no we can't but they'd had a rough time of it since Big Mac had left. They'd missed him something awful and now there was trouble with some family named MacDoogle. A MacDoogle boy wanted Treva MacDonald for his wife and there had been big trouble over her rejection of him.

They'd even come to blows once or twice over the situation and it had progressively gotten worse. Bitter feelings had erupted into harsh threats and it wasn't getting any better over the course of time. The MacDoogles wouldn't take no for an answer. Justin got upset when he heard the report. He was all for going over there and teaching them a lesson, but cooler heads prevailed and we talked about it.

The main push from that point on was for Mr. Harry MacDonald to come with us back to America and escape all the persecution that the MacDougals were heaping upon them. We laid out the picture of our new business venture and how we planned to establish it in California. The family was impressed at Harley's accomplishments in America.

Harley told them of the rich soil in the Sacramento basin and of Mabel's family and their farm on the American River and how with a little water it could bloom into a Garden of Eden. How crops would just pop out of the ground. The family was all for it but Mr. Harry was a stubborn man and didn't want to leave the home place. The farm that they lived on had belonged to his father and his father's, fathers for four generations.

Even though his son was going to set him up on a better piece of land he didn't want to leave the farm and have it just lay idle while he was gone to America to have a long look around. While they were gone someone might come in here and steal them blind plus the weeds would take over the farmland.

Harley said it wasn't in his father's nature to give anything away for free even if he was going to get something better. Harley told me that he felt like he was a quitter if he left the home place and that wasn't part of his personality.

Now that the family knew the whole scoop they were part of the friendly persuasion that finally swayed him into leaving Scotland. But only if he could get his brother to live on the home place for a year or two while he was gone, at least until he could see if the State of California was all we said it was.

For the next couple of days while the family was packing their belongings Harley and JJ went to see his Uncle Hubert MacDonald a half days ride from their home place. The fellows were back home by nightfall.

The very next day at noon Uncle Hubert, his wife and kids came rolling in on a two-wheeled cart. The MacDonald brothers came to an agreement, the farm would be rented for five years and if Harry MacDonald didn't return home, the place would transfer to Hubert MacDonald lock, stock and barrel. They would get the whole ball of wax if Harry MacDonald stayed in California longer than that period of time.

For the next two days we moved things to the Downey Cruiser and prepared to leave Scotland in our wake. I'd watched Hubert MacDonald when Harry proposed to let him have the family farm. At first he thought he was just joshing him and a smile broke out on his face. But once he got the drift of what was going on, a look of astonishment took control of his face and he stood there with his mouth open.

While looking around I saw Justin Jenkins standing behind Harley's sister Treva and she had her hands in his. What was that all about? Has the love bug been nibbling at ole JJ too? As I thought about it I decided it was a good match. If it hadn't been for Mabel's little nudge I would have missed it completely. That awesome wife of mine saw a lot of things this ole English kid missed all together.

Harry MacDonald was hesitant about getting on board the Downey Cruiser and had second thoughts about leaving solid ground, getting on our little tub and crossing all that water to America. He had to be nudged and pushed but finally he gave it to the Lord and moved on his own.

Once we cleared the shoreline we hit the breeze and set sails for America. At first the water was calm and that was good and I saw him settle down. But once we were under full sail there was no turning back. We had a destination in mind and everyone was anxious to see the Promised Land

Like myself, I hope the MacDonald's family's hopes and dreams turn to reality once they land on that California coast. If these close friends of mine have anything to say about it they will. My desire for them is that they be as close to us as my adopted family is. Ole English needs as many relatives as God will send his way.

Five years ago I had no one anywhere to call family and now my adopted family is growing by leaps and bounds. Oh how blessed I am!

After the first day out the water became rougher than a cob with waves twenty feet high, that is when Harry MacDonald was ready to return to Scotland. But Mrs. MacDonald and Harley took control of the situation and finally persuaded him to tough it out like the ladies were.

Mr. Macdonald was the only one on board ship that wanted to return to England, well maybe the men down in the hole did but they had no say about it. Even the ladies, in his family aboard ship, wanted to continue onto America. They had made the move off the small farm and were looking forward to a new home in California.

I hope they all feel that way when we round the southern end of South America.

His Scottish pride fought with his fears and after a few days aboard ship he let his good sense over ride his worries. The man barfed most every meal over the side. Tom said, "He's only feeding the fishes, they need to eat too."

Justin Jenkins reveled to us that he wanted to visit his family on the way through. So once we docked on the east coast Harley and him rented horses and headed west into Pennsylvania.

While they were on their mission of mercy we took in the sights of the town. This trip was the first time I'd ever seen the east coast of the Americas. Every other time I'd been locked up down in the hole of the ship.

We topped off our load, buying things to sell in the mining camps and to the regular citizens in California. I'm glad everyone decided that we would build our business in the Sacramento and Frisco area. Every other area on the east coast was a mystery to me. I could settle anywhere and I could adjust to any place we went as long as my wife was happy there.

Sacramento is where her family lives so that is where she wants to be. Now that no one wants me strung up on the gallows and they had stopped chasing after me, we could at this time live any place we wanted to. I must admit because of Mabel, California is now home sweet home for me.

Ten days had passed and Big Mac and JJ returned to the ship. The two brought along Justin's sister and it looked like Harley had already taken a liking to her. They were a good looking pair and I hoped they were right for each other. On this trip home from England both JJ and Harley had found female companionship and the duck was happy for them. A man isn't complete without a good woman to be with.

This time of year it was cold outside with some gray snow on the ground. But it wouldn't be long and spring would put some warmer weather on us. I bet the days are pretty nice out in Southern California and it wouldn't be long before miners would be up high fooling around in the water looking for gold.

FRISCO BOUND

The day we pulled out of port and set sail south it was really nice out and I was glad to be on our way again. Things went well until we started around the cape and the rough seas hit hard. Harry MacDonald wasn't sure this was worth all the farmland in the world. He heaved all he ate and tried to throw up his insides, besides. The guy was white as a ghost for a week. Everyone else aboard didn't feel all that good. The waves seemed to come at us from every direction at once. Our new captain was equal to the task and we lost no one making the trip through that wretched place.

The shanghaied crew suffered the worst. Once we reached the other side he let them clean up their nasty mess in the hole. I didn't envy those men in the least for Harley and I made the same trip when we went east and it wasn't a picnic in the park.

The weather was warm from Florida until we reached Baja California then it started to cool down a bit. This trip was like heaven for my wife and me. We had all this time together with nothing to do, but we kept occupied. Everyone was anxious to get to work on our new enterprises.

Aboard ship the carpenters were busy finishing the living quarters for the men and passengers. The captain's quarters were already pretty nice and he said to wait until the crew and passenger's quarters were finished.

What a difference between Tucker Meredith our present captain and Nelson Rodgers who cared not for human life. Tucker thought of his men as more than just trash while Rodgers held them in low esteem.

Justin Jenkins' family had no idea what had happened to him. They didn't know if he was alive or dead. He just up and vanished one day on a trip to the east coast. They wanted him to stay home but he didn't feel that he could with all he had going on in California. JJ also had his eyes on Harley's sister Treva and the boat trip showed it plainly. Harley was a little more reserved but you could see love was there also.

Justin deposited a good chunk of cash in his folk's bank. It would make their lives a whole lot easier for them. He tried to talk them in to coming to California but all their kinfolks lived in that area and they weren't willing to give them up. JJ left three younger brothers at home but Donna his only sister took a liking to Harley and came along with them.

Justin had made it quite clear to his family that we had a ship and they could ride it to the west coast to live or visit any time they wanted to. All they had to do was let us know by mail that they wanted to come see us.

Tom and Mary had posted letters to his folks in Maine and let them know of their where abouts and filled them in on all that Dick and he had gone through since leaving home. The correspondence they sent to Maine was more like a book than a letter. Tom let it be known that they were welcome anytime they wanted to come west.

At first JJ was flabbergasted at all the chickens the MacDonald's had up on deck in cages. When he asked

Mabel about it she said "I think the Scotsman is going to be a chicken wrangler when they get settled down in California."

Well to each his own I guess. You can take the Scotsman out of Scotland but you can't take the farmer out of the landowner. Whether they know it or not there is a great demand for eggs on the west coast, so in reality that might be a very good investment for the Scotsman if they can somehow get them all the way to California alive.

After rounding the cape we fought a stiff head wind for three days. And then a gentle south breeze filled our sails to capacity and we made excellent time. We were all anxious to sail into San Francisco Harbor. As we sailed north we could see the snow caped Andes Mountains way off to the east.

Captain Tucker Meredith made good time on this trip and it wasn't long and we were sailing into San Francisco Bay. The docks there were beehives of activity, as we off loaded the merchandise on board. Shop owners were eager to purchase fresh and new supplies for resale

We stayed aboard ship until we had horses and wagons rounded up and ready to shove off for Sacramento. Harley and JJ would stay in Frisco with two carpenters and build a huge warehouse for our future supplies, coming into California, and keep the supplies we couldn't move with us by wagon. Folks from all over the Frisco area were already moving onto the dock area looking to acquire much needed supplies.

Harley and JJ purchased a building lot just outside of town but close to the docks and the carpenters began construction of a large warehouse for our use. Even before we started those wagons east Captain Meredith was sailing up the bay, headed north to pick up some building lumber for our use and for resale.

It was rumored that up north there was plenty of lumber to be had if you had the where with all to haul it. If only John Sutter had finished his sawmill on the American River there would be lumber in this area. But he had no way to finish it without help. His hired crew was up in the mountains looking for gold. I hope we didn't run into that kind of trouble.

Two of our carpenters stayed in Frisco and two went with us to Sacramento. Our plan included a warehouse in both places. We'd made the most of our journey home from England and it looked like the supplies we were moving east would fill the bill. It staggered me to look ahead and see all the work that was staring us in the face. Work didn't bug us all that much for we were eager to get started.

The snow-covered mountains and the empty land that stretched out for miles captivated the MacDonald's. They saw the rampaging streams and rivers making their way to the ocean and wanted to know if they were like this all the time.

We informed them of how the rivers got this way and said later on this summer they would slow down, after most of the snow had become water and had ran its course. Then next winter there would be a snow build up again and it would start all over again next spring.

Two long hard days found us in Sacramento. We went to the land office to buy a track of land and found what we wanted, three hundred and twenty acres of land on the American River for a warehouse and a place to pasture our mounts.

A six-man crew shoved off for the mountains to cut aspen poles so we could build corrals and enclose the pasture for our animals. The carpenters set about laying the foundations for the huge warehouse. And as soon as that was under way we started a boarding house for our gang to live in until we made other arrangements.

Our home for a month was our wagons on our land outside of town. In the mean time the Downey Cruiser came in with a load of lumber. That was a product that was in high demand by everyone and as soon as it was off loaded in Frisco, Captain Meredith headed north again to replenish the lumber that people rushed into buy.

We scoured the area asking folks about Dick Ames. No one knew for sure where Dick was. He'd been playing cards quite regularly and was a big loser. Someone said they thought he might be in the mountains looking for gold again. Well I hope he's doing well up there. We wish only the best for him. We need him to come back for he was a part of this enterprise. We asked several men heading up there to tell him we were back and needed him to come down and lend a hand.

When Captain Meredith returned with another shipload of lumber we picked out what we needed and rushed him off to the west coast of South America to pick up more supplies. For now the area needed food staples. Later he would get things that were needed in the mining fields.

Businessmen in Sacramento were running low and were hitting our new warehouse hard. We hired flat boats to bring our building supplies up to our little farm on the American River and we started a lumberyard there and sold plenty of building supplies.

Aspen poles were arriving by water as men pushed and poked the poles down the river when they got hung up. The men labored all the way down here from the Sierra Nevada Mountains so we could have poles for a rail fence.

Two men were looking for a stake so they could return to the mountains and seek for the allusive gold. They stayed with us and helped us build our fence for a month or so and said they would be back this winter to help us.

Then we hired four other men that were looking for the same opportunity. They wanted to get a stake and return to the mountains. After a night on the town the pole prodders headed back into the hills to poke and prod a lot more aspens our way. Some folks wanted the larger aspens poles to build shacks for livestock and chicken coops around town. We tried to make them available to them. Things were really jumping here in Sacramento.

As one crew worked building the warehouse we had another crew raising our boarding house. The girls were anxious to get inside and have some space to themselves. In the tents sometimes the dust covered everything and made a mess and no woman wants that.

The building game was in full swing with the new supply of lumber and larger aspens in town. Folks everywhere had hammers, saws' and axes' making a sweet sound in town and our small settlement was starting to grow by leaps and bounds.

We hung onto our lots on Main Street and were pressured many times to sell. We had no plans for them at the present time, but might need them in the future. Our family group was growing by leaps and bounds and we had no idea what most of them might want to do with their lives in the future.

About two months after we got back to the continent, on a Saturday, a dozen miners came riding into town. They had been chasing four robbers and killers. The men had killed some miners for their gold up in the hills. One man had been wounded and had lost a lot of blood trying to escape the vigilante's pursuit. They were positive they were in town somewhere, but no one had seen a man with a gunshot wound or bandages. Our crew kept their eyes peeled and saw nothing out of the ordinary. We had our suspicions but couldn't prove a thing. The miners insisted that they were in town someplace and wanted some short order justice.

To see what we could find out we sent to Frisco for a gambler to help us. He would play cards in the Bull Dog Saloon and see if he could hear anything. We had to agree to take care of his expenses that he incurred and pay him two hundred bucks for a week's work. This fellow was the best or so I heard.

We all kept our eyes opened and the girls would walk around town looking for whatever they could see. One day as they made their rounds they saw a small piece of cloth with dried blood on it. The material was almost burned up on a burn pile. They hustled on back to the boarding house where we were working and showed us the bloody clue they had found. Several houses used that same fire pit so we set up guards that could keep an eye out for something that would give us an indication of who had left the rag. When someone would burn things or toss out cans we'd have someone inspect it for anything unusual.

After five days of this without another lead we decided to get the sheriff to help us search each house. Early one morning we put our plan into motion. Our miner friends couldn't help for they had gone back to the mountains to play in their little streams.

With the men we could gather together at the first house we found no one home, the second we rousted out two men. The men weren't very happy about being awakened so early in the morning. In those two places we found nothing that would raise a red flag. The third place was much the same. The fourth house no one would come to the door but tried to send us away.

We made it plain that we were the law and wanted in. When we persisted a slug punched a hole in the front door and it whizzed by my head. That's when glass broke at the side of the house as Harley hit that front door and it came off its hinges. Men raced inside and soon had four men subdued and face down on the floor. One fellow had a shotgun wound in his shoulder and arm. It got to bleeding in the scuffle that ensued and blood soaked the bandage over the shotgun wound. Before the sun had cleared the treetops the four men were sitting in jail. The sheriff got a young deputy off to the mining camp, for them to send down their witnesses to finger the prisoners we had in custody.

The fellow lit a shuck out of there right after the judge bound the prisoners over for trial. The trial would be as soon as the miners got into town. The trial had to be quick for the miners couldn't be away from their claims for very long. People were quick to move in on claims that didn't have someone looking after them.

The gambler man left town without taking any of our money. He said with all the money they gave to him, at that card table, he didn't need any of ours. Those guys in there have more money than sense. Anytime you want my help again just give a whistle.

In a week's time they found the four men guilty and sentenced them to hang by the neck until they were dead. The judge wanted to send a message to all that thought about living by the gun and not by the sweat of their brow.

The vigilantes were in town for the trial and would be back for the implementation of justice; those boys needed to see them swing. The sentence was to be carried out in ten days at ten o'clock in the morning. It was to be a spectacle and every business would be closed up all morning long. All commerce would cease and everyone was invited to come and witness the execution.

DICK AMES

Five days had lapsed sense the sentencing and in the middle of the night gunfire broke out in the street and woke the whole town. There was an awful commotion down by the jailhouse. In my mind it was a jailbreak and someone was trying to spring the convicted criminals we had housed there. It came to mind that someone was freeing the men that we had convicted and hot lead was going back and forth as men on horseback made their get-a-way.

We lost the prisoners we had in the jailhouse, but one of the men that sprung them loose was down in the street with a bad wound and to my astonishment the wounded man turned out to be Dick Ames. We wondered where Dick had been all this time. He'd just disappeared into thin air and now he shows up with a bullet hole in his back from one of the men he was helping.

A man on the street said that Dick's friends shot him in the back as they were leaving town. I'm mighty glad Tom was out of town tonight for this would be devastating to him. I called the boys over to where Dick lie dying in the dirt. Dick was still coherent and asked, "how long you fellows been back in town." He took a deep breath and continued. "Is Tom in town with you guys?"

"We've been back home awhile Dick. We've been getting our business up and going around town. Tom is with his wife out to his in-laws." We gathered around his prone body and took a seat in the dirt and continued the conversation.

"How in the world did ya shake free from that noose? I thought you boys were goners for sure. I wished I'd gone with the guys to help spring ya loose. Maybe I wouldn't be where I am now. I've made some bad decisions in my life and lately they were just downright dumb."

The doctor came a running up the street. He took one look at Dick and shook his head. I got to give the man credit he didn't give up. First off he tried to stem the bleeding and had his wife hold one bandage tight to Dick's back. He administered laudanum to Dick and in a little bit Dick settled down. You could see the hard pain ease up some as we talked.

"Dick, how did you get in this fix, I thought you were way above this kind of work?"

English, I got to gambling way too often while you fellers were away so I decided to get back up in those hills. While I was up there I got to chumming around with the fellers you folks had locked up down here in town. When they were out on their little excursions I kept myself to the grindstone grubbing around, looking for gold.

When one of my fair weather friends got locked up some of their friends talked me into helping spring them loose. All I was supposed to do was hold the horses while they did all the dirty work. How lacking in judgment it was, I had no business helping out crooks. Those same sorts of men caused us all that trouble back when we first got here." He took a deep breath and said, "I'd sure like to see Tom again." That boy sure turned out to be a fine upright gentleman and I'm sure proud of him. Ma and dad would be proud also if they saw him. I would say that I think he is a good man.

"Dick, my friend you did right by him, you would be proud of him if you could see him now. Tom has become a real man, someone to ride the trails with. He holds up his end of the work and is a real asset to our business. Tom is a man to take with you if you need help in any kind of a situation. That wife of his has made him happy. It sticks out all over him; you did right by him Dick. He's a happily married man and has his head on straight. You would be proud of him if you could see him."

"English, this fellow that leads the gang that shot me has a brother or someone that lives here in Sacramento." His breath was coming harder now and the pain was increasing. He fought the pain and started again. "The gang leader is called Woody Williams. I don't know if that is his real first name or just a nickname, but he has a relative here in town somewhere. He's a big wig of some kind. You boys be on the lookout for him he's got ambition and big objectives for this town. They will do whatever they have to, to achieve their goals."

Dick was struggling to get out what he wanted to say so we kept our mouths shut and let him talk. "You tell Tom I love him and that he is a good friend and a brother? Oh Lord do I wish he was here. Tell him I've missed him a lot."

"We will let him know, Dick."

Dick acknowledged the statement and lapsed into mumbling. I did make out a couple words, He said, "I'm sorry Jesus pleases forgiv—"and the rest became garbled and we didn't understand what he said, but Jesus did for He knows the intent of the heart. In less than a minute Dick was off to see his maker. The doctor stood up with a sad look on his face. "Well there is a man that knows for sure if there is a heaven and a hell." "Well at least he went prepared for whatever lies ahead of him in the great beyond."

"Do you fellows want me to notify the undertaker or will you take care of it yourselves?"

"Thank you sir but we will do that; we want to thank you for what you did. Do we owe you anything for your services here tonight?"

"Ya have your ladies send over a couple dozen of them fresh eggs tomorrow and we'll call it square."

"Thanks doc, we do appreciate what you did for Dick."

"You're welcome Mr. Drake." Him and his wife turned and ambled on down the street. They still had blood on their hands as they left. The duck thought to himself I'm going to do something nice for that young man

Harley and JJ looked sadly at me. Justin said, "I'll get a horse from the pasture and go out to the farm and inform Tom of his brothers passing. You guys need to get Dick off the street so the undertaker can get him cleaned up. The girls are going to want to see him in the morning."

"JJ, don't paint a dirty picture for Tom. Say good things about Dick. He'll find out but let it be someone else that digs up the dirt." Later as Harley and I came out of the undertaker's parlor we saw JJ riding up the street headed for the Firth's farm. We gave him a wave as he rode on by.

It's a mighty sad day for me. Dick got himself into a real mess by hanging out with a bad element. Six months ago he wouldn't have given those men the time of day. But being alone like he was for all that time, made him seek out company that wasn't what I would call good citizens.

He would not ride with them when they did their dirty work but he did allow them to talk him into helping out.

Now he's dead and they are free to do their foul deeds. The longer I live the crazier life gets. The good thing is that I felt comfortable that Dick had made it into heaven.

We would have to do something about all this. Dick was a first-rate friend, a self made man. He was a comrade in arms and we went through thick and thin together for a long time before he decided to strike out on his own. A lot of water has passed under the bridge since we first met on that boat.

The next day Tom Ames came back to town with Mary. Justin rode in with them and we all went over to the undertaker's parlor to see Dick's body. Dick had a pleasant look on his face and that helped Tom a lot. Tom shed a few tears and that got the ladies to crying. It wasn't very long and a tear slid from my eye socket making tracks down my face and then dropped off my chin onto the ground. As tough an outfit as this was their hearts were still tender toward friends.

We didn't want to fill Tom in on what had happened but he persisted until he knew it all. Then he wanted us to take up the trail of them that had used Dick, shot him and then left him to die in the street. This was a sad time for our group. My hope is that we never have to put a close friend in the ground again at least not for a long, long time.

After we'd laid Dick Ames to rest, the remainder of the day was spent getting ready to pursue the murderers. We had three mountain men in our employment that we convinced to go along with us. We made them a deal they couldn't refuse.

Herbert Wesley, Walter Wayne and Warren Stubblefield, these three men had been in the Sierra Nevada Mountains before gold was discovered. They wondered why so many men had invaded their territory. At first they kept moving deeper and deeper into the mountains to have some peace and quiet.

Finally they talked with a couple of men and then tried their hand at digging up gold. They'd run out of money and came down to Sacramento to get a stake, so they could try it again. They were trackers and knew those hills fairly well. Rick Larry who worked in our pack train business was a shooter with a long gun so we asked him if he would go along. He knew people up here and that would help us.

We promised to give them some time to check out some of the mountain streams for gold as we moved around. We didn't think this would be a one week deal and we packed accordingly. There would be eight of us to take up the cold trail and follow it until a debt was paid to Dick.

Those robbers and no good murderers didn't care a whit about Dick. They just used him to get what they wanted and for no reason put a slug in him and left him to die in the street. To me that is about as low down mean as a man can get. They must believe in the saying 'dead men tell no tales'.

I spent the night with my little woman. The two of us went out to eat and stayed close all night. We knew we'd be apart for quite a spell and we took advantage of our time together.

The sun was peeking over the Sierra Nevada Mountains and driving every bit of the early morning shadows away. We were at the town limits trying to follow the vanishing tracks in the sand. Once they left the road it got harder and harder to distinguish the hoof prints in the deep grass and they finally disappeared altogether.

We had the general direction they were going so we held to that course and headed into the mountains. Our plan of attack was to question anyone we came across and find out what they had seen or heard. We asked many, many times if anyone knew a Woody Williams without an affirmative answer.

At every mining camp we saw we would visit with them and find out what they knew of people in the area being robbed. Secretly I was enjoying the trip being out in the mountains and seeing the majestic vistas. Once in a while we'd see smoke drifting skyward from some miner's campfire or a deer scrambling up a small ravine headed for cover.

Birds were a sight to see like the Mountain Jays or a covey of western quails taking flight or listening to their lovely three-note song. In camp at night the coyote would serenade us. Yes, this was a great time for me. With all of God's wonders all around us it made you want to relax and fish some mountain stream. We still needed to be on our toes for the outlaws must suspect that someone might be hot on their trail.

Those boys in the past didn't abstain from killing those that got in their way. They would surely kill to stay free. We must be alert at all times. Being alert is why we see so many of God's magnificent creations all around us. If a twig was moved by the wind someone in the outfit would see it.

Close to a month had gone by and we didn't have clue one as to their where abouts. With Rick Larry's experience as a muleskinner and working in the mountains, it made it easier talking with people. Rick knew a lot of folks and where most mining camps were and we systematically went from one mining camp to another asking question.

As we searched out every draw, ravine and canyon it took us some time. Along the way we took time to look for gold for that was the promise we'd made to the men that came along. If a stream looked promising we'd dig out our pans and work it for awhile hitting the high spots as we went. We picked up very little yellow stuff in our travels.

We'd been out over a month when we got into a small valley with a tiny creek, it was so small you could jump across it, but there were a lot of yellow nuggets showing in the gravel in one spot. We worked that creek for a week and pulled out about an eight quart pail full of gold.

They wanted to stay on and work it until they got it all. Because of their handshake agreement they got ready to leave. You've got to give them credit they worked it until darkness called a halt to their operation. They worked on us to let them stay, but in the end they got ready to leave. The gold we pulled from the water we gave to the four men that were along on the hunt.

They figured they could return in a few weeks and pull the rest from the streambed before winter. Those four boys were as chipper as a squirrel in nutting season. By law the fact that they were in our employment made the claim ours but we settled that right off the bat with a letter that said it belong to the four of them.

With all that gold on the pack animals those four boys were making plans for their future. They reminded me of the five of us when we first hit pay dirt back on Falls Creek. That was a time when life was oh so sweet, not that it wasn't sweet now, but life wasn't so hectic and demanding way back then. Would I want to go back to that time, I don't think so, not without Mabel in my life.

A week later we rode into Teeter Creek Camp. A man had come down out of the hills last night saying that several men had jumped their claim killing three of his friends and he got away by the skin of his teeth. He was out of camp hunting for meat when they rode in shooting. They saw him but he made good his getaway.

We left for Teeter Creek camp with four extra miners on horseback. We rode up to his claim area and dismounted as the mountain men Walter, Warren and Herbert on foot moved into the mine area to scope out the land. As near as those boys could figure it out there were about eight or ten men that did the killing, after the killers did their dirty work they rode upstream and up and over the divide.

Herbert Wesley took the lead and tracked them down into the next valley and then off to the north and east. We were getting further and further away from home as we attempted to run these buggers down.

They'd killed three more men while doing their dirty work. It looked like they hadn't given up the owl hoot trail. Apparently they weren't concerned about being apprehended. Now that we had some fresh tracks to follow we would make it hot for them if we could ever catch up. Two long days later they killed two miners and ransacked another camp. This time no one made it out alive.

We had closed the gap between them and us; our gang was on their trail from first light until we couldn't see the tracks anymore. We made no fires now. We were eating cold food so as not to tip our hands and let them know we were closing in on them. The following night just before dark we saw horsemen off in the distance that looked like tiny ants. We saw them for a couple of minutes and they rounded a high bluff and disappeared from view. We decided to send four riders on ahead to see if they were our men.

The rest of us would stay on the tracks. Rick Larry our packhorse man, Herbert Wesley the best tracker, Tom Ames and Harley MacDonald went on ahead to scope out the group. As dawn came on the scene and darkness turned to pale gray we stood and watched for a sign from the men that rode on ahead. Before the sun lit up the landscape a small fire off in the distance told JJ and me that they were on the outlaws' tracks.

Saddles were cinched up tight and the packhorses were loaded. The crew didn't wait for me but took off like a big bird in a windstorm. This ole wrangler brought up the rear with ten horses in tow. Keeping up with them while dragging packhorses along was almost impossible but this foot-dragger did catch up about the time they started into a canyon.

The canyon floor was a magnificent place. It was as pretty as a picture. Up ahead a ways was a beaver dam with small trees along the water's edge. Several ducks skimmed the top of the water as they hurried to leave. Birds of all kinds flew in every direction and ground squirrels scampered to and fro among the rocks. A big buck burst from a clump of brush and headed uphill in a frantic scramble to gain concealment.

As we climbed higher all that was heard was the clank of horseshoes on stone and saddle leather as it creaked under us. A little further along we saw ten horses tied to some saplings. Taking in the hillside we saw men moving higher into the rocks.

Our guys took off moving on foot as fast as they could go. I moved up the canyon fifty yards and dropped the lead ropes and on horseback started up the creek singing to the top of my voice. It wasn't long and I saw men scrambling for cover and their weapons. The first shot from the miners was a warning shot which ricochet off a large bolder and whined off into the distance.

This ole packhorse wrangler unloaded leather in a quick hurry and hid behind that same huge rock. From there I could see both sides of the canyon and the outlaws' horses. I could see our guys moving in above the claim jumpers as the killers were systematically shoving lead toward the miners below.

That's when the miners started moving higher up into the rocks. As that scene developed I had less and less places to hide and finally decided to vacate the premises. As ole English was making his move Tom and the guys up above started laying down a line of fire on the outlaws and I started my move up the opposite side of the valley.

It took some time to get above the miners but finally I did and snuck down behind a miner and held him so he couldn't shoot at me, He put up quite a resistance but I talked to him as he fought back. As I talked he slowly stopped struggling. Then I informed him that several of the shooters on the other side of the canyon were trying to help them.

Finally he got that straight and one by one he began to tell his friends not to shoot at the men that were higher up on the other side of the canyon. Once they got that worked out the outlaws couldn't fire with any effectiveness and soon started to pull up stakes and move on out of the canyon.

That's when this sorry excuse for a wrangler got to worrying about our pack horses for they were tied to a bush down below with no one to watch over them. They would be easy pickin's for anyone that saw them.

It took a moment or two for our guys to figure out that the outlaws were on the move again and that is all the time those scaly wags needed to get to their horses and waltz right out of our little trap. Those unscrupulous varmints mounted up and high tailed it down the trail at full speed trying to get clear of those rifles that sent hot lead a chasing after them.

While those dirty rotten scoundrels widened the distance in their hasty retreat. Ole English made his way down to where the miners were coming out of concealment. Those ole boys believed me but were a little bit hesitant about having me in their midst which was wise. They have no way of knowing if this was an elaborate trick, by the outlaws, or was someone really coming to help out in a pinch.

As we talked the guys mounted up and hit the trail after the scum bums that left without saying good-bye. I quickly cautioned the miners about the outlaws' operation and then headed down the canyon, rounded up the packhorses and took out after our gang.

As this ole knot head gave chase he decided not to even try to catch up, but just hit an easy gate and follow them to their destination, this would leave the pack horses in good shape for a longer run if needed.

This ole dude was moving at an easy lope but too fast to enjoy the scenery on the way down, all those riders up ahead of me were riding at a reckless pace. The ground of the canyon floor was torn up by horseshoes and it was easy to follow.

Once they cleared the small valley they cut to the right and headed north. The pack animals were under a lighter load than the riding mounts and didn't work hard at all as we followed at a slower pace. Every horse in our string was a fine nag and you can bet your boots later on they would be fresher by a heck of a lot.

This eagle eye of mine could see our guys off in the distance ever once in awhile. Mostly I saw their dust, there were two dust clouds moving away from me. I'm thinking those creeps up ahead of us just might have bitten off a little more than they could chew this time. "Lord, will you protect our crew and watch over us until this is all over?"

All day long we stayed on their tracks. At creeks and streams I took time to stop, rest and water the mounts for I knew the outlaws and the guys wouldn't take the time to rest and water their fur balls. By this it insured that these mounts would be fresher and able to travel further.

After leaving the third stream, way up ahead I saw something half way up a steep incline. I wondered if it might be a horse that had gone down and as we progressed along the tracks I could make out a horse lying flat in the dirt. That ole hay burner had given his all in their attempt to get free. I saw no one in the dirt so I assumed a friend had taken him aboard and they were riding double. That spelled big trouble for those two.

By a little creek the guys were waiting for the remounts. They had their mounts stripped of saddles and gear as I rode in and unloaded leather. We all commenced to pull packs from the semi-rested pack animals. It took but a moment to make the exchange and they were off and moving again.

Ole English had to reload the tuckered out mounts. He took his time so they could get a little more rest. We didn't need a dead or played out horse on our hands. At first we all walked, then trotted for a while and after a bit this ole pack man mounted up and broke into an easy gallop and kept it there for a spell then alternated walking together with them and trotting.

The tracks of the single horse that was double mounted were plain in the sand for he was about done in. No horse could take the abuse, which that horse was taking and survive for long. Two men riding double were just too much punishment on this trip. From experience this ole boy knew that sooner or later that bag of bones would be down and men would be putting up a fight.

It wasn't but a mile and I could see that poor mount down in the dirt. Higher up in the rocks there was a battle going on. Tom Ames, Rick Larry, our mule skinner, and Herbert Wesley had them nailed down and were working their way into a position to put those two outlaws out of commission once and for all.

As I rode up Tom waved me on so I stayed on the tracks of the main party and headed northwest in pursuit of them. The horses Tom and the boys rode were dead on their feet. My job was to keep these horses as fresh as possible so I couldn't even think of catching up to them.

I heard sporadic gunfire behind me as I kept to my course. As I was about out of earshot the rifles went silent all together. Before I pulled out of sight the guys back there looked like they might have shot the two dudes in the rocks. Apparently those men on the dodge had no desire to give up and rot in the Gray Bar Hotel back in Sacramento and after those scum balls killed Dick Ames we weren't going to ask them first.

Up ahead I could see no one not even a dust cloud in the sky. There was a bluff that jutted out a ways and they must have gone around it and had moved on out of sight.

When I rounded the bluff off about five miles I could see a cabin under an overhang of a cliff. From here it was quite a pleasant sight to behold.

When I was about three miles from the homestead I saw horses racing off to the west. The outlaw gang had out maneuvered us royally. The treacherous no good thugs were making good their escape on fresh mounts. They even drove their exhausted mounts ahead of them as they made their way west.

This was the end of the line for us, for our fur balls had about killed themselves today and the ruthless ruffians were now on fresh animals. With that view in my noggin I slowed the pack train to a walk and got off and walked with them. No sense sapping every last ounce of strength from these bags of bones. It would just take them a lot longer to recover.

As I eased into the dooryard the guys were sitting under a big ole cottonwood tree. Their worn out nags were being led around by Harley in a small corral. You could see that the guys had fussed over them for a bit and Harley was putting them away. We all knew the race was over for now. It would take a day or two to get the horses ready to make any kind of a trip. That wouldn't hinder the outlaws for they had fresh mounts to ride.

After hellos and a little explanation I turned my pony around and headed back the way I'd come. I needed to see if Tom and the boys needed any help. When I got back to the Bluff that jutted out I saw them coming a long ways off and I stopped to wait for them.

They had no prisoners in toe so that meant only one thing they were both deader than a mackerel. Rick Larry recognized one of the dead men as one of the convicted murders that escaped from jail.

We walked our second class and mighty tired out ole transportation all the way back to that house under the overhangs. The little place was a smidgen rough on the inside and out. I wondered if they had killed the folks that built this little place. Right now I wouldn't put it past them.

The next day we located what looked like five fairly fresh graves out back away from the house. It sure looked like someone was out there under the sod and pushing's up daisies.

We spent three days at that place babying our tired out ole hay burners and getting them ready to carry us out of here. I was proud of the job they'd done for us. Those ole crow bait nags were well worth what we spent for them.

After three long days of doing nothing much on the fourth day we started out on their tracks and followed them southwest toward Sacramento. This whole she bang seemed like an exercise in futility. Or should I say it was like banging our heads against a brick wall. The one thing we did do was put the gang on notice that the law-abiding citizens were fed up with their kind of antics and they'd better move out of the area.

This is where our mountain men earned their money for they had to hunt hard to stay on their tracks. The wind had filled their tracks in some. If it hadn't been that there were so many horses running with them it would be nigh on to impossible to track them. I'm sure those boys, on the dodge, were still making better time than we were today.

The first day down the trail we camped on a good size stream and low and behold our muleskinner brought out some fish line and we had trout for supper. Wow did they ever taste good, will wonders ever cease.

After three days of dogging their tracks we saw a place where they were going to bushwhack us, apparently they thought we were coming right behind them. At that point we decided that they were headed for Sacramento so the mountain men and our packer stayed on their tracks while Halvey, JJ, Tom and I headed for home.

We gave them the best mounts to ride and two pack horses with camp things. They were not to engage the outlaws but to just make sure that they headed for Sacramento. Four days later we were back home with our women. Tom with Mary Ellen, the guys with their sweethearts and of course Mabel and I found each other's lips as soon as we met.

Right off the bat we alerted everyone we came into contact with to keep an eye out for several men riding into town. We knew that the ones that had been convicted of murder probably wouldn't show themselves openly among the population.

The following day some of our men hung out around town waiting to check men coming into town. But that my friend was a near impossible job when new people were coming and going all the time. We told them to keep an eye out for men that looked like they'd been on the trail a long time. Sad to say that fit more than half the men that came through here.

On Saturday the mountain men drifted into town and we had a confab. They'd lost the tracks twenty miles outside of town. The outlaws cut loose of their extra mounts somewhere along the way. They found some of the nags outside of town eating grass near a stream. They put the extra mounts in the horse barn on the American River for safekeeping and warned our stable hands of the situation. They were to report to one of us if anyone came sniffing around or asking any questions. If no one came to claim them we would just add them to our string of horses.

Rick Larry, our mule train packer, stayed close to the Floyd Williams' place for I'd not forgotten what Dick Ames had said before he died that the leader of the gang was a Williams and had relation here in town. I had a sneaking suspicion that there was a connection there. Whenever someone suspicious walked into the Bull Dog Saloon I had Rick mosey on over there, and have a beer and look around.

Rick had been at the trial and got a good look at the men that were found guilty of murder. Of course he didn't know any of the men that had broken them out of jail. We were sure that it was all interconnected. It all seemed like they fit together and the men kept coming back to the Sacramento area even though it was a hot place for outlaws to be. How was Floyd Williams getting all the money to build his businesses? He'd never filed a claim or spent any time in the gold fields since he came into this area. Folks said he didn't look like he had a large supply of money when he first came into town.

In two short years he owned the Blue Bell Hotel, the Bull Dog Saloon and now he'd expanded again into the Williams Livery barn. He seemed to have his hand in all the things that were going on in this area. The man was closed mouth and as wily as a weasel.

I've got to be careful for men could say the same thing about the four of us. It might look to most folks that we were trying to take over the town. Our group had businesses going on all over the place. Most residences knew we'd struck it rich and knew about the gold we'd packed into town from our mining camps last year.

Somehow we had to find the men that rode away from that ranch house under the overhang. The murder of Dick Ames had Tom in a quandary; he couldn't comprehend why anyone would want to kill his brother after helping them spring their comrades.

Dick somehow got caught up in their imaginary friendship and didn't see that these men of the West were cunning and was just using him to achieve their own objectives, but that still didn't explain why they would kill him. Dick didn't always do the right thing but he was loyal to a fault and always wanted our friendship to continue. Had we been here he would never have gotten mixed up with that gang of cut throats, thieves and murders.

TOM AMES

I've been the best of friends with English, Harley, JJ and my brother Dick Ames for quite a spell now. Dick is gone and that leaves a hole in my life and our organization. Treva and Justin have talked about marriage and they are only waiting for this mess to be cleared up. Harley has talked with Donna, Justin's sister, about her hand in marriage and it looks like wedding bells for them also.

I'm sorry to say the West had a sprinkling of bad men throughout it and one day those kind of men will be history, I hope. A week has gone by and we have had not a clue to the where about's of the men that killed my brother Dick. We chased those boys out of the hills an apparently they didn't come into town but turned off somewhere along the way.

Nigh on to a month has passed without any luck and this ole boy took it upon himself to go over to the land office to check out the land records to see if the Williams' boys had filed a claim on a piece of land somewhere out in the countryside. As luck would have it the land office clerk remembered Floyd Williams filing on a piece of land out east of town somewhere.

"Mr. Ames, it is out in the country somewhere, let me take a look."

If it hadn't been for all the trouble that Floyd Williams had caused the clerk and us when he built on our property on Main St. and then refused to get off or pay up, the going to court and all, those things had imprinted Mr. Williams on his mind and he wondered at the time if he was trying to turn over a new leaf. Was the guy on the up and up or was it just another way to break the law.

"Mister Tom, I believe Floyd Williams finished building a house on the property well over a month ago or at least that's what I've heard. I ain't been out there and haven't talked with anyone that knows for sure if he has a house built on the property or not. I can show ya where his place is located on the plot map; Tom do you think they might be mixed up in something illegal out there?"

"I can't say for sure Mr. Glenn but we are checking out every lead we get. Mr. Glenn, please don't spread this bit of news around until we have time to check it out."

"Got ya Mr. Ames, mum's the word."

I left the land office and hurried back toward the boarding house. The building was two story and rectangle with windows in every room. I must admit the ladies had a good plan for that place, to me it looked great. You can bet it was a credit to Main Street.

Every one of us lived in that boarding house except Harley. The MacDonald's family were living on their own piece of land outside of town. They had a house up and were living in it. Harley had ordered farm equipment for them in New York City and it would be here by spring.

I found English, Harley and JJ in the dining area of the boarding house having coffee. I got a cup of the black stuff, sat down at the table and revealed to them what I'd found out from my little trip to the land office. Right away we started making plans to go out there and have a look around.

Arthur and my in-laws were in town so we enlisted the three older boys Aaron, David and Rusty to give us a hand with our plan to investigate the Williams' Farm. Our plan was to go out there early in the morning and just spy out the place. At this point none of us wanted any trouble; we just needed to look around.

Our mountain men friends and our muleskinner Rick Larry were back up in the Sierra Nevada Mountains working that little stream for all it was worth. Before they left they staked out four mining claims at the land office. The boys were hot to trot and eager to hit the breeze on out of here. They wanted to pull some yellow metal from that tiny creek bed before winter sets in. To tell you the truth I wish they were here right now to lend us a hand. But those guys were hard at it up there in those hills.

Arthur and Harley tried to persuade the sheriff to form a posse and go along with us but the guy was way too busy to be going on another wild goose chase. He said, to my three friends, "you have no real evidence that the men that killed your friend Dick are even in the territory."

Arthur got on his case with a lot of urging and almost threats and the man finally did relent and sent three deputies along with us to give some semblance of authority. He called us all in before we left town and quickly administered the oath of office, to us, just in case there might be one of the convicted men at the William's farm. For laziness this law dog took the cake.

Mr. Frith insisted that he go along and took the oath with us. Art and I tried to talk him out of it but it was like talking to a brick wall. Dad just wouldn't take no for an answer. English told him, "If it comes to a shootout, it's your job to hold the horses."

When I heard it I knew English was just whistling in the wind. No way was Mr. Frith going to let us take all the chances and him set back and just watch. That ole boy was a good man and a real fighter. Mr. Frith didn't get where he is today by sitting back and letting someone else do the dirty work for him.

Our aspen pole pokers were down from the mountains and were lounging around town. Plus one of our fence builders was interested in going along. With a money incentive they decided to take the trip with us out to the Williams' place.

That made fourteen of us that were loaded down with firepower. Everyone had two rifles plus a shotgun and the four of us had revolvers. This ole dude carried that revolver rifle that I bought on the east coast. English was the only one that was anywhere near proficient with a revolver handgun. That ole boy had a God given gift with about anything he put his hand to.

The Williams' place was on the river at the mouth of a stream. They had built a large house on a low hill. Tactically it was built like it should be. We approached the house from the west. Our whole gang came shanks mare (on foot) down river to a place about forty yards from the house. The high riverbank covered our approach.

There was a lone horse tied at the hitching rail out front. The beast had covered a few miles already this morning. There were nine nags in the corral. Ole Tommie boy wondered how ole English was going to handle this operation. Our play it by ear plans from the beginning was to just wait until we checked out the circumstances then make our final plan of attack.

First off Arthur spread us out along the river and the stream's bank, from our position we had the house covered good and proper. There was no way they could get out of that house unless we let them.

English and two deputies return to our horses and leisurely rode up to the front door like they were going to ask for directions. The problem was three or four men answered the front door and just opened up on them. At the first sound of gunfire all heck broke loose at the house and in the dooryard.

In the action that started I saw Art snake out that colt from leather like greased lighting and started blazing away. He fired two times before an outlaw's bullet impacted him and he staggered backwards off the porch into the dirt. His third shot hit the porch roof as he was going down. The two deputies caught the shotgun blasts and I knew they were dead before they hit the porch floor.

Man-oh-man I think ole English might have met his maker this morning. As the three downed men cleared my line of sight, my first shot took someone in the shoulder and spun him around and out of sight. Then I grabbed the second rifle and looked for another target. Someone broke a window and I put a slug where I thought he was. That place was crawling with all kinds of critters bent on killing us.

With my shotgun resting on the riverbank and one eye on the house I reloaded my weapons, slid two percussion caps into place and was ready to go. The shots from the riverbank were sporadic. I checked and couldn't see Arthur anymore and that worried me some. I hope he didn't make the second member of our gang to be killed, first Dick and now Art. Both men were good men to know and I loved both quite a lot.

The lawmen were in plain sight on the porch steps. Why had the men in the house just opened up on them? If we let anything happen to Art, Mabel will take us to the wood shed and it won't be fun. I sure hope Arthur hasn't bought the farm here today. (Died)

The shots from the house came slower and slower. Had we killed off a few of them skunks? Were their numbers about depleted? Our guys kept their heads down and that gave them in the house no targets to shoot at. We depended on English for information as to whom and how many people were in the farmhouse. He didn't have a chance to figure out anything for us before the shooting got started and he went down in the first wave of shelling

It looked like one of the Frith boys by the creek bank had taken a slug, but he was okay or it looked like he was from here. His papa was a working on him. Off and on a rifle bullet was fired our way. We also sent a bunch of lead up their way. Mostly we kept our heads out of sight.

We heard some splashing coming our way, I looked up and saw Mabel and Mary headed straight for Big Mac and I could hear her ask about Arthur. Harley sent her over to me, that big chicken. I was worried enough about Arthur and I didn't want to get a tongue lashing from Mabel too.

When I explained it to her I got the surprise of my life for she didn't argue a bit but jumped up out of the water and headed for the house waving a white hanky. I hollered for her to stop, but she didn't break stride. That woman had her mind made up and kept on moving. She walked right straight up to the porch and gave a yell. "You men in there where is my man?"

I could hardly make out what they said over the noise of the river behind me.

"Someone fell off the porch, lady and we don't know where he landed."

"You men in their hold your fire I got to look after my man."

"Well lady, tell that to those men out there."

She turned and looked right at me and said, "Thomas Ames don't you dare shoot until I get my man out of here. Do you hear me?"

It's funny what men will do for a pretty woman. I'll tell you something there ain't no way this ole geezer was about to shoot at that house with her there, later maybe but not now.

A slight movement caught my eye off to my left, then I saw Mary, my wife, getting up out of the river and she headed for the house. Her ole bunkmate bit his tongue and looked toward the house. Mabel was dragging Art out from under the porch where he'd crawled after being shot.

She opened his shirt then tore off a piece of her petticoat. Mary checked the deputies. Then help pack the bullet holes in English and did the same thing on the backside and then bound the wounds up tightly. From my spot at the riverbank Arthur looked real bad and the deputies weren't moving at all. I assumed that Mabel and Mary would bring that tough nut back this way, but they started east toward Blue Water Creek.

While Mabel was doing her thing no shots were fired. The men in the farmhouse were fortifying the house; you could hear a lot of commotion inside the place. It sounded like they were piling furniture and other things against the outside wall as a barricade. Apparently they had a reckon bar and were pulling up floorboards so they could get below ground level.

I thought to myself this was smart on their part. This maneuver would make it harder for us to dig them out of there alive. We had them hemmed in good but we would have to go to extremes to pry them loose and I didn't want to lose any more men if I could help it. It might come down to burning them out of there, I hope not. But we couldn't lose any more men to those sidewinders. (Rattlesnakes)

I sent Mr. Frith to give the gals a hand as soon as they both got clear of any danger. Off across the creek a ways, just over a low hill, stood a wagon she'd brought when she came out here and that was their immediate destination.

Mr. Frith was helping Aaron get to the wagon with his wound. They walked up river until they were close to the wagon. Then they hopped out of the river water and moved weak kneed and erratically toward the ladies. Once they arrived Aaron sat down in the shade with his back against a wagon wheel. The trip had taken the starch right out of him.

The ladies were just about to the wagon themselves. Apparently they had medicine there to work with. My father in-law and the girls loaded English and Aaron into the wagon and the girls both took a man and went to work on them. Mr. Frith had helped the two ladies as much as he could and was now headed downstream toward us.

Some dirty rat from the house took a shot and the slug just missed my head and plowed into the tree next to me. It didn't take very long for this ole hound dog to duck his head down out of sight. Right away I moved to a better location one that they hadn't pinpointed yet.

Whoever fired that slug meant to do me bodily harm. I laid my rifle on the riverbank and looked for a target to lay waste. To keep them from zeroing in on me I kept moving from place to place along the riverbank. I had both of my rifles up on the river bank in different places.

I kept putting my head up in several different places along the bank to have a look around. I hoped this would confuse them and they wouldn't know just where I'd lift my head next. I located one fellow and my rifle slug put daylight clean through him. I didn't know for sure where the slug hit him but that shot was true to the mark and I saw him disappear from view with a jerk.

Deliberate, sporadic gunfire continued for the better part of an hour, with no let up in all that time. I never saw another soul to shoot at. But some of our guys had sent lead bullets up there anyway, that by chance they might find a home in flesh.

By now no one was shooting. We had come to a stalemate and those ole boys in the house seemed content to keep their heads down or were they peeking through the cracks or bullet holes in the walls. An hour had gone by and we were thinking of burning them out of there and were getting ready to put fire on the roof.

A white rag was protruding through the front door so I hollered up to them and asked, "What do you men want?"

"Gentlemen, we would like to talk."

"We tried that and you killed the two deputies and maybe even Mr. Drake."

"We know that now but we thought they were here to do us harm. They started right in to bad mouthing us and threatening us with harsh words.

"Did you have to open up on them? Were the words hurting you? Did you need to kill them?"

"If you remember right Mr. Drake shot first."

He was first to shoot but it was still in self-defense. "Sir, we saw it and if he hadn't fired when he did he would have been dead on the porch like the deputies."

"Hey down there you fellows got us all wrong. We purchased this property to start a farm, not trouble. We got families back East we plan to bring out here when it gets a little more civilized. When your man came to the house we were afraid he was going to harm us."

"Listen that is just a bunch of hogwash and you know it. That story won't hold water with me. There is a whole passel of men in there and only three men were standing on the front porch without a gun in their hands and that doesn't pose a threat. To me, what you did was out and out murder."

"If that is true why did we let the misses help them? You got us all wrong Mister, we are peace-loving men. A couple of our men thought your party was a threat to us. We saw your men hiding along the river and getting ready to lay siege to us. Sir, it looked that way to everyone in here. So what did you expect us to do, set on our hands and be killed?"

"Sir, if you give yourselves up we'll haul you into town to a trial and let them decide if you are guilty or not."

"We know your court system and we don't want to be railroaded. We're good citizen and aren't interested in a trip to the slammer and then a necktie party."

"If you don't want to come out what is the alternative?"

"Back off and let us breathe a little more freely and we'll give you an answer."

"You up there, we aren't leaving but we'll give you an hour to make your decision. For one hour no one will fire his weapon at the house unless you fire first." For the next half hour there seemed to be lots of commotion going on inside the house. At the end of an hour I hailed the house again.

"Well what have you men decided in there? Hello the house, what have you decided." The answer was slow in coming.

Hello out there, we haven't come to a final decision but we're close. Could you give us a little more time to persuade the holdouts to give up, for we all want to do the right thing?

"OK a bit more time won't hurt anyone." Was I going out on a limb for these guys? I really didn't want any more of our men hurt. We'll have time to do our dirty work later on if it comes to it.

The thing that bugged me is why were they making so much noise in there? Were they making the place more defensible? Maybe, but our next tactic was to make the house a torch and then pick them off as they came out. Once the place started to burn it would be mighty hot inside.

JJ and Big Mac gathered around to discuss what could be going on inside the house. The general consensus was that they were not going to give up but put up a fight.

The builders of the house had excavated the yard up around the house. The ground was flat up close to the dwelling then dropped off as it moved away from the house. Did they have a cellar in that place is that where all the fresh dirt came from?

That gave birth to new thoughts. With our postponement were we giving them a chance to fix up their defenses? I sure hope not. It could spell big trouble for us later on, but burn it we would. They still had a little time on their extension but this ole nut was getting mighty nervous about the whole thing so I gave a holler up to the house and there wasn't any answer to my calls.

Over by Blue Water Creek I saw movement. It was Justin Jenkins and he was headed for the end of the house. He made it without a shot being fired. He had some kind of a torch in his left hand. The torch wasn't lit but he was in a position to set the house afire if it came to that. All he had to do was light it and toss the thing onto the roof. Those wood shingles would burn hot once they got started. My hope is that they'd come out a-shooting and this thing would get settled right here and now. But whatever happens is all right if we can put these murderers away for keeps, whether it's from a bullet, fire or a judge's rope.

I gave another holler up to the house. "Hello the house." We got no answer from the prisoners, so I did it again. "Hello the house." Then gave the go ahead sign to JJ and I saw him dig a sulfur match out of his vest pocket, light the torch and give it a fling onto the roof.

The fire spread out on the wood roof and slowly ate into the wood and turned it black. The flame set there and dug into the wood and slowly took root and grew. Hey you in there come out with your hands in the air." When JJ got back to the creek bank and under cover, I gave another shout up to the house and there was still no answer. JJ did a good job, the roof was burning quite well and the slight breeze fanned the flames. The house was in the grasp of the fast growing flames.

Fifteen minutes went by and still no life came from the burning house. The dwelling had to be filled with smoke by now so I said at the top of my voice, "if you come out with your hands high you will be taken prisoner and allowed to stand trial."

Now ole Tommie boy was getting worried, had they gotten out of the house somehow? No it wasn't possible we had the place covered like a blanket. We could see all four sides of the house and no one had left the building. So what is the deal in there? Had they somehow shielded themselves from the heat and smoke, is that possible?

I had to have a look see so I went over to where Harley and Justin were by the creek bank and got my revolver rifle that Justin had borrowed. That would give me six shots if I needed them. The long barrel would give me some accuracy if I needed to shoot.

JJ said, "I'll go with ya, Tom. I'll cover your back." Up and over the bank we went and headed for the house on the dead run weaving like a snake in the grass. We reached the sidewall of the house without incident and that was a relief. We made our way to the front door and jerked it open. The black smoke came pouring out and we couldn't see anything in there.

No lead came our way and that was a relief but also posed a problem. Were they in there, were they dead or had they somehow escaped from that inferno? The heat forced us back away from the entrance and as we backed away from that inferno, the dead deputies came along with us. I put my hand on the outside wall and the boards were hot to the touch.

No way could they be in there and still be alive so what was the deal there? We called the men up from the river and creek. They approached the house but they were cautious as they came. The last thirty yards they came like the devil himself was after them. With our backs to that warm wall we discussed the situation.

We all searched the area. We spread out and it wasn't long and Harley yelled. "Hey you guys come take a look at this." He was standing between the outhouse and the house. Look here the sod has turned brown between the house and the small shed. As we approached Harley said, "The sod has been picked up and re-laid between the house and the outhouse."

We three approached the small shed that was just over the hill with lots of anxiety. Harley jerked the door wide and backed out of the away. We were ready for any type of trouble but none came. The place was empty. The outhouse was a one holer with lots of room for hand tools and such; there were handsaws and hammers. There was about anything a person would need to build a house.

In the floor was a trap door that wasn't completely shut. Below the trap door was a tunnel that led back toward the house. The loose sod outside covered a tunnel they had dug to the outhouse. There was a small door out the backside of the shed. It couldn't be seen from the water's edge.

Now we knew that the men were not in the burning house. They had escaped through the tunnel and this little exit door. There were drops of blood on the floor and on the back door of the shed. It appears that one or two of these scoundrels were wounded.

Their operation was well planned and executed and now they are nowhere to be seen. We spread out looking for any sign of them. Over two hills we located an empty corral. The chickens had flown their coop and were nowhere to be seen. Ma use to say, 'he, who fights and runs away, lives to fight another day' well those little rabbits must really believe that saying for they were gone.

Any of those unlucky stiffs back in the burning abode will need a wooden suit to wear before we stick them in the ground. That won't be today; today we have tracks to find and to follow. The three of us returned to the house fire and peeked inside. By this time two sidewalls had fallen in and we located three dead bodies in the red hot ashes. As near as we could figure it there were about six men still on the run.

With two of our riders involved in taking the wounded men, the women and the dead back to town that left us with eight men to pursue those killers that were on the run. They were all good riders and most were good shooters. Most folks out here were not good riders although everyone could ride a horse for a half a day without getting sore.

Harley, JJ and I went over to see how bad Arthur and Aaron were. Arthur didn't look all that good to me his face and hands were an ash color and he looked like he might kick the bucket at any moment. I worried about him. Mabel looked like she had been dragged through a knot hole backward.

Those two always looked good together even when King Arthur was out of it. JJ asked one of the men to go to town and bring back the doctor, then asked Mr. Frith to go with the wagon and help the women as they took the guys back into town. This would get him out of harm's way. "Dad, look alive out there for the gangsters are still on the loose somewhere and they might not treat you to kindly if they catch you."

Everyone else was chomping at the bit and ready to get with the program. We now had eight good men left to ride herd on the six outlaws. Dad Frith and our fence builder would make the trip into town and then return to give us a hand.

Everyone wanted to be on the move, so we got straddle our mounts and hit the trail. At the hidden corral we picked up their tracks which headed east toward the Sierra Nevada Mountains. Within a mile they had entered Blue Water Creek and we followed it upstream for ten miles riding each bank east toward the mountains until we came to a fork in the stream and saw no hoof prints that we could follow.

We split up and four each took a stream and headed toward the foothills after about five or six miles we returned to the fork and headed downstream toward the American River and the burned out farmhouse. Talk about wily; these men were as sneaky as a snake in the grass. We had traveled over twenty miles and never saw a hoof print, after they entered the water and now we were right back where we started from.

We ended up back at the cabin we'd fought over just a few hours ago. All the walls had fallen in and burned. We were back where we started from at the American River. I sure wish those mountain men were with us right now. These boys sure had talent for finding the slightest disturbance in the soil.

We had to make a decision on which way they might have gone, in the direction of Sacramento or toward the mountains. We opted for the mountains and headed upriver in hopes they'd gone that way. About an hour before dark a stream came in from the northeast and we sent four men to check it out. About an hour after dark they came riding into camp without any news to help us. Those slime balls had somehow vanished into thin air.

We'd gone up river for about four miles and saw nothing. We'd traveled quite a few miles and we hadn't seen anything, not even a track since they had entered the water. This whole deal had me baffled to no end. What had happened to those polecats? Did we miss where they came out of the water or had they stayed in the water all this time? Had they come out of the water one at a time, no I don't think so, for we were looking and saw nothing.

From the Blue Water Creek and that cabin had they followed the water toward Sacramento? As I think about it they may have gone west for medical attention, they did have walking wounded in their party. When we got back to the burned out house on the American River we saw the two men we sent to town plus another; the fence builder, my father in law, Mr. Frith, and a man that I didn't know, they were waiting for us to return. Did they know something we didn't? I asked, "How are Arthur and Aaron?"

Dad said, "The doctor said Art will make it and Aaron is okay." He then pointed to the spot, the exact spot where they'd come out of the riverbed. It was right where our horses came up out of the river on to the riverbank, just before we got on their trail. Those dudes were crafty. They let us come up out of the water and after we were gone they came up on the bank right where we had exited the stream.

The third man with Dad was a wagon master from the east. They'd come into Sacramento just after we left the other day, the man was also tracker.

Those boys made a fool of us and sent us on a sure enough wild goose chase. Well we never said we were trackers and I guess it shows. Once the town's people found out about our lack of skills, it was better than a year and we still heard about it.

The new man showed us how the outlaws kept their tracks in our tracks when we left the hidden corral. He showed us how they struck out across country until they hit an east west road. We had played the fool ever since we got to Floyd Williams' farm. We have two men burned badly, by a bullet, and two more were dead. We were always two steps or more behind them all the way.

We played the fool real good for them; they had us dancing on the end of a string like a puppet. Well no more from this point on we're going to plan our moves a little bit better. This new man knew his business and we got on their tracks and followed them west.

The men we pursued must think we had lost them for good and we would have if it hadn't been for my father in-law and the wagon master, Ken Bentley. Finally we had someone in our party that knew how to follow a cold trail. Arthur Drake was pretty good but the rest of us had our problems.

We were eleven men strong traveling on their tracks. Mr. Ken Bentley took control and very soon we were moving westward. Those no good thugs we chased came to a stream got in and followed it from the American River for a mile or so and then came up out of it and proceeded toward town.

They then crossed the American River and kept on going past Sacramento toward San Francisco.

We took some time and stopped at our barn, by the river, and picked up fresh horses to see us through to wherever those hard heads were taking us. Three of our hired men, that worked at the farm, saddled up and rode along with us. We had thirteen good men on fresh horses ready to run the outlaws down.

Toward the middle of the next afternoon Mr. Bentley came back to where Harley, JJ and I were sitting our horses and said, "Boys, somewhere along the way we've lost a man. There aren't six men any more in that group we are following. Somewhere along the way one man slipped away from the rest.

Probably back at the stream where they crossed the American River just north of Sacramento. I'm sorry I was so long in finding it out. What do you want to do now?"

"Ken, I think they're headed for San Francisco so let's split up and seven of us high tail it for Frisco, do you agree."

"I think that's a wise decision. Pick seven of the boys and strike out after them the rest of us will chase them to ya."

"Mr. Bentley we've got to make sure no one else slips away like that one did or after awhile we could be all alone out here. If they do that stream or river trick again ya got to make sure they all come out the other side. Let's give chase to the bunch ahead of us for now and find the other lost soul later on."

Harley stayed with the trailing riders while Justin Jenkins, five others and I hit a smooth easy gate on out of there. We took off making lots of dust as we moved toward San Francisco. It looked like the killers were headed for

Frisco; if they get in there before we do we could lose them for good. None of us could recognize any of the outlaws or their horses accept maybe one horse.

When they left that cabin, under the cliff, over a month ago someone in their outfit rode a dapple gray with a good size white spot on its nose and face. If we saw that critter we would know him with just a quick glance. Horses that looked anything like him were few and far between. If he could run he would be a swell mount to have in your stable.

EL CERRITO

We rode through the night and came into a little burg called El Cerrito just east of Frisco Bay. We parked our nags at the hitching rail in front of a cantina with four other nags. Right there for the entire world to see was that bald faced horse. Five of our men stayed to keep an eye on that gray horse.

JJ and I rode on down the street to the marshal's office, went inside to talk with the law dog on duty. The Sheriff was Spanish. I wish our man up there in Sacramento was as willing as this man was. We showed our badges, told our story and he was on his feet and ready to go. The man hailed two men out in the street with badges on their shirts.

We warned them that these outlaws were killers so beware. As we neared the cantina I waved to our men on the opposite side of the street to come follow us. Three men stayed outside with the horses. Two men at a time spaced about a minute apart followed us into the building. This ole law dog was a mighty efficient man. With eight of us inside the building the Marshall said, "Who do those horses outside at the rail, belong too?"

A man at the bar said, "They belong to us why do you ask?"

"Well senor they look like they were rode a long ways and no one is tending them and that doesn't set well with me. If they belong to you fellers you better send someone out to take care of them and give them some water before you guys guzzle down any more booze in here.

They grumbled a bit but one man sent two others out to take care of them. I knew that when the two men touched the reins the guys out there would take control of the situation.

The Marshall moved up to their side and ask chummy like, "where you boys from?'

"We've been in the mountains to the west doing some prospecting for gold."

"Did you hit the bonanza up there, senor?'

"Not hardly; we got enough for a boat trip back to New York City is all. It's time to go home and see our families; this place will kill ya if you stay to long."

Just then one of the marshal's men came in through the bat wings doors. And everyone started to close in on the three remaining men. That's when the marshal asked the final question, "Are any of you men wanted by the law?"

The leader who I assumed was Floyd Williams' brother' for he looked a lot like him, started to protest, but before he could blink several weapons were in their faces. Quicker than you could say Jack Robinson they were disarmed and on their way to the gray bar hotel right here in town.

One man in our party was at the trial, three or four months ago, and he identified three of the men in the group. Three of this bunch was already convicted of murder. The other two he didn't know. Let's hope those miners in the hills can recognize the other two.

At this point we don't know who the man that split off from this group earlier was, but we had an idea who he was. But thinking ain't proving it.

The sheriff sent a deputy with us back to Sacramento to make sure that everything was on the up and up. We were glad for the company. In two days we were back in Sacramento.

Man-oh-man was it good to be back home again. My wife Mary met me as we dismounted, that sweet lady was still in love with me and was I ever glad. This ole saddle sore dude found his arms full of a beautiful woman. Oh it's good to be back home again where folks loved you for who you are.

"After some sweet kisses she said, "Tom honey, Arthur is going to make it. He is taking a little nourishment now. Art was shot twice, once in the hip and one time high up on the left side of his shoulder. The doctor is encouraged about his progress. Aaron Frith is back home and moving around. He's his ole cheerful self again. He had a deep crease under his arm that bled like a stuck hog."

We talked for a spell in front of the jail. From up the street we saw Sacramento's barely credible law officer coming our way. It was getting to the place where I didn't want to even talk to him but he was our sheriff and we needed to keep him in the loop, if possible.

"Howdy Tom, I see you got your men that broke the law. You deputies did a good job and I'm proud of ya. People will soon get the message that you don't mess with the law in this part of the country. The law is efficient down here and they will land in jail if they mess with the sheriff in Sacramento.

Gee-will-akers, this ole boy takes credit for everything that gets done in this area. Well let him have the credit, we don't need it. Our credit goes to Jesus anyway.

Mary tugged on my arm and we started for the doctor's office to see English. I turned my head back to the law dog and said, "see ya later marshal." I grabbed my wife's hand and we ambled on up the street. Glanced to our right and saw Harley, Donna, Treva and Justin Jenkins going the same direction we were to see how ole English was.

Earlier Harley, Justin and I talked about Floyd Williams and if we had evidence enough to bring him to court. How did that man change stolen gold into cash? He had to have a source somewhere. At this point no one could connect him with the wild bunch down at the jail. Was he going to get off scot-free? We tried to get the men in the gang to connect him to the crimes, to no avail. His men seemed faithful to him.

Arthur wasn't up to a bunch of talking; in fact he was out of it most of the time so we never talked about the case around him. The doctor said, "Let him have his rest."

Mary said, "no one seemed to have missed Williams the day you men were rousting them out of that house on the river. I'm not sure we can make anything stick to him. The man is as slick as hog fat and has himself covered pretty well; nothing seems to stick to him." Two miners told the marshal they were with him in a card game that day, after they said that the men bought food and other things that they needed and disappeared into the hills.

They told the sheriff their story and left for the gold fields the next day with all new rigs. They had new horses and pack mules and all kinds of supplies. We got a list of things that they got from the General Store. Those two panhandlers somehow struck it rich right here in town. The horses and mules came from the Williams' livery stable. The holster said they paid hard cash for the whole she-bang.

There was one of those new photographers in town and the mayor got Floyd Williams to pose in front of his saloon and hotel. He told him it was to promote Sacramento. After the photographer developed the glass negatives and made pictures from them he gave us a copy of those new fan dangled pictures.

Once we acquired copies we sent two men out to investigate every assayer's office in the district. We needed a face for men to look at. Mr. Williams could use a fictitious name to turn their stolen gold into cash. Many, many people did not use their given names out here. Names didn't mean a whole lot in the West. Out here everyone looked at the man not the name, if you turned over a new leaf out here that is who you were.

The first day in our investigation we hit pay dirt. Courtland, a small place to the south recognized him. They said he exchanged gold many times in the past. They wondered about him but had no complaints so they did nothing about it. The man said he would come up to Sacramento to testify at the trial, of what he knew.

That was the first shred of evidence we had against Floyd Williams but it was a long ways from incriminating him. We needed a whole lot more than that or we were just barking up the wrong tree and we knew it. He could say I had the gold before I came into town and we couldn't prove differently. We wracked our brains to come up with something more.

To our surprise two of the mountain men and our ole muleskinner wandered into town from the Sierra Nevada

Mountains. Those men were quite wealthy now. That little tiny creek didn't run out of yellow stuff but turned into a huge vein of gold. The one mountain man and two others were guarding the claim right now. They brought a massive amount of gold into town and turned it into a chunk of money.

I was proud of the boys and how it turned out for them. Those men couldn't thank us enough. You would think we were their very best friends in the whole wide world and maybe we were. For sure they held us up in high esteem.

After a week, Arthur was up and making some sense of our conversation. As we talked he listened and said, "Floyd Williams was in the house when I was on the front porch. He was the first man to shoot me. That man is as guilty as sin. Isn't he locked up, down at the slammer with the rest of them?"

"No my friend, until now we had no hard evidence to hold him." With Arthur ready to testify the whole thing was now coming together. It looked like the end was in sight with ole English ready to give his testimony.

The trial for the gang was day after tomorrow. With this new evidence the sheriff took three deputies and tried to pick up Mr. Floyd Williams. The man must have smelled something for he disappeared. We scoured the town to no avail. Now where did that rascal go? He told his help he was taking a boat trip back East to see his family. Could we believe that.

Was he going to let his brother hang and him skip out on them? Someone had hired a good lawyer to defend the gang. Maybe that is all he figured he could do. The men that checked out his story couldn't find anything out about him. They traveled to Frisco without any leads.

Two dozen miners were in town for the trial. The vigilantes, the witness and several men that came for the entertainment, all came in to see justice done. They wanted to see if Sacramento would foul it up again. Two of the jailed men were already convicted of crimes and had the death sentence hanging over their heads. The other three soon would have.

We were going to post night guards outside of the jail at night, but the miners took care of that. The deputies and the miners were now providing security for the town. Everyone gave their testimony and the verdict was guilty as charged. They were sentenced to death by hanging; the judge said in five days.

The posse has been scouring the countryside looking for Floyd Williams without success. The word was out and everyone was on the lookout for him. Would he really let his brother hang? What else could he do at this time? The day before the hanging people were coming in from everywhere and the town was filling up.

All the guards were alert, for Floyd Williams might be trying to spring the gang loose before they swing. Everyone in our town felt they needed to see these bad boys dangling from the end of a rope. Floyd was out there somewhere and he didn't seem to me like someone that would forgive real easy.

It was about three in the morning when it broke loose. Five men hit the jail trying to free the men inside; without success I might add. In fact only one man got away alive and he was running for his life. The posse chased him out of town and four horsemen were hot on his tail. Once they were clear of town, Sacramento settled down and went back to sleep, if that was possible.

At four-thirty JJ and I were watching the lockup door from a dark doorway across from the jail. We saw two men sneaking up Main Street. Mr. Williams was in the lead. The light was on in the jailhouse and as soon as they were inside we high tailed it for the front door. Just as we reached the boardwalk a big boom sounded from inside the jail.

We hit that door at full speed, it flung open and hit a man in the back and drove him into Floyd. We were ready for anything and as they tried to bring their weapons to bear we both fired and killed Floyd in his tracks. He ended up graveyard dead right there in the lockup. His helper collected lead in his chest right where he lay.

My first thought was I hope this ends it once and for all. I didn't realize how tense I really was until I sat down and started to shake all over. "Lord, please take this nervousness and tension away from me. No way do I need the shakes."

In but a moment or two the place started to fill up with curiosity seekers and they wanted to know what happened to the dead men. They saw the dead deputy, Mr. Williams and his sidekick. The man with Williams, someone in the crowd recognized him. The stranger was always hanging around in the mining camps without any real means of support or at least none that people could see.

The young man looked like a greenhorn to the West. The man that recognized him thought someone was staking him with necessities for a share of what gold he might find once he got in the field. This maneuver was done once in a while to help new men out.

In fact English did it sometimes if a man was a good worker and had integrity. What could anyone offer the dead man to get him to do this dastardly deed and immediately my mind scrambled back to Dick? The outlaws back then only offered him a little friendship and then killed him out there in the street for no reason at all.

With that thought of Dick something came up from down deep inside of me and I broke down and sobbed. I got outside and cried for my dead brother and almost instantly felt a hand on my shoulder. Looked up through blurry eyes, there was my woman showing just how much she loved me

Those loving arms of hers encompassed me. Then her head rested on my shoulder and kissed me on the cheek and neck. "I thank you Lord for this wonderful woman of mine." Her love is not a fleeting thing; it stuck closer than feathers to a chicken. I said, Honey, "I love you." That's when she snuggled up even closer and said," I know Thomas."

THE HANGING

Sacramento has geared up for the hanging today and businesses are raking in a bonanza with all the people in town. Miners were out in full force to see if justice would be carried out here in town.

Mabel, my loving wife, helped me into my good clothes and Tom and Harley helped me down the stairs and out into the fresh California sunshine. The warm sun was up a ways in the clear blue sky and it felt wonderful on my stiff ole body. Mabel held my hand as we ambled up Main Street.

After a very short walk, my knees felt weaker than a new born kitten so we looked for a seat to sit in and rest for awhile. People got up and gave us their chairs and Mabel thanked them. My thoughts jumped to the Downey Cruiser and the men our gang had shanghaied back in England.

Our Captain Tucker Meredith said he let them escape over in the Orient. Now they thought they were fugitives from justice and would be on the run like we were; even though we had no thought of pursuing them. In the back of their mind they must always be on guard.

There were saddle horses and horses harnessed to buggies and wagons tied to the long line of hitching rails on both sides of the street. It looked like everyone in the district that knew about the murders was here to see justice done. With rigs lining the street you could see both horses and people stirring the dust while walking up and down Main St. The boardwalks and the streets were filled with milling people.

I watched a few slow moving clouds drifting across the clear blue sky and every once in awhile the clouds' shadow would glide across Main Street. Off to the west I saw a big black bird circling in the sky looking for a feast. What did they call that big bird out here? I think it was a condor or something like that.

My sweet wife, Mabel, sat next to me and we held hands in silence. With the short rest I had regained my strength so we thanked the good people and got up and moved on toward the hanging area. This trip was exhausting me. The guys had chairs set up for us in the shade of a good size tree. The scaffold was barely a hundred feet in front of us. The state of California was handling the hanging.

All five men would hang at one time. I wondered what would happen to the businesses that Mr. Williams had established here. Auction sale is my guess. A cheer went up and people were standing and stretching their necks to see. What was going on down by the jail house. Me, I didn't give a hoot.

The prisoners were being led to the scaffolds and allowed to have their final say. One man got salvation before he went to see his maker and I was glad of that. The rest died in their sins and that made me sad. The Methodist Minister had worked with these boys and thank God one will meet Jesus on friendly terms.

Their faces were covered with a flour sack and they were led to the hinged part of the scaffold and nooses were put in place. A man underneath was taking up the slack in the long rope and then gave it a jerk.

My eyes went skyward before the hangman's ropes started their jobs. I closed my eyes and saw my life back in merry ole England and how God led me to California by way of ship and ultimately to Mabel the love of my life. God does have a plan for our lives if we will allow him to work in it. Most men and women think they have it all worked out and don't allow Jesus or the Holy Spirit to work in their lives.

Mabel and the wee one in her tummy, big Mac, the guys who helped to form and shape my life so God would find me acceptable to him and all my wonderful family that is what is on my mind as I looked skyward.

If you listened hard you could hear the men on the end of a rope struggling to survive. That is what I saw and what I heard as those men went to meet their maker. Ole English never did look at the men on the end of the rope. I didn't want that imprinted on my mind, but I had to get this part of my life settled once and for all and I did. To tell you the truth I felt numb and cold all over. Why do men want to live like those men over there did? That I'll never know. I'm just glad their mothers and their families aren't here to see this and I shook inside. "GOD be merciful to me a sinner."

In the next few years things went well for us and our enterprises expanded. We were a big reason that Sacramento became the capital of California and we really celebrated when that came about.

I lost Mabel when she was fifty years old and that was a big shock to me and our six kids. With Mabel gone I felt like I'd lost my good right arm. When you think of a helpmate she was the best and I loved her with all my heart. I didn't think I was ever going to get through that loss and to tell you the truth I never did completely. How do you replace a woman like her? The truth is you can't.

That time by myself made me realize that I need Mabel's family in my life and we drew closer. It is easy to let close relationships kind of unravel and drift away. Dad needed help and all of us men made sure he got the help he needed with his crops and around the house. We all went out there once a week to help. Our big family was a loving family. My good friends helped me get through that rough time after Mabel passed away.

I went over to the east coast looking for a good woman and it took me about two years to find a lady that fit my needs. We were wed in California where all my friends were. This sweet lady was a good woman but she couldn't replace the wife of my youth.

Every one of us four and our wives lived to see the new millennium arrive out here. You might say we grew up with California and we are proud of how it turned out.

We are all over seventy years of age and busy every day.

The mountains in California are still just as beautiful as they were when we first landed here so many years ago.

The End

Arthur Drake a teen gang leader, in London, crosses the line and had to flee England. Shanghaied he spends over two years aboard, a ship the Downey Cruiser. Art and four friends escaped into California and ends up in the gold fields in 1848. Being one of the first they struck it rich. Art finds and marries Mabel the girl of his dreams but their road isn't an easy one.

The Captain of the Downey Cruiser recaptures Big Mac and Arthur in Sacramento and in irons they are taken back to England to be hanged. Mabel and friends sail aboard a fast clipper ship and arrive ahead of them and help them escape the noose.

In their absence things in California have gotten worse. A spree of murder and thievery plague the mining camps of the Sierra Nevada Mountains. Art is seriously wounded as they try to bring law and order to the area. I submit to you "English" for your reading pleasure.

I enjoy writing and have completed thirteen manuscripts. A professional reader has encouraged me to seek publication and I have three books in print. My fictional writing is based on historical facts, and a vivid imagination that I received from my mother.

Book one-	LAKIN
" two-	BLUE RIVER
" three-	SHORTY
" four-	ENGLISH

In London, England Arthur Drake was the leader of a ghastly gang. Art did as he darn well pleased and whatever seemed right in his sight. Thievery is how Arthur and his gang made money to live on. With him it was always the big "I" that ruled him until the Bobbies tried to arrest him.

Art dug up his savings and headed for the harbor and boarded a ship bound for America. The crew saw money change hands with a Bobbie and they knew Art was in trouble. Out to sea Art's life of leisure came to a sudden end and for two plus years he was a crewmember aboard the Bounty Cruiser.

One night in 1848 off the coast of California Art and four friends jumped ship. The California gold rush was just starting. In a card game this English kid won a gold claim with a cabin on it. When they got to the claim it was nearly worked out so they started looking for greener pasture.

While hunting for food Art saw three miners killed in the next valley to the north. Later the same dirty rotten scoundrels tried to kill the five of them. In two days they were attack and fought them off. They hadn't found any yellow stuff yet and already gangsters were out to kill them for whatever they had.

Because they weren't lifting any yellow metal from the creek three of the boys wanted to check out the dead miners' creek operation. Harvey and Arthur stayed in Falls Creek and worked their way upstream. Above the falls they struck gold and tried to entice their friends to leave their operation, over the ridge, and come along to help. One friend Justin Jenkins did come with them.

Back at their dig, they ran smack dab in to their former attacker. In the rain the boys rousted them out and sent them packing but just before dawn the claim jumpers returned. The three sailor boys were ready for then and ran them down and put them out of business once and for all.

All summer long Art and his friends filled bag after bag, with gold, and hid it away from prying eyes.

While Justin and Harvey went for supplies for the winter Arthur had trouble with a big mama grizzly and met Mabel Frith, his wife to be, her brother David Firth had a degree in mining and Arthur picked his mind and later put it to good use. The Firths moved on and English lost track of them. The winter weather was more than the ex-sailors bargained for and they struggled to make it out of the mountains alive.

Once on the flat land below they encounter a bad bunch and put their rifles to work. They decide to winter in Sacramento away from trouble, where they located their two friends, the Ames boys, and the Firth family. The Firths own a farm in the Valley but someone was living in their house and would not leave. Without any law the five sailors and the Firths go out there and force the intruder to leave.

Arthur and Mabel Frith get hitched, in the spring, and the six of them head for Falls Creek and dig out a lot of gold. Miners were swarming into the valley but Art and the boys had filed on their claims. Men even tried to work their claims and a dispute arose. The group got a little testy and Art and the boys ran them off. Once the creek was worked out they gathered all the gold they'd hidden in the ground and started for town.

Back in Sacramento Tom Ames and Mary Ellen Firth get hitched and everyone in the group is hustling to clear out of California and go east. The Captain of the Downey Cruiser was looking for them but before they could leave Harvey and Arthur are snagged and whisked off to San Francisco and put in chains in the hole of the Downey Cruiser. They survive the rugged trip back to England. The poor food the captain bestows on them made it iffy. They end up in a dungeon in the tower of London to wait for their trial.

In a surprise twist Mabel and Mary go to work to save their necks and free them from a hangmen's noose. The group purchases a small ship with the gold they dug out of the ground and with their families all travel back to California together.

A man in Sacramento and his gang are leaving a trail of death and destruction in California. The miners form the vigilante group and give chase. Part of his gang was captured with Dick Ames, one of their close friends, were killed. Dick's brother Tom Ames finds out the gang has a house built on a farm northwest of town and with a large posse they surround the house.

English hires a few good men and they give chase. Arthur, under a flag of truce is shot down in cold blood. The outlaws allow Mabel Drake to remove him and another man to a wagon and then she moves them both back into town.

Back at the hideout the outlaws make a clean get-a-way. The gang has a hidden tunnel out to the toilet, they escape and their tracks lead a ways from the house. They follow them and apprehend them in El Cerrito near the coast. The outlaws were all tried and sentenced to hang.

When all is said and done Art wants law and order to prevail, in California, but he doesn't want to witness anyone being hanged, so he looks toward heaven as the trap door falls.

Printed in the United States
By Bookmasters